P9-DNG-251

It's all for the love
of horses —

Best

Rita Cleary
November '93

SORREL

SORREL

Rita Cleary

Santa Fe
New Mexico

© 1993 by Rita Cleary. All rights reserved.

No part of this book may be reproduced in any form or by any electronic or mechanical means including information storage and retrieval systems, without permission in writing from the publisher, except by a reviewer who may quote brief passages in a review.

First Edition

Printed in the United States of America

Library of Congress Cataloging-in-Publication Data
Cleary, Rita, 1941-
      Sorrel / Rita Cleary. — 1st ed.
          p. cm.
      ISBN0-86534-191-5 : $12.95
      1. Frontier and pioneer life—Montana—Fiction. 2. Horses—Fiction. I. Title
PS3553.L3916S65   1993   92-43522
813'.54—dc20   CIP

Published by   Sunstone Press
                Post Office Box 2321
                Santa Fe, NM 87504-2321 / USA

To Senia Hart
my
Montana mentor

CHAPTER 1

The arctic wind heaved snow down from the mountaintops and onto the rolling flats in the valley, piling the drifts roof-high against the western slopes and sweeping the eastern faces almost clean. Nan Fletcher huddled in her cabin of lodgepole chinked with shale and daubed with prairie clay. The Fletcher cabin, tucked into a curve of Rock Creek, down in the valley, bore the brunt of the early October storm. Nan felt every log tremble with the first mighty gusts, then watched quietly as the snow began to rise like a tide in a marsh, gradually filling the spaces between the grasses, spilling over rocks, erasing the last vestiges of man and beast, and evenly covering the land. Joey slept soundly, thank the Lord. She had stoked the fire and now waited for her mate. He had been gone two days. But she was not afraid. She had seen the storm on the horizon and filled the wood box herself. It had actually been a pleasant two days. But soon, Bo Fletcher would return. She wished sometimes he would stay away, disappear into the wild lands like so many men, good and bad. Yet she had her doubts about whether she could handle a homestead herself, a woman alone with a six-year-old son.

Bo never let her forget her six-year-old son. What a joy he had been when newborn, a tiny bundle who slept through the night without croup or cries, who lay placidly content in his cradle and let his mother regain her strength rapidly. But six months passed and he did not sit up. At about ten months, when other babies were standing, he sat. And how he crawled. He would haul himself around by shoulders and arms, dragging his skinny legs behind. At about sixteen months he walked. It was a stiff, lock-kneed stagger, not the eager bounce of a normal toddler. Nan knew something was wrong and knew that that something could not be hidden for long, not here, on the frontier, where physical strength was so necessary to survival and so admired in the minds of men.

She remembered those few happy months after Joey was born, how proud his father had been of his firstborn son, when all he expected was an infant's trusting smile. Then, slowly, the realization had crept in like a deep freeze after the first spring bloom. Bo had revelled in thoughts of bouncing a son on his knee, of wrestling and scrapping as all boys should with their fathers. But Joey was thin, his movements feeble. Joey could just about walk. And sometimes he would fall hard. Once he fell near the pump by the corral, cracking his head against the corner of the watering trough. Bo was with him and rushed him immediately back to the house. The wound was superficial, but it was a head wound and blood gushed menacingly from a gash over his eye. Nan had bathed it, stopped the bleeding, and it had healed over quickly. But it had left its scar. That was when Bo's silences began.

Joey was only three when it happened, but he was so small he looked more like two. She had heard his scream from inside the house.

"He slipped." Bo had never been a man of words. His face was white and expressionless like the snow.

"He doesn't walk well." Nan stated the obvious lest she sound accusing.

"I was right back of the fence." But Nan knew his thoughts had not been on the boy.

She remembered how quietly he had held Joey while she worked over him. Only his eyes portrayed the shock and disappointment. Right then he knew. The boy was only a shadow of the strapping son his father had wanted. Nan would always remember the look in Bo's eyes. The grief and anger would come later. But they never came, at least not on the outside.

Bo was a model father from then on. He'd ride Joey around the homestead on his big muscular shoulders; he'd gently take the boy by the hand on the rocky path to the barn; he'd sit him astride old Blazer, the swaybacked plow horse, on trips to town and he, himself, would walk the twelve miles each way. He'd tell stories at bedtime and tease the youngster until they cried laughing. He'd croon him to sleep. He even carved a whole army of toy soldiers equipped with cannon and horses from a choice cedar tree in the garden. But there was no rousting, no physical horseplay. And all the while, he avoided Nan, and she had stopped even suggesting that they try again, that Joey should have a brother or sister to play with and work with and care about him. But Bo didn't even talk to her.

And so her life went on, and Joey's. Bo Fletcher spun his cocoon. Physically, he performed all the man's work around the homestead. He'd wake at dawn, when the first light struck the corner of the cabin's small window. He'd stoke up the fire to warm the room before Nan and Joey got up, and then he'd trudge out to the lean-to barn to milk Tess, the cow, and feed old Blazer. Summers, he'd turn to haying or hoeing before breakfast. In weather like this, he'd first chink the ice off the watering trough and check the wood supply, and after breakfast, shoulder his Kentucky long rifle and go hunting. Nan knew he was hunting more often lately and for longer times, yet he was bringing back no more game than he used to. He also ran some trap lines and these he would check almost daily except when it stormed. She'd tried gently to ask why he was gone so long and where, but she was basically trusting, a true frontier woman brought up to stand loyally by her man. And as more homesteads filled the prairie, game animals retreated and men had to penetrate farther and farther into the wilderness.

More and more frequent were the physical separations. Gone was the zest, the camaraderie, the close and intimate evenings on the settle by the fire. Gone were the struggles and dreams and desires and doubts that men and women share who work together so closely and so hard. Gone were the eager calls for help in planting a new fence post or plowing through an especially big chunk of hard pan, when even a man's brawn needed the little extra edge that a woman's added strength would give. How long since they had felt the happy fatigue and exhilaration of a difficult chore completed together? Worst of all, Bo no longer wanted her as a woman.

The "bench" was a level space of green, low-shrubbed table land, tucked into the foot of the mountain that overlooked the homestead from the western slopes. It was Bo Fletcher's first stop on his hunting treks back into the maze of canyons that rutted the mountains behind his cabin. Here, an enormous pine had uprooted in last winter's storms and here he would sit for hours alone. He would look down upon that cabin, the work of his bare hands and of his wife's. Here, he could keep his distance, removed in the mountain's stillness. His home no longer beckoned him. Its demands were extreme for this simple, honest, and hard-working man: a faithful wife who bore him only a runt. He loved the boy and he loved her, but that was what Joey was, a little runt, like the smallest, most feeble of the litter. He had wanted her so desperately, the most beautiful, in his eyes, certainly the best dancer in all of Cedarville, Iowa. They had come west together, encouraged by the promises of the Desert Land Act, bursting with the optimism that drives men to strike out and discover. They had mastered the forests and the plains, the dust and mud, the boredom of the trail west, to lay claim to this, their own 320 acres. They had built a home, fenced and plowed. They should have had a parcel of strong sons and daughters to carry on after them. And now this.

Bo Fletcher put his big hands over his eyes. "Why?" This was the question he had submerged deep within his consciousness. He had worked so hard. Now, he could only stare at the site below him, aware of an emptiness in his groin. He had done no hunting today. He didn't want to. And he hadn't checked his trap lines for days. His feet were cold. His ears and the tip of his nose were white with cold, close to frost-bitten, his lips blue. Elbows and knees ached like a cat's in a cage. The wind was picking up. He should be getting home. Dumbly, he roused himself, pulled his buckskins around him and started toward the fork in the trail. The way down was steep, waylaid with rock and scrub. He cursed. Another way opened smoothly in the lee of the wind, into the protective depths of Deer Creek Canyon. Bo had never followed the ramblings of Deer Creek all the way through to the other side. Rumors said that this was the escape route of Chief Joseph and the Nez Perce from the hammering of General Howard's cavalry in 1877.

The canyon mouth yawned amid tumbled rocks, some shale, and a few bright aspens that still held their yellow leaves. Only a few flakes filtered through the rocks over the rim and touched there. Out on the open slope, the blizzard was starting to blow. Bo turned to the canyon. Yes, he could wait here, find a quiet cave, doze, think. The trail down from the bench was already too treacherous. His muddled thoughts crowded good judgement. He might slide, break a leg, lie exposed for days before Nan found him. Better to stay here until the storm broke. He checked his pack. He had a few days supply of jerked meat, a couple of dried biscuits. There was water enough from snow melt and he could still find a few dry branches for a fire before the snow got too deep.

Just beyond the aspen grove, under an overhang of rock, he gathered some deadfall and built a small fire. It felt good. Slowly, he planned how to best be comfortable and weather the storm. He collected spruce boughs for bed and blanket and more deadfall to keep his fire stoked through the night. With the butt of his rifle he dug in beneath the overhang well beyond the reach of wind and rain. He chewed a few mouthfuls of jerked venison and lay down.

Somewhere, in the darkness, an owl hooted. Some snow slid from a limb. He heard a faint rustling, some animal disturbed in its flight from the storm, just like him. Then quiet. When he lay his head upon the branches, there was a vague pounding, and nearby, the earth was trembling ever so slightly. A horse was coming from the interior of the canyon.

The horse's rhythm was uneven. He had either been ridden very hard and was near falling, or he was picking his way along the frozen and rutted trail. Mountain-bred mustangs were adept at choosing their footing. The horse rounded the last outcrop of rock and juniper and came dimly into view. It was a handsome animal, close-quartered and muscular, deep red sorrel in color against the blue green background of spruce. But Bo didn't notice the horse at first. He had drawn his rifle and looked down its sights at the rider, a broad shouldered man whose head drooped down almost to the pommel of his saddle, dwarfing his otherwise considerable height. The horse, sensing danger, stopped short about fifty feet away and the rider did not move.

Bo cocked his rifle.

"Speak up mister. Who are you and what do you want?"

The man's head seemed to nod slightly but there was no answer.

"I said who are you?"

In the silence that followed, Bo looked at the horse. It was as fine an animal as he had ever seen, a mare about sixteen hands high, very big for a mustang, with flashy markings, four white stockinged legs, and a perfect blaze down the center of its finely chiselled head. He could use a horse like that. He could breed her to that stallion of Jarvis', maybe even beget his own stallion and start a herd. There was a good future out here in the horse business.

The man groaned. Bo tightened his trigger finger and took a tentative step forward. Then another. The rider just sat there, slouched. Then Bo saw the dark streak down the length of the horse's shoulder. Sweat? Slowly he approached. The horse stood warily, ears pricked forward, but let him approach.

"Easy lady, easy now, good girl." The sound of a human voice was reassuring to the animal. Bo saw the thong tied around the rider's thigh, the thong that held him securely in the saddle. This man had tied himself on and that dark streak was blood.

Bo put one hand on the rein and with the other touched the crusty stain. It was blood all right and it had congealed and dried. The man had lost a lot of blood and lost it many hours ago. He was in a very bad way.

Gently, Bo led the horse into the lee of the rock. The mare hesitated, sniffing the fire, but came ahead at the urging of a human voice.

"Come on girl, easy does it." The mare was not easy with human contact, she had probably been handled and broken only recently.

With his Bowie knife, Bo cut the thong that held the man astride and caught the huge frame that slid limply from the saddle. There was a powder stain that blackened his bleached sheepskin parka on the lower left and another on the left shoulder. This man had been shot twice at close range. He had probably been moving to the right as the bullets were fired, escaping the mortal wounds he could have met with if the bullets had hit another four inches to the right. Still, he had lost lots of blood. The freezing temperatures had helped stem the flow just in time. He could have bled to death. He should have been dead.

Bo laid him gently on the spruce bed he had prepared for himself. He laid back the jacket and unbuttoned the shirt. There was a nasty hole in the left abdomen. The shoulder wound was less serious, the bullet having scratched a deep furrow in the muscle and gone right through. Bo melted snow in a piece of damp bark, and, using his own neckerchief, soaked it in the near boiling water. When he laid the scalding rag on the side wound, the man twitched with pain. Bo got up to loosen the cinch and tether the horse. When he came back, the man was conscious and staring at him through piercing brown eyes.

"Don't worry, mister, I ain't one of them." The eyelids flickered painfully. "What happened?"

He cradled the head in the crook of his elbow and lifted a cup of melted snow to the dry lips. The few drops of moisture must have been reassuring.

"Ambushed," the voice cracked, "over by the Yellowstone. Horse, they wanted my horse."

"She's a fine one, she is." He glanced again at the beautifully conformed animal. "You have a name?"

"Wendy, folks call me Wendy." He struggled with the words, then added as if he was used to explaining, "That's short for Wendell." Then his head lolled and he passed out again.

Bo was no doctor. He had always depended on Nan for that. Her mother had been a nurse in the War Between the States, and had taught her many a valuable lesson. And this man needed more care than he could ever give out here on the mountain. Maybe, with the horse, they could get down before the real onslaught of the storm. The horse was strong, well-fed, and seemed sure-footed and mountain-wise. As much as Bo resisted going home, he could not leave a man to die.

He led the horse alongside and pushed his arm under the man's shoulder blades. Again the man came to and groaned.

"I'm taking you down, mister. I've a cabin and a wife and a boy down there. They'll do more for you than I ever could up here. Think you can make it?"

"I'll make it."

Bo heaved the long frame into the saddle, climbed up behind him and wrapped them both in a huge slicker. He headed the mare up through the aspen, around the outcrop, and out onto the bench. The blizzard hit them head on. The old pine log was nearly buried, and the wind was driving the snow before it like an unrelenting overlord. The horse lunged through the drifts and strode eagerly across the smoother levels. Icicles formed on her nose and on the brims of the men's hats. The horse trod bravely on, seeming to sense the switchbacks in the trail and avoid the edge, where the mountain dropped away.

The snow was two to three feet deep when they reached the valley floor. Bone-chilled and exhausted, Bo had no idea whether his companion was alive or dead or half frozen. He smelled the smoke from the chimney at the homestead. The horse sensed it too and broke into a trot. When Bo reined in to steady the pace, the mare simply shook her head and lurched forward with great bounds through the drifts. Bo clung to the saddle and braced the limp form in front tightly against the horse. The mare ran straight for the cabin.

CHAPTER 2

Wind and snow muffled the sound of hooves, but Nan heard the scuffing on the porch as Bo dragged the injured man to the door. She felt a pang of fear, then recognized Bo's familiar voice.

"I've got a wounded man here. Hurt pretty bad." No emotion in his voice, just a statement of fact, cool and fluid as meltwater from the mountain.

She rushed to lift the bar from the door. Two human forms slumped into the room.

"What happened? You've been gone so long..."

"Found him coming out of Deer Creek Canyon. That's his horse outside."

They laid the stranger on the bed and Nan helped her husband to the fireside settle. She turned to the stranger.

He was a big man. He wore faded blue britches and a buckskin coat, buttoned tightly over a blue checked shirt, and, under all, the ubiquitous union suit so necessary for warmth on the western plains. His hat was sturdy brown felt, broad brimmed and turned down. It was a good hat and had held out the snow. His brown hair was wet, pressed down against his temples, because of his own sweat, not melting snow seeping through the hat. His face was flushed in spite of the biting cold. Nan felt his cheek. He had a fever.

She unbuttoned the buckskin coat and gasped. The bullet had ripped a piece of flesh the size of an apple from the man's side.

It was a gaping, ugly wound. Pieces of blue cloth stuck grotesquely to chunks of flesh. She felt Bo's hand on her shoulder.

"He'll not live."

"But we can't just leave him." Her eyes searched her husband's for some vestige of warmth and human sympathy. He stared back.

"Nan, we've already one sickly in the house. We don't need two. If he lives, even then, it's a long winter and if he dies, it means we've worked and fed an extra mouth for nothing."

"Joe's weak, not sickly." Nan snapped back aware that Joey was listening. "We'll make do."

Nan had not come west without courage. You just did not let a man die. Survival was too important.

"He'll live, Bo. Bring the bed closer to the fire."

It was a plain, simple statement, not a question, and it came as confidently as the spring rains follow the thaw, even though she knew her husband was of different mind.

A cauldron of water was already beginning to boil on the stove. Together they stripped off his grimy, bloodied clothing. Nan worked first on the shoulder wound where the bullet had gone right through, and Bo helped carefully. But when she laid back the shreds of cloth from the side wound, the sight was repulsive. The flesh had been ground to a pulp and the bullet was lodged some two inches deeper, in tough muscle tissue. It had to come out, and it best come out while he was still unconscious. Nan laid her emotions aside and steeled herself for the job that lay ahead. Bo backed away.

"I'll see to his horse." Bo headed for the door.

"No." Nan looked at her husband. There were dark circles around his eyes. His cheeks were veined and raw. He needed sleep; he needed the ministerings of a wife who loved him. He needed it in his heart as much as this bleeding stranger lying there on the bed. But he didn't seem to want any of it.

"I'll go. The knives must be clean anyway."

She dunked her best kitchen knives into the water to boil, wrapped a shawl tightly around her and opened the door. The wind hit her like a battering ram as she stepped out. The horse was there, head tucked, rump to the wind. She grabbed a rein. The mare followed willingly across the snowswept yard and into the stable. She stood quietly by while Nan cleared hay and harness from the extra box stall, stripped her of saddle, bridle and bedroll, rubbed the crusted snow off her shaggy coat, and bedded her down. It was dark in the barn, the only light glimmering from a faint lantern, so Nan didn't notice the quality of this horse. And not knowing how she had carried two men through a raging blizzard down a treacherous mountainside, Nan had no idea of the animal's strength and stamina. She picked up the bedroll, took the lantern from its peg, extinguished it and started back for the house.

Bo was waiting at the door for her as she came in. The man on the bed was breathing evenly now, but was still unconscious. The knives had been boiled. Joey slept soundly in their one other room. She laid out all her tools and got to work, holding emotions at bay, aware abstractly and exclusively of extracting a bullet, of picking out the impurities, of cleansing and closing, stitching and healing, of the stilted breathing, and weakened pulse of this man, conjuring up all her mother, the nurse in the Civil War, had told her.

Bo watched while she worked. He was a proud man, proud of his wife of many talents, proud of the way she coped, but also somehow childishly jealous that all her concerns were not for him. Minutes slipped by. Bo dozed. Suddenly, she sat back. The movement woke him.

"Finished?" he asked.

"Yes," her voice trailed off.

"You need rest," he said, and he pulled up their largest, most comfortable chair. Their bed was already occupied by the stranger. She laid her head back, pulled a blanket over herself and slept. Bo rolled the stranger's bedroll out on the floor near the fire and also drifted off, but slept fitfully. Twice, during the night, he heard the stranger moan. He was regaining consciousness. Bo Fletcher went back to sleep.

At dawn, he was up, dressed, and, as usual, stoking the fire. Nan stirred and the man on the bed was breathing evenly now. Bo would see to the animals first. He dressed and went out. The snow was three feet high against the door. He took up his shovel and started the long task of breaking a path to the barn.

Joey awakened next and came scrambling in expecting to smell bacon frying and coffee brewing. He was a friendly boy in spite of his frailty. He loved people, the few he had met, and greeted everyone with an open innocence only a small boy would dare. Others sensed the sincerity in him and reciprocated. And he was cute as the dearest little boy in the old rhymes, with a sprinkling of freckles across his nose, large expressive dark blue eyes, and a shock of reddish brown hair that tumbled aimlessly down over his brows.

Today, he found the whole cabin rearranged, and stopped and stared. His mother sat slumped and still asleep in his father's chair. And the big four-poster was shoved directly in front of the fire. He paled when he saw the sleeping form of the man, but his childish curiosity prodded him on. It was not his dad. It was a man whom he did not know. How still he lay! Joey put out a hand to touch the calloused hand that lay across the sheet. It was warm. He touched his cheeks and an eyebrow twitched. The eyes opened suddenly in an uncomprehending glare and focused piercingly on Joey. They were a deep midnight blue, almost black. The child drew back. Then the man smiled.

"What's your name?" His voice rasped and he added, "You live here?"

"Yes sir." Joey was always respectful. "I came for my breakfast but my mother is still asleep."

They spent the next few minutes just looking at each other, not talking at all, just acclimating to the idea of having another person nearby. Joey didn't want to wake his mother; the stranger didn't want to scare the boy. Both were glad to have company and they grew more comfortable in each other's presence.

"Your Dad bring me in?" He coughed and stopped, another lull.

"You was hurt pretty bad." Joey looked at the pile of soiled clothing tossed in the corner, the blue shirt with the massive brown stain that was this man's dried blood. He was confused. Should he be frightened or horrified or just plain surprised?

"I was shot, boy." From the look on Joey's face, he knew Joey had never seen a shooting. "It isn't nice." He took a labored breath. "Your Pa, a good man, he brought me in. Name's Wendy."

The stranger's breath was coming harder now. It had been a strain to talk, but also a comfort. The boy just sat and listened without judgment, without question. When had Wendell Morgan last talked with anyone at all? Ever since he had left the log house behind the stockade, back at Fort Laramie, Wyoming, there had always been suspicions; he had always been watching what was behind him; he had always been so careful, not to reveal too much. Now, it was different.

With his own dad, he had headed for Deer Creek with five hunters on his trail, been ambushed, shot, and had escaped under cover of night. The canyon trail had been treacherous, but it was the only route that would confound the trackers. They'd not given up. They'd come after him. He had holed up in an outcropping of rocks and shot two of them, one who crept up on him not twenty feet away, and another who foolishly exposed himself from behind his rock cover. Then he was shot.

There were still three left when the snow started. Beautiful snow. It had erased the marks of his passing, wiped the earth clean. With two wounded and possibly dead, the remaining three pursuers would never chance entering the canyon in a blizzard. The blizzard and the canyon itself would probably kill him and them too, if they followed. They had not known how desperately he would push on, how he had willed himself to survive in the worst of weather on a treacherous trail. They had not known what a powerful animal he rode. And now that the snows had come, the canyon was sealed until spring. He was on the other side. Pursuit was no longer possible.

Wendell Morgan lay his head back against the pillows and closed his eyes. All he wanted to do was sleep.

Joey put his hand on the muscular arm.

"Mister, you hungry?"

Wendy Morgan opened his eyes, "S'all right, boy, later."

Quietly, Joey walked over to the fire. He bumped a log with a poker and watched the sparks leap up the chimney. Then he looked at the sleeping form of his mother. He was brimming with questions he wanted to ask her, but she was so still. Where was his dad? He could ask him if he were home. He dressed himself in his denim pants and shirt, tugged on his tiny boots, and walked to the door. Someone had left the door unbarred, maybe his dad was home and had risen early and gone out to check the animals. Joey heaved at the heavy door, which swung back slowly, and looked out.

Snow was everywhere, about two to three feet deep on the flats and drifted deeper, much deeper, against the buildings. Some flakes were still coming down and the sky glowed a deep, gunmetal gray. Joey loved the snow. This was the stuff you could mould and build and throw and roll around in. It acted on him like a powerful magnet. Out the door he went, not even looking back to close it. A narrow path had been cleared across the yard to the stable and Joey stepped out. His progress was slow: he marvelled at the sheer whiteness, picked it up in his bare hands, felt it, tasted it, studied the individual crystals. Gradually, he crossed the yard in short, careful steps, always very careful of sliding or falling because of his weakness.

At the barn, Bo was forking hay to the cow and Blazer. Joey ran to his dad and threw his arms around his legs. The big man stopped what he was doing and tousled the boy's hair.

"Daddy, Daddy!"

Bo quietly stroked the boy's head.

"I'm here, son. Came back last night."

Joey already knew. He saw the other horse. The mare was rested now, awaiting her generous portion of hay and she thrust her fine emblazoned face over the partition. Joey hobbled up - he had never seen such a beautiful horse - but at his sudden movement, she shied back.

"She has to get used to us, son. I don't think she's been around people all that much. Pretty, isn't she? Come on over here and get a closer look."

With slow, even movements, Bo lifted the log that barred the stall entrance. He would soon need a real door - this animal was smart and would too easily learn how to slip her nose under the bar and escape. She could produce all sorts of trouble loose inside the barn. He would start on the door tomorrow. Now the mare faced them squarely, backed up into the far corner of the stall, watching. She snorted when Joey walked in.

"Just introduce yourself boy. She'll come around more and more each day. You don't force a lady like this."

"Is she afraid of me, Dad?"

"No, keep your hands low, like this," and he stretched out a hand palm up. The mare approached warily.

"She just has to build her trust. Takes time." He nudged the small boy forward toward the waiting horse.

Joey offered a hand. The mare sniffed and moved closer, less threatened by the boy's small size, but wary of his jerky movement. Because Joey was weak, he seemed gentle. He leaned back against the partition logs. She would get used to him.

At the house, Nan woke up groggily. She had dark circles under her eyes and had not really slept soundly until near dawn. Carefully, she dusted the wrinkles from yesterday's dress and pushed the unruly wisps of hair back behind her ears. After all, they had a guest in the house. She lifted a pot from the hearth, ready to start breakfast, when she noticed the man on the bed. He was breathing evenly and seemed to be more asleep than unconscious.

Had the fever broken? She put her hand to his brow. Wendy Morgan tensed and opened his eyes.

Nan felt the need to explain. "You were shot. You had a fever. I took out the bullet."

"Ma'am?" Wendy hesitated, uncomprehending.

"You were shot," she repeated, "here," pointing to the shoulder bandage, "and here." She indicated his side.

His brown eyes flicked downward. Then they fastened on the strange woman. He thought back to the boy and to the man on the mountain - this must be the mother and the wife. She had a calm, oval face, with blue eyes and soft brown hair. She was smiling slightly and looked faintly amused.

He shifted his shoulder and gasped in pain, embarrassed at his display of weakness in front of this woman.

"You're laughing at me." He looked directly into her bright blue eyes.

"No," she looked straight back at him, "You hurt badly, but you won't admit it. And you'll hurt more. We've nothing here for the pain," she hesitated, "but we'll do all we can to keep you comfortable." She placed her hand on his good shoulder. "You will survive, you know, and I'm very glad for that."

She smoothed his pillow. His lips closed in a firm, thin line. His teeth were tightly clenched but he wasn't complaining. This man had endured pain before. He closed his eyes again but she knew he would not sleep. For the next few days he would feel the sting of those bullets many times, like a malignant fiend poking and probing and never letting him rest. He would probably lapse into merciful unconsciousness again and hallucinate.

She wondered what kind of dreams a man like this would have. Would he dream of his youth and his longings? Would he dream of his efforts that failed or succeeded? Wendell Morgan was an odd name. Where was his home? Did he have one or was he just another drifter, content to ride on to the next mountain on the horizon? And who had ambushed him and why had he been shot?

The water was boiling now and she added the rolled oats. Breakfast was usually some soft porridge of mashed grains along with slabs of ham or bacon, a loaf of sourdough bread, cups of steaming, black, frontier coffee, and warm milk. She laid out wooden bowls for Joey and Bo and looked toward the stranger.

He would need to drink to keep the fever down, then to eat. He was resting now, and as much as she hated to disturb him, he had to replenish his strength. She filled a mug with water, went over and touched his arm. He stiffened and looked back at her.

"You must be thirsty. I'll help you up. Come on and drink this." When he started to move, she thrust her free left arm under the pillow, cradling his head. The movement was automatic but when, suddenly, his whole body arched in a spasm of pain, his head thrust against her breast, and she was holding him as a lover would her most beloved. The spasm passed. He drank from the mug and sank back down.

The episode had shaken Nan. Even in his worst moments, she felt a strength in this man and a need. It had been a long time since she had felt that in any man. At least the long winter months would be less lonely. She walked back to the hearth to finish preparing breakfast.

Wendy Morgan followed her with his eyes as she moved about the cabin. He was very weak, and the sight of this woman's lithe and graceful movements eased his confused thoughts. He watched her pull Joey's boots off after he and Bo came clattering through the door. He watched her spoon out portions of oatmeal and slice the ham. He was aware of her hands as she wiped them on a corner of her apron, those same hands that had cleaned his own wounds and cooled his brow. She offered him more water, and he drank, this time less painfully. And he chewed a bit of the ham. The boy brought him food and straightened his blanket. He was definitely her boy, same pale brown hair, same blue eyes, same tilt to his nose and depth to his eyes. Some of his movements almost paralleled hers, but less gracefully and with a certain masculine deftness. But there was something different, too, about the boy. Wendy was too tired to pinpoint exactly what that was.

Bo sat quietly on the bench eating bread, jam and sipping coffee.

"Nothin' in the traps yesterday. Animals all holed up waitin' for the storm. Nothin' to hunt either."

Nan withheld comment. There were still two deer left in the smokehouse and a haunch of elk that Ludlam had given them when they had rescued that mongrel from the wolf pack. Fool dog was ready to take on four of them to protect a skunk he had killed. Nan had simply fired two warning shots over their heads. The gunfire and the scent of man were enough to make them scatter fast. But that old hound would not leave his kill. He had lived wild for too long. She had returned him to Tom, proud as a new groom sweeping his bride over the threshold, with a mouthful of skunk. She giggled at the memory. After that, they had all needed a good bath, and it had taken four washes to get the smell out of her clothes. Still, Tom had been grateful and had brought them meat from his kill, the most welcome gift he could think of.

But this was just the start of winter, and sooner or later they would need meat. Bo would have to go after it.

"Weather's clearing. I'll go see to the barn. Chores to do." He went out again. Nan nodded and let him go.

CHAPTER 3

The sun came out by noon and spread a sheen of silver across the snow. Joey went out to play and came in for lunch crinkle-eyed and almost blinded by the brightness. Bo turned out the two horses. The mare kicked up the snow, nuzzled it, and nipped at poor old Blazer. Old Blazer humped his back and let fly his two rear hooves in her direction. He missed, but he was feeling very spry. That ugly mongrel of Tom's showed up again and chased both horses, yapping at their hocks until the mare almost caught him broadside with a flashing hind hoof. He yelped, ran off to find an easier target, stole Joey's hat and one glove, and knocked him over into two feet of snow. Joey came screaming into the cabin. Wendy was the first to see him covered with snow from head to toe. It was the first time Wendy had laughed as he struggled from his bed to brush the snow from Joey's shoulders with his good hand. Joey wiped his tears from his eyes and stripped off his wet clothing. The dog had only been trying to tease. Wendy had tried to explain.

"I hate Joker!" was all Joey said.

Wendy didn't argue. Tomorrow, maybe, Joey'd understand. But he wondered why the boy had been knocked down so easily.

Nan went out to the small corral and watched the horses. It was the first good look she'd had of the mare. She was standing there in awe when Bo walked up.

"Pretty, isn't she?"

"Like a picture."

"I been thinkin'," and he hesitated, looking over at his wife out of the corner of his eye, forming in his simple mind what he thought her reaction should be, "Wonder who he is...how a drifter like him could come up with a horse like that. Only people have bloodstock like this one is that Meachum outfit or outlaws. Least, the only people I know." There was a turbulence building inside him and yesterday's concern for this wounded man out on the mountain turned to vague suspicion here in his own home.

"What do you mean, Bo?" Nan looked back at him with a tinge of apprehension in her brown eyes. "You think he's a thief?"

"Well, he was comin' through that Deer Creek Canyon, and we all know who lives on the other side. He got shot up pretty bad. Somebody was chasin' 'im for a powerful reason."

"Bo you're accusing him of stealing."

Bo stood there, elbows spread on the top rail, chin cupped in his hands. He stared straight ahead.

"Yeah, horse stealin'."

Nan knew what that meant. Horse and cattle rustling was a hanging offense. If they were caught harboring a horse thief, they could be treated to the same drastic fate. At the very least, their reputation as a hard-working, honest, and neighborly family could be ruined.

"Let's go ask him." She whirled around and started back to the house. Bo shrugged and followed, knowing the stranger would only deny it.

Joey was playing with sticks from the wood bin and Wendy Morgan was propped up on two feather pillows when she flung back the door. He shivered at the sharp gust of arctic air that flooded the room. This was not the calm and soothing woman who had eased his pain. This was a determined and forceful personality who knew exactly what was required of the moment. Bo stumbled in behind her.

"Mr. Morgan," she began, "my husband thinks you stole that horse."

Bo gaped wide-eyed at her boldness. To accuse a man openly of stealing a horse meant a sure challenge, very likely a gun duel. It was the worst blot on his good name short of shooting him in the back. Joey stopped playing, sensing the gravity of his mother's words.

Wendy Morgan's face blanched. Never had he been accused of a crime in his life. His instinct was to draw a gun, but his guns were stashed in the far corner of the room and he was very weak. He couldn't reach for his gun and he didn't want to, not in front of this lady. Lady, yes, that was what she was. She had strength and dignity, and she had brought him back from near dead. She deserved a true answer. But her husband, as far as Wendy was concerned, deserved a gun duel for drawing such impulsive conclusions. "Ma'am, that's my horse. Just look at her brand. You haven't seen a T-bar in these parts. My Pa and me we registered that brand and raised her and her dam, and a bunch of others in Wyoming. My Pa, he was sergeant at Fort Laramie, charged with training remounts. Every once in a while, he'd get a good one and he'd get permission from Colonel McTigue to breed them. You can wire the Fort from Red Lodge if you like. The Colonel isn't there any more, but Major Belden'll remember us."

Nan faced him squarely. "And where's your father?"

"Dead." His eyes held her gaze.

Bo came up beside her, chewing his lip. "Likely story, no one rides a prize like that, leastwise not through Deer Creek in the dead of winter."

"The dead of winter only just started." Morgan had the strength to defend himself.

"Convenient, eh? Hide your tracks real well. No posse'll chase you through a storm like that." Bo pivoted on one hip and stalked out into the snow. He'd had the last word, but he was annoyed that Morgan could speak up so well for himself, make him look light-brained in front of his wife. He was beginning to wish he'd let the man freeze out there in the canyon. Could have grabbed the horse and nobody the wiser.

Nan stood in the doorway holding Wendy's gaze.

"You believe me ma'am?" He hunched his shoulders and winced. "I want you to believe me, ma'am, but there's no way I can prove it. Pa died. I'm here looking for a place of my own with some good pasture. Gonna find who took my stock and get them back, a prime stallion and more mares. That mare had more heart than all the rest. She just kept goin' and we outran them all." He paused. "Wire Laramie. Ask Phil Belden about Tooker Morgan. That's my Pa. It's the truth. I'm not lying."

"Mr. Morgan," Nan began, "my husband is frequently very quick to judge. As for me, I want to believe you. You sound sincere.

You look honest. But if you'll forgive me, I will reserve the right to wire Laramie and this Major...what did you say his name was?"

"Belden, ma'am."

"Yes..." she hesitated, "meanwhile, you are still a guest in this house, and Joey seems to like you."

"Thank you, ma'am."

Just then, Bo clomped back in, picked up his rifle, and started back out. He kept his eyes on the floor.

"Got to check the trap lines." He walked out.

Joey broke the stillness in the room. "Mr. Morgan, I believe you," he said bravely.

Bo walked out to the barn. Out of habit, he threw a saddle over old Blazer and started to pull the cinch. The old horse's swayed back seemed to dip even more from its weight. Embarrassed and jealous, Bo just wanted to get away. Trap lines were an excuse. The snow wasn't slippery, just deep. The horses had kept their footing, kicked, and bucked all afternoon in the corral. You could travel safely. The wind had whipped the surface smooth on the ledges and flats and a good horse could manage a trip to town as long as he stayed out of the canyons.

Bo's thoughts focused - a good horse. He stopped what he was doing. The mare, rested and fed, stood quietly in the next stall. He could borrow the mare. After all, Morgan wouldn't be riding for quite a while and that fine animal would get out of shape. He took the saddle from Blazer and placed it carefully on her muscular back. She was eager to get out and tugged him through the open doors. He mounted and together they headed out across the flats.

The going wasn't bad. The wind had died almost completely and the noon sun was at its zenith. Bo would never have attempted Deer Creek Canyon, but this road, the long way around into Red Lodge, was easily passable. The mare's long, sure stride swallowed the miles and soon he had covered a good half of the ten miles into town. Gradually, he mustered his thoughts and brought his shredded feelings under control. He formed in his mind a purpose for the trip. He would go to Red Lodge. He would send that wire. Nan would see that he was really only thinking of their welfare. And so he rode on, the bright red horse casting a handsome shadow on the new-fallen snow.

CHAPTER 4

$\mathbf{H}$arv Meachum pulled up. His horse stumbled on the frozen ground. Slim Halloway and the Indian reined in behind him. There were three of them left. Of the five men who had started the chase, one was dead in the brush behind Bleeker's Rock and Tag Meachum they'd left alive, gunshot and probably half frozen by now. The two extra horses waited with him about five miles back down the trail. "Time to quit, boys. Canyon'll git 'im, most likely. Hair-brained kid, going off down the Deer Creek like that, in the snow. Damn horse'll probably slide right off the rim."

His two companions looked at him and nodded. Harv Meachum was a big man, the oldest of the Meachum brothers, which, in itself, carried its store of prestige in and about Red Lodge, Montana. He was also a man of very real physical strength, six-foot-four in his stockings and weighing about 260 pounds. He rode a huge bay mustang gelding of close to seventeen hands. His friends used to say that the horse was part Percheron and that only a workhorse could carry the man. But they never said such a thing to his face,because Harv Meachum only laughed at his own jokes. His sense of humor did not match his size. He was, however, a man of big ambition. When old man Meachum had come to the territory in 1868, he had brought along his six sons. Harv was twenty years old, and Tag, the youngest, was six. The old man, a southern aristocrat, or so he claimed, from Lexington, Kentucky, was long on pride and short on temper. An avowed Confederate, his prime bluegrass pastures had maintained as fine a herd of Kentucky thoroughbreds as existed south of the Mason-Dixon Line. During the war, cavalry requisitions had devastated his finest stock. But the old man was no less a gentleman than he was a horse trader.

He rounded up his best yearlings together with his six sons and sent them to find new pastures to the west. They crossed the Mississippi at St. Louis and stayed with fellow southern sympathizers in Missouri, near St. Joe, during the bitterly cold winters of 1866 and 1867. Then they moved farther west. And Harv matured here among southern sympathizers who had lost all to the whims of war. He resolved early to get it all back and more.

At first, old Meachum had stayed behind, trying to hold on to his land and rescue what shreds were left of his livelihood. Finally, in the summer of 1867, he scraped together what funds he could from the sale of his property and came on to join his boys in Missouri. He would start over out west. Together with the horses, now valuable and saleable three-year-olds, and some five hundred head of cattle acquired along the way, they crossed the plains.

They settled a stretch of grassy foothills just north and east of the Yellowstone. This was Indian country but there were ancient burials there, so the native Crows stayed away. The Meachums held their customary range tenaciously, sometimes by agreement, sometimes by force. Everyone thought the irascible old man was building his plantation all over again. In fact, that's just what Harv intended. It was Harv who was doing the building.

No one dared ask the good Colonel why those homesteaders moved out so quickly just a few years before the Northern Pacific railroad arrived, or why the Crows let Meachum cows feast freely on the rich reservation grasses, or why the Indian lands were suddenly appropriated and shrunk to half their former size, to great Meachum benefit. And nobody ever asked him how his four teen-aged sons had managed to survive such a cruel war when so many other southern families had lost their sons. Anyone who owned such beautiful horses was a man of substance and beyond reproach, no matter where he came from. The past remained unquestioned. The Meachums thrived. Harv carried on.

The surveyors came later, looking first for a way around Granite Peak to route the railroad, then for coal to fuel the railroad. Meachum land was covered with it, and the family grew richer by the minute. Old Meachum was a politician, brought up in plantation salons. Horse dealing had taught him how to sell rice to a Kansas wheat farmer. He could bluff the smoothest riverboat gambler. He could harness his temper like a mule team to an ore wagon when he wanted. Whatever he said was sure to please at least on the surface, but his deeds often contradicted what he said. Harv handled the killings and the hazings, and Harv hired other men. The Colonel remained comfortably proper behind the walls of his rambling ranch house. Then he died.

Harv, as the eldest son, took over the sprawling Meachum ranching operation and budding mining interests. For ten years he had consolidated his father's far-flung holdings, but he was not nearly as discreet. Harv was brutal and direct. Idolized by his younger brothers, he was accustomed to getting what he wanted, and getting it promptly. The very day Old Meachum died, he dismissed all hands whose loyalty was even mildly suspect. Even old retainers who had been with the family back east, like Jerry McGowan, his father's cook, and sixty-year-old Mrs. Gertrude Simpson, who had endured the grueling trip west and kept house for his father ever since his arrival in old Coulson, before Red Lodge ever existed, had to leave. She had started the three youngest on their reading and writing, and had probably accommodated the old man in more intimate ways.

Harv hired gunmen in their stead. Then, like a hound tracking coon, he began expansion of the family ranch. It was fast becoming an empire. Honest homesteaders, many of whom were immigrants who spoke little English, cowed easily. First, two barns burned. The homesteads happened to lie between two Meachum claims. The owners had been absent at the time and there were no witnesses. But many people who held land between or near Meachum holdings left for uncontested claims farther west. A few diehards were found dead, all victims of convenient accidents.

Zeb Heidelberger fell from his buckboard on the way into town through Boulder Basin. He must've landed head first on one of the very boulders that the basin was named for and lay there for days, unconscious, until the wolves got him. They found him after two weeks.

Tink Crowley simply disappeared. He left home early one morning to check some trap lines and never was seen again. Even his horse never came home. Rumors started that the two of them, horse and rider had slipped on a rock slide and fallen off a ledge. But no one knew which ledge. He left behind no children, a widow whose shape could compete with the best of barroom nudes, and his farm, prime gamma grass pasture that bordered George Meachum's canyon corral, where he was trying to mate a newly-imported Kentucky thoroughbred stallion with mustang mares. Mares in foal needed more grass and water than his little canyon could supply.

The next brother was Moses. Mose, only a year younger than Harv, had spent his youth in the shadow of the dominant older men. Mose Meachum was a sickly youth who had depended on his more powerful brothers to fight his battles for him. Several inches shorter than Harv and thin, but with powerfully muscled shoulders, he still was not a small man. He had a pale, scrawny look with narrow appraising eyes that peered from under bony brows and squinted from a suntanned and wind-cracked cowman's face. He'd somehow overcome the coughing and wheezing that kept him abed many times when the family had first arrived - the clean dry mountain air would do that for a man - but now he clenched a grimy corncob pipe perpetually between his teeth. There was still a dependence within him. He was a scheming, careful man with a canny intelligence and an innate sense of self-preservation that went unnoticed by his brothers. Mose Meachum did what he was told, and he was usually told by Harv and George, but he resented it.

George Meachum was a handsome man. Tall and broad-shouldered, he was muscular but not brutish like his older brother. His hair was sandy blond and so was the drooping handlebar moustache that he kept meticulously trimmed and combed. His skin was bronzed and smooth. But his best feature by far was his eyes. They were a deep liquid brown and they seemed to have a pleading quality, like those of a puppy looking for a treat. He dressed himself carefully in fine suits, kid gloves, string ties, and expensive planters' hats ordered from St. Louis. When he pulled on the brim to tip his hat over those piercing eyes, women found it very hard to say no to George Meachum. And Harv Meachum decided that the neighborly thing to do was to send George Meachum calling, and so ease the pain of the grieving widow Crowley.

No one knows what kind of promises Tink Crowley made to his intended when he asked her to marry him, but, Irishman that he was, they were probably full-blown with velvet and gold leaf. Mrs. Brenda Crowley was a very appealing woman. Many a man must have promised her comfort and leisure, but Tink had struck gold. It was a wonder that she had believed him. But she had come east from San Francisco to the wilds of Montana to marry him and he had spent the very last of his diggings on the biggest blowout of a wedding Red Lodge had ever seen. The whole population along Rock Creek was invited and they all came from miles around. Then the happy couple had retired to a 160-acre homestead like everyone else, and Brenda found out too late that she had to work right alongside her husband to make the farm pay.

She'd already decided that this was not the way she intended to spend the rest of her life when, suddenly, Tink was gone and George Meachum was calling. No one recorded how often he visited or how long he stayed, but the two of them were robust, attractive, and free, and the matrons of Red Lodge made them the nectar of backyard gossip. Tales of orgies flourished. Brenda Crowley cared not a whit what they said. Promptly, she abandoned the farm, came into town, and married George Meachum, no questions asked, and with the full-blown blessing of Harv. That cemented the Meachum claim to the Crowley homestead. After that, the Meachum name inspired an unspoken fear. Harv Meachum had never been crossed. And now the railroad needed the coal that his lands produced. He had powerful friends all along the line and even in Washington. He ruled Park County.

Then there were the twins, Dancer and Gabe. Dancer was a nickname for Daniel, because he was the only musical member of the family and drove his father and all his brothers crazy with his constant rhythmic tapping and footwork to match. Harv and George hated it, but he was their kin. Once Dancer had almost run off with one of those theater troupes that was passing through to entertain the miners. He would have been a natural on stage, easy with people and he really did have a natural talent and passable good looks. Still, no one could beat George for looks. Dancer's sandy blond hair wasn't quite so blond; his jaw was square but without the cleft; his moustache drooped and his shoulders slouched, but just a little, and his eyes, although blue and friendly, lacked that piercing depth that made women melt. With the ladies of Red Lodge, those who could let their baser feelings show, George always came first. Dancer was a near second, but still second. Dancer learned early to give way to George and Harv, except when he sang, and then his deep melodious baritone held everyone enthralled. Harv and George had actually encouraged him to go with the theater people, but he was young then and didn't have much of the ambition of his older siblings. Home was too comfortable, and he had a girl he was seeing down at the Elkhead Saloon. So he stayed.

Gabriel, his twin, was big and broad like Harv. Gabe had sandy hair and brown eyes like his twin, two ugly scars down the side of his left cheek, and a nose that swerved to the right side of his face. In profile he was not at all bad looking, but full-faced, everything seemed out of place, as if some huge fingers had crudely destroyed the symmetry nature had intended. Gabe resented his ugliness, the result of a fall from a corral rail when he was just seven, into the pen of some wild yearling bulls. He had pulled himself out, but not until hooves and horns had done their gruesome work. Now, he refused to work cattle. Gabe Meachum was a fist fighter even before he was a gunfighter. His face showed it. But it also earned him the respect of the burly miners who worked the local coal deposits. He was mine foreman and crew organizer. It was a shoestring operation but not without potential. The coal had to be packed by mule to Laurel and that cut profits. But the railroad was getting closer. George kept him informed. Meanwhile, as the nearest source of coal for this stretch of the Northern Pacific, the mines ran nicely in the black.

Then there was Tag, their baby brother, who was twenty-four years old and younger than the twins by eight years. Taggert Meachum was the one person who could inspire something like love in the bosom of tough, hard Harv.

CHAPTER 5

Harv swung his big horse abruptly around and jogged down the narrow trail. Let the horse thief die. For the moment, he was stopping the chase. Two men were down. Snow was blowing and it was bitter cold.

"Got to pick up Tag, bring him home," he was muttering under his breath to his horse. The footing was slippery, but the ground was not frozen and some traction was still possible. He dismounted about a mile farther down.

Slim Halloway and the Indian followed a few paces behind. Tag Meachum was lying, facing the trail, against an outcrop of rock. The two horses stood ground-hitched about ten feet to his right. Their ears perked when they heard the approach of the three horsemen.

Harv was the first to reach his brother. "I'm here boy, we'll git you home." Slim and the Indian rode up as Tag shivered convulsively.

"Got to warm him first, Harv. The boy's cold." Harv grunted. The Indian dismounted and started to gather kindling. Slim untied his bedroll. He walked over to Tag. Harv was still talking.

"You listenin', boy? You can make it home. We'll warm you up, but we got to pack on outta here. Grady's dead. We gotta git you home."

"Harv, you can't." It was Slim talking. Harv looked up at the scrawny older man. He didn't like being crossed. But there was no threat in Slim Halloway, either in his raspy voice or in the casual way he simply stood there chewing his wad of tobacco, gazing at Tag. Then he took his bedding and quietly laid it over Tag. It was only a flesh wound and Tag had been bleeding, but the real threat was frostbite. The Indian had already started to build a small fire and together they pulled the younger brother closer in. Gradually, Tag stopped trembling. Slim moved back toward his horse to get his cup and melt some water for the wounded man. Deliberately, he turned his back on Harv, knowing that on at least one occasion Harv had shot a man in the back, a man who had crossed him. But Slim had worked for the Meachums for close to fourteen years now, and he was good with a gun and loyal to his employer. He also knew that there used to be a certain bond between Tag and Harv Meachum. It was a pity that Harv had never learned to express his gentler feelings. Slim had watched Harv squelch those feelings. He had seen Harv Meachum grow tougher and gruffer all those years. Now there was no changing him. Lucky for Tag that before those fourteen years, Slim had spent six with the U.S. Cavalry at Fort Laramie. No Cavalryman would ever leave his fellow hurt and alone in the wilderness, prey to the wolves and weather. But Harv would.

Slim pressed the cup of warmed melted snow to Tag's lips. Harv still stood close by, watching. Suddenly, the Indian appeared from behind the rock with an armload of dried branches and spruce boughs. He said nothing, but calmly started to build the skeleton of a rude shelter near the fire.

Alone in his decision to return immediately, Harv picked up the reins of the dead man's horse. He pulled himself up on his own big bay.

"I'll bury Grady on the way in," was all he said, and he leaned forward, giving his own horse his head and pulling the riderless horse behind him. Slim Halloway and the Indian watched him go.

Harv pulled up next to the contorted body of Grady. He looked down callously at the glaring eyes and twisted legs. One of the many young men of the wilder west, Grady had a natural talent for a fast draw. He had lived by his gun. Harv had hired him for his gun. And that was how he died.

The body was now deep-frozen in the position of its last breath. Harv relieved the corpse of its two guns and belt half-full of ammunition and rolled it over until it was hidden beside a big spruce deadfall.

"Waste of time trying to dig a hole. Need a couple a miners an' a double jack to break through that ground." He mounted up and rode away, thinking about how he would tell the hands why he had come back alone, without Tag, whom he'd left wounded, without

Grady, whom he had left dead, and leading an empty horse. At least he had the horses. Boys would run them back to George's herd.

Harv Meachum rode right up to the barn door and yelled for the stableman. Willie, stablehand and blacksmith to the Meachum riding stock, swung back the heavy doors to let Harv ride right into the wide aisle. Willie was fat, taciturn, and generally disagreeable, but he knew his job and there was not a finer shoer west of the Black Hills. Promptly, he took the two horses, handed Harv a lantern, and led the horses into the stalls.

Harv stomped through the powder snow to the ranch house door. He stepped in and brushed the flakes from his shoulders and hat. Mose sat on a settle by the fire, pipe clenched between thin lips. He wheezed and looked up at his brother.

"Where's Tag?"

"He caught one up by Blecker's Rock. Slim and the Indian are bringing him in."

"Oh. Not dead, I hope?"

Harv shook his head.

Mose was leaning back resting his head on the leather-backed chair by the fireplace. His legs were stretched out and his feet were propped on the dull brass fender. He chewed the end of a smoldering pipe. He was studying his brother, waiting. A portrait of their father glared down from above the mantel. He would have to tell Mose what happened. Harv knew the story of the escape would be all over the bunkhouse by dusk. Mose was tight with the gun hands. "You catch the bastard that shot him?"

"We chased him bleedin' halfway up the Deer Creek. Canyon'll finish him even if we didn't."

"Right." He hesitated. "What you gonna tell the boys?"

"Tell 'em? I'll tell 'em he's dead in the Deer Creek, if you don't tell 'em first. If he don't bleed to death, he'll freeze. If he don't freeze, that horse will slide right off the rim."

"Reckon." That was all Mose had to say. He went back to chewing on his pipe, his breath audible and even. The gun hands were tough, especially that kid from Texas named Hendl, friend of Grady's. A man was only surely dead when you walked up to him and put a bullet between his eyes. The gunmen would know that even though he'd been shot, Morgan was alive and riding away, when last seen. Hendl would know. And one of their own was dead. They'd miss him. Big Harv would have to do some commandeering if he was to keep everybody in line. In the morning, Harv Meachum rose early. Today, he would have to convince his hired gunmen of the success of yesterday's pursuit. He dressed in a fine dark grey suit, white shirt, and string tie. Harv Meachum disliked fancy clothes, unlike his father who always stood out, tall and straight, immaculately tailored, a tribute to his years in uniform. But Harv Meachum had learned the value of a prosperous appearance, and of maintaining his position as cattle baron, mining mogul, and head of Red Lodge's wealthiest family. Growing up, he had bullied his way to family dominance. Today, he still commanded. His was the largest outfit of hired guns in the territory. There were those who were hired for other skills, like old Luke, the blacksmith and stable hand, and Slim Halloway, who could break the most hot-headed thoroughbred. Most had at least a smattering of horse and cattle sense, but all could shoot fast and hit what they were aiming at. They were a very tough crew. There had been bunkhouse brawls and shootouts right there on the ranch. Men had died. The old Colonel would never have permitted such behavior among his troops. But Harv's guns and Gabe's fists had always bested the worst of them. Today would be no different.

Harv clomped down the oak staircase across the hall and into the dining room. A big cowboy breakfast was spread, sweet rolls, a big loaf of sourdough bread, a steaming pot of hot black coffee. Gabe, Mose, and Dancer were already there. When Harv entered, they all looked up. Harv pulled back his chair at the head of the table and clapped twice. Ruthie, the Indian cook, came in carrying a platter of eggs, refried beans, and home fries. She set it in front of the men and retired promptly and quietly into the kitchen.

Breakfast proceeded like a eastern company's executive board meeting. Only George and Tag were missing: Tag for obvious reasons; George, because he was living in Billings with his new wife. No one missed Tag. He was only included because he lived there. Harv would have to talk to George later. George had a very cordial relationship with the railroad directors, and was always included in the family plans.

Gabe spoke first. "Mose says you got a horse thief yesterday, but he got Grady first, an' shot Tag."

"Fool kid, he was drivin' off some of George's prime stock. We brought most of 'em back, but he lit out down the Deer Creek ridin' a prime sorrel, two white stockings in front and a blaze."

"Shame to lose prime stock," that was Dancer, "You thinkin' a gettin' it back?"

Harv could become very impatient trying to explain things to

Dancer that would have been obvious to anyone else. "Dance, you look out the window this mornin'?"

Dancer turned and stretched out a long arm to pull back the lace curtain. A slice of dazzling white light penetrated the room.

"Yeah, snow. You ever ride into the Deer Creek in the snow? And blizzard snow at that! Canyon'll be brimfull this mornin'. Likely ain't nothin' left to get back after the Deer Creek in a storm." This was Gabe talking. He stuffed a bite of eggs and home fries in his mouth and added, "What about Tag? He didn't come in yet."

"He will. Slim and the Indian are nursin' him. He'll mend, but somebody ought to teach that kid how to shoot. Too much book learnin'll get him killed someday."

"You gonna tell the boys what happened to Grady? Hendl and Murph will want to know." Mose was asking.

"Yeah, after breakfast, and maybe we should give Grady a big send-off, make the boys feel important, readin' from the Good Book an' all. Have to keep the coffin closed though. I ain't diggin' him up. Dancer, you git into town, you know the preacher. You oughtta be able to fix things real proper. Tell 'im how Grady was a first class hand and how sorry we all are to lose 'im. 'An tell 'im there'll be money enough left over for an organ or even a stained glass window if he has a mind. All he has to do is recite his Bible." Harv, Mose, and Gabe were all thinking that this should be a simple enough job for Dancer.

Dancer finished his meal, pushed his plate away, and stood up. He was glad to have an excuse to leave. "I'll go saddle up."

"And take Hendl with you."

That would leave only Murph for Harv to deal with and make a suitable impression on Hendl. Those Texans always hung together and the others always followed their lead.

The other three were quiet until Dancer had gone out. Mose chewed his grub slowly like he chewed his pipe. He picked a rind of bacon from between his teeth with the pointed end of his knife. Finally, he grumbled, "Hendl should see Dancer gits his chore done. Better tell him to keep an eye out for that red horse." He stopped and waited until they were all staring his way, still casually picking his teeth. "Just in case."

"I just might do that." Harv snapped back.

Gabe said nothing, but decided to go with Harv when he talked to the hands.

They finished breakfast in silence.

CHAPTER 6

Back at Bleeker's Rock, Slim Halloway was thanking the Lord that if he had to get stuck in a blizzard with a wounded man, that he had the Indian to help. Nothing like an Indian for knowing how to live off the land, especially in winter. Just now the Indian had returned with a squirrel he'd killed. Not much, but better than jerked beef. The Indian had rigged quite a cozy shelter and fed Tag some shaman's brew that seemed to revive him. He bathed the bullet hole and packed it with fresh dry moss. Good man, the Indian. Tag's shoulder wound had bled freely. A little rest and warmth and a break in the storm, and they could head home tomorrow. But it would be a cold, cold night, and no Indian could improve on that.

In the morning, the youngest Meachum looked better. Slim rolled over and added a log to the fire. He'd left the log within arm's reach last night so he could stoke the fire without getting out of his bag. It was bitterly cold. The Indian's shelter had kept the snow from them and from their fire, but now the snow in the branches above the fire was starting to melt and drip. It was time to move. The Indian was already gone, probably scouting the way ahead to see how deep the drifts were and how best to avoid the stinging northwest wind. Just then the Indian returned, this time with two big snowshoe hares. He took out his knife and slit and cleaned the hares, slicing juicy slivers from the carcasses into the frying pan. Slim smiled.

"Couple a bites and you'll be chasin' grizzlies again."

Tag grinned, a good sign.

Slim reached for the frying pan and laid the rabbit fillets neatly side by side. The meat sizzled and cooked quickly. Its aroma revived Tag's appetite. With his good arm he took his portion and ate. Then he gulped a large mug of bitter coffee. He was feeling better, much better.

Tag Meachum was really a likable man. Shorter than his brothers by a few inches, he was still close to six feet in height. He had a wiry build, a thick crop of auburn hair, brown eyes, and the tanned complexion of a man who had lived a large part of his life out of doors. He had never really fought alongside the older Meachums. That was probably why he was lying on his back right now. He had never learned to fight and he had only vague memories of Missouri and no bitterness at the family's loss. Most of that had occurred before he had really matured enough to be considered a man, and he had been late maturing, attaining his full height at the ripe age of eighteen. He had spent his youth at the Meachum Ranch, doing boy's work, light work. He exercised the blooded saddle stock, ran errands, hayed and watered in the barn when he was needed, hung around the bunkhouse absorbing every phrase the more experienced hands uttered. And he read books. He had gone to school.

There were not very many books at the Meachum Ranch, but Tag, unlike his brothers, loved learning and had received daily instruction from Mrs. Simpson, his father's old retainer and housekeeper. His talent pleased his father, who knew that good brains were required for the success of any family enterprise. But that very same intelligence set him apart from Harv, Mose, and Dan, who were not so endowed. He could not escape the embarrassing designation of baby or wimp. Still, Mrs. Simpson had struck an effective partnership with the Colonel. Between them, they encouraged Tag, and Tag responded, because through learning, he could focus his beloved father's attentions on himself. Otherwise, as the youngest, he could not compete with Harv and his bigger and stronger brothers, since he had precious little of the physical toughness that old Meachum admired.

The Colonel placed orders for shipments of books from St. Louis and once even from New York, until the Meachum Ranch possessed one of the finest libraries west of the Mississippi. And Tag read them all. First came the classics, translations from the Latin and the Greek, works by Homer, Virgil, Pliny, and Caesar. Then there were batteries of lesser known works, histories, religious treatises and some philosophers, mostly English. There was a huge family Bible and an equally huge unabridged dictionary. The Colonel would have liked all his sons to have learned what this great wealth of printing contained, but only Tag complied. But then Tag, a slight child, and the little brother, was never quite included in the rowdier pursuits of the other five. And this worried the Colonel.

Tag was naive, ingenuous, and content to remain so. He had not gone along on the more violent undertakings, was not as keenly adept with a gun or as battle-wise and hardened as the rest of the clan. It was not really surprising that he was the first member of the family to have been wounded in one of these contests. In his ignorance, he had probably stuck his head out above the rock, trusting too much in the good will or clumsiness of his opponent, or in the immunity of youth, and gotten shot. At least it was not terribly serious. He was going to live. But he would be forever suspect by his brothers when under fire. The sun broke brightly over the horizon and warmed the earth.

"Leave now," said the Indian, who had gulped his breakfast in just a few bites and was saddling the horses, collecting all their meager belongings, making ready to break camp. Slim got Tag to his feet. He was a little weak, but he had suffered more from the cold and exposure than from the bullet. They mounted up and headed for home.

About half way there, Slim pulled up and quietly looked at Tag. It wasn't like Slim. Slim liked to talk. But for years, Slim had ridden alongside the Indian, a very private man.

"Lead on, Bull." He didn't question the redman's judgment.

Slim liked Tag, and remembered the old man's concerns for his youngest son. Tag's horse, knowing the quickest way to the barn and out of the freezing temperatures, started to pass Slim, but the Indian swung his horse to block the trail. He lead silently and they followed. But he stopped before they came within sight of the town.

"Mr. Meachum, I'm thinkin' you be better off in town for the time bein'." Slim looked back at Tag. The Indian had edged his horse into some cottonwoods at the side of the trail and had disappeared.

"That old preacher a yorn, he'd take you in," Slim hesitated, not wanting to explain his reasons entirely. "I'm thinkin' his house be in town an' near to the doctor an' all."

Tag, who had been gritting his teeth against the pain in his shoulder and the cold in his veins, looked blandly back at the older man. He was surprised. But he knew that Slim must have very good reasons for such a suggestion, reasons that at the moment, he was too tired to penetrate. And on the surface, Slim's remarks made sense. He needed a doctor.

He nodded his approval and they proceeded on down the road to town away from the ranch.

CHAPTER 7

Dancer Meachum, Bill Hendl, and the man they called Murph let their horses jog aimlessly into town. Bill Hendl, a twenty-three year old Texan, had signed on to the Meachum outfit at the same time as Grady (also a Texan) and was just as good, maybe better with a gun. Murph was a surly black Irishman from Kansas. A loner and close-mouthed, rumors trailed him. He was a dangerous man. He and Dan Meachum stopped at Parson Bowden's bungalow, surprised to find four horses out front at the hitch rail, one of them Tag Meachum's. Bowden answered their knock, explaining that Doc Zilka was tending to Tag. He'd be delighted to make the funeral arrangements, but right now he was busy. They rode on into Red Lodge to spend the afternoon at the Elkhead Saloon until the Doctor finished. The Indian disappeared into the hills, never eager to be spotted off the reservation. Custer's defeat was raw in the memory of most folks, no matter if he was a Crow whose relatives had warned Custer not to advance.

Now Red Lodge had been a cowpuncher's outpost up to a few years ago, a lonely little cabin on the stage route between Billings, Montana, and Meeteetsie, Wyoming, where stage drivers dropped the mail at the Meachum ranch for all the outlying settlers. Then the Northern Pacific Railroad arrived in Billings and then the town of Laurel, and rich coal deposits were discovered. Men worked hard, lonely hours, dripping with sweat in the stifling mines, and when they got paid, they played. Cowboys, on payday, grimy from weeks of dusty riding, joined the miners in wild nights of revelry, drinking, gambling, or out and out brawling. Rose McCartle's Elkhead Saloon was just one of the various establishments that catered to these needs.

When Dancer, Hendl, Murph, and Slim dismounted, there were a half dozen horses at the hitch rail, fuzzy ungroomed animals, hidden beneath the coarse matting of winter coats. And there was one sleeker animal, a big sorrel, who stood a good hand above the rest. But Dancer had his mind on a girl, and on an afternoon and evening and maybe a whole night with Rose's girls, so he only gave a peripheral look at the horse. Some vague worry kept tickling the back of his mind.

Slim had just come from chasing a "thief and murderer" and Bill Hendl had trailed with Grady for just shy of two years. He and Grady had worked together for a big Texas outfit near Mobeetie, when Hendl had gotten some liquor into him. He was a mild-mannered man when sober, but unreasonable and stubborn, even violent when drunk. There was an argument over the cards. Hendl drew faster, and this, with two other rumored instances of shootings in his past, was enough to saddle him with a gunman's reputation. He had to leave Texas. Grady, no amateur with a gun himself, stuck with his sidekick. Both of them had arrived in Montana, reputations in tact, and signed on with Big Harv Meachum for gun hand wages. Now Grady was dead and Hendl was a vengeful and unpredictable man.

Hendl looked hard at the horse, then at Slim who was staring straight ahead. But Bill Hendl's sharp eyes had glimpsed the few seconds of stark surprise that wrinkled the old man's face when first he had spotted that horse. Slim was a careful man, but not quite quick enough to fool Bill Hendl.

Dancer stepped up on the boardwalk and pushed through the swinging doors. Amelia Craven looked up from the blackjack table and smiled. He winked back, and reaching up with his right hand to tip his hat, he suddenly whipped it off and threw it at her. She ducked, squealed, and headed for the bar. A man always had to buy a girl a drink first.

Bill Hendl and Murph had not followed Dancer into the Elkhead. Hendl had spotted the big red horse immediately, dismounted, and stood, hat pulled over his eyes, a lanky form wrapped in the envelope of his sheepskin parka. He turned his back to the wind and pulled up the collar, but still did not go inside. That was the horse, the one the thief had ridden into Deer Creek Canyon, the thief who had shot Grady. Why didn't Slim Halloway speak up? Must be getting soft in his old age. No matter, he was going to find the man who was riding that horse. But first he needed a drink. Slim followed warily. Murph stayed outside.

Hendl went into the saloon quietly. He stood for a moment near the door and scanned the room with pale, intelligent, blue eyes. Smoke from the wood stove in the center of the room and from the pipes and cigarettes of the clientele made him blink. The saloon was crowded. The weather had driven cowboys and miners indoors. There were three ongoing poker games, mostly miners playing. "Miners," he thought, "who strike it rich quick and gamble it all and end up broke and start all over again...fools!" He, himself, was earning more than they were and his money was coming in steady and he was squirrelling it away. A gunman never foresaw his own gruesome ending. There was a crush two-men deep at the bar, mostly cowboys with a sprinkling of homesteaders, and they were drinking. Then there was a mixed group, cowboys and miners, over at the end of the thirty-foot bar, near a couple of tables, the piano, and the girls.

Dancer was with this group, well out of pistol range, and Hendl nodded to him as he elbowed his way through the crowd at the bar. He ordered whiskey. He downed it and clapped the shot glass back on the bar signalling the bartender for another. The bartender placed a bottle in front of him.

"You see the man who rode in on that big sorrel?"

The bartender knew Hendl was no stranger to liquor. He also knew who he worked for and why he was hired. And he had an idea of where Hendl was leading with this little chat. He answered with a question.

"You think I go outside in this weather?"

"Big horse, two white stockings in front, two in back."

"Mister, they can come in here struttin' like a pigeon or crawlin' like a worm. All I do is pour the drinks."

"Yeah, well the scum that's ridin' that horse is a thief. That there's Mr. George Meachum's horse." Hendl looked menacingly at the scruffy collection of men in the barroom. "An' the man who rides that horse shot my buddy, Matt Grady." He was nearly shouting.

The bartender eyed him carefully. Men were easing away from the bar. Conversation in the immediate vicinity had come to an abrupt halt. Accusing a man of horse-thieving was reason enough for drawing a gun. A murder accusation meant sure shootin'.

The bartender broke the silence. "Mister, you take your trouble outside. Then you an' that blizzard can stir up all you want."

An old grizzled cowpuncher from one of the poker tables had sidled up to Hendl. Slim Halloway had seen about enough bloodshed in the last two days, more than he had seen in his first thirteen years with the Meachums. He had just come from fetching Doc Zilka to the Bowden bungalow to tend to Tag, and he had watched Grady die. It had been a horrible ending, even for a gunman, Grady gasping for breath and gagging on his own blood. No one should have to suffer that much pain.

"Easy, Hendl," the old man's voice was grating but somehow soothing, and he was not afraid. "What's this about a horse. That there thief was gone yesterday in the Deer Creek. He ain't comin' back and neither is his horse. I saw 'im."

Hendl was grim, "That horse is out there at the hitch rail and you know it. I seen 'im and you seen 'im or we seen a ghost...Halloway, you old enough to know better. Ain't no such thing as ghosts. Only Injuns believe in ghosts."

"Well, then, let's go take another look." Slim knew Hendl was grieving in his own blind way for Grady and knew he was drinking. He could ease him away from the bottle, ease him outside to where Murph could get him back on his horse and out of town before he could no longer stand up.

He put a skinny arm around the younger man's shoulders and steered him toward the swinging doors. Murph was there but so was the sorrel horse, big and red, two white stockings on its forelegs and two more behind.

"That the horse we was chasin'?" Hendl phrased the question but he already knew the answer. Slim hesitated. He'd never been easy with words.

"It's her, but lotsa horses look alike." Slim had spent the good part of the previous day tracking that horse, studying not just the white stockings and blaze but the configuration of her body, the ripple of her muscles, her bone structure, and her way of moving. He remembered the confirmation of a horse the way some men remembered the proportions of a woman. Somehow that horse had come through the canyon even though Harv Meachum had declared it impossible, and Harv was an excellent tracker. This was the same horse right here in Red Lodge.

"Lotsa horses don't look like her, old man. I'm goin' back in there." Hendl was drunk, and he was mad. He shoved his way back to the bar and to his bottle. Tilting the bottle up to his whiskered lips, he took a long swig. Droplets of yellow whiskey trickled down his beard. Suddenly, he turned around, braced his back casually on the bar, and rested his two elbows on its rail, pulling his shoulders up and back, and exaggerating their width. His gun hand was free. "Who here rode in on that sorrel horse?" Nobody answered. Hendl persisted ever more loudly, "Whoever came in on that sorrel horse is a thief and a murderer." It was an ultimatum.

Slim did not go back to the bar but slipped quietly outside. He buttoned his parka, pulled on his gloves and hat and was walking across the street to his own horse. He was looking at his boot toes, preoccupied, when a shoulder brushed against him. The old man stumbled and caught himself. "Sorry," he mumbled almost instinctively.

Two bloodshot brown eyes squinted back at him almost as surprised as he was. The wind whipped a couple of strands of brownish hair across the stranger's tired face. He too, muttered an automatic apology through a wad of homespun scarf wrapped around his jaw. He continued on across the street, swung a set of saddlebags across the rump of the big sorrel horse, ran a hand down her neck, and climbed the two steps to the saloon door.

The encounter jolted Slim from his own musings enough to make him notice that this man didn't really resemble the man they had chased yesterday. And he certainly didn't look prosperous enough to own that horse. He could have sworn that the Indian had winged the thief, maybe twice, yet this man was walking briskly, obviously unhurt. Still, he was tending to the sorrel horse. Maybe Murph could figure it out. He was too old. He shook his head, trying to make some kind of sense out of the events of today and yesterday, when the stranger stepped through the door of the saloon. All Slim wanted was to avoid any more trouble, especially shootin' trouble.

"I ain't waitin' for Hendl this time. Or Murph," he muttered, unhitched his own mount, and rode away.

Bolen Fletcher had a lot on his mind, and but for this he probably never would have left the red horse standing out in the bitter cold. At least he could have hitched her across the street out of the wind as Slim had hitched his horse. Such a horse should be at the livery stable.

But Bo Fletcher was confused. He spent a wakeful night and a worrisome day and now that he was in town, he had second thoughts about having ridden that fancy horse. He was still angered and jealous of the care his wife had given Morgan. His disabled son, his wife's dutifulness, his struggling homestead, his debts, his dreams, and now this other man in his home, all these jostled together in his mind like marbles in a tin can. He wasn't himself, hadn't been himself in a long time. He wanted to go home, yet events at home disturbed him.

He looked at the swinging doors, stepped up and pushed his way through. Just one drink would make him feel better. He could relax, maybe talk to Nan, play with Joey again. The last thing on his mind was the big red horse.

Hendl had just issued his challenge for all to hear. Vaguely aware of some voice inside talking about a horse, Bo Fletcher stumbled three steps into the saloon. Cigar smoke made his eyes tear. It was dead silent. As he came in, all eyes focused upon him because his was the only movement in the room. "That's 'im. I seen 'im ride in." It was one of the miners, anxious to get the shooting over with and get back to his card game. Another whiskered player chimed in. "Yeah, me too, I seen 'im too."

"You got a gun mister? I don't draw on an unarmed man." The bold, drunken Hendl was looking at Bo, who was still blinking dumbly, trying to accustom his sleepy eyes to the indoor gloom. Bo had a gun - most western men always carried one - but it was half hidden under the folds of his parka. He was lowering his hand to unbutton the bulky parka. All Hendl saw was the movement of Fletcher's right hand. He drew and fired. The bullet took Fletcher in the center abdomen, a vicious wound at close range, tearing away his middle. Bo hunched in shock, suddenly aware of what was happening. Now his hand reached belatedly for his gun. He was bringing it up to aim when Hendl fired again. This time the bullet hit Fletcher in the chest, just below the collar bone. Coughing, Fletcher fired and fell sideways, spurting blood. His shot slammed into the floor.

CHAPTER 8

Joey had drawn aside the faded curtain at the cabin window when he heard a horse's soft patter on the packed snow. He had just glimpsed the mare jogging out of the yard and his father on her back. His mother was busy at the hearth and Wendy Morgan was asleep, so he kept his knowledge to himself. How many times before had he seen his father ride away?

The afternoon passed slowly. Joey went out to the barn. He enjoyed the company of the animals, and carried feed to Bessie and Blazer. But he did not linger in the yard in spite of the new-fallen snow for fear that the mongrel dog might come back. The afternoon was bright, even in the dusty barn, where the sun sent a splash of glittering light across the shadows through the big door. It was even warm, sitting there in the sun with the barn cats soaking up its warmth and rolling playfully on the dusty floor. As the afternoon wore on, Joey managed to milk the cow. He was slow and methodical, but his weakened touch was gentle and the cow cooperated. Simple tasks were tough for Joey, but he would compensate for his lack of strength by having his tools close at hand, and methodically and meticulously going about his work. He took great pride and joy in this.

Nan stayed in the house. Winter, for her was a time of household bustle. There were socks to darn, clothing to wash and bread to bake. She kept a pot of stew and a kettle of water warm on the wood stove and swept yesterday's accumulation of mud and melted snow from the raw plank floor. How she had insisted on that floor before the first winter - most homesteads were without them and virtually impossible to clean. And it was one more insulation against the winter cold.

Wendell Morgan slept for several hours. When he woke, she saw him following her with his eyes. Momentarily, she tensed, then ladled a cup of soup, carried it to his bedside, and lifted his head in her arm again to drink, just as she had the night before. He swallowed the broth eagerly now and took a few bites of the stew. Swallowing the stew was painful and he choked.

"I'll get you a pillow."

Nan slipped gracefully through the door to the next room for Joey's pillow. Morgan watched her dreamily. He had sensed the absence of her husband, although she had not mentioned it.

Just then, a cold gust blew in as Joey opened the door, carrying his pail of milk. Morgan shivered. Movement still hurt. Carefully, Joey placed the pail inside while he struggled to close the door.

"Sorry. Where's Mom?"

"In here," Nan called from the back room. "Mr. Morgan needs another pillow." She walked back across the room toward the sick bed, smiling. "And he would probably be warmer in the back room away from that door."

"Mom, Dad's gone again." Joey was biting his lip. He didn't want to seem the weakling in front of his new friend, Mr. Morgan.

Nan finished fluffing the down pillow and easing Morgan up higher in the bed, and began spooning him mouthfuls of soup. Morgan glued his eyes to the wall, a stranger embarrassed in the middle of another's family trials.

"I know, Joey. I know."

"And Mom, he didn't take old Blazer. He took Mr. Morgan's horse."

Nan stopped. A spoonful of soup splattered across Morgan's blanket.

"I'm sure he had a reason Joey."

"If he didn't, that's stealing, isn't it Mom?"

Silence hovered, a choking, smothering cloud.

"Joey, I told him to take the horse." It was Morgan, this stranger, in his feeble voice, permitting Nan to regain her composure and restoring Bo Fletcher's respectability in the eyes of his son.

The day wore on, Morgan sleeping fitfully between intense moments of awareness, watching the woman in the still afternoon, studying the worry lines at the edges of her eyes, the furrow when she wiped her brow, and even a tear that somehow escaped all her brave efforts to bolster herself and her son. She was waiting for the sound of hoofbeats on the snow, for a "Halloo!" from her man, the same deranged man who had brought him out of the storm and had accused him yesterday of theft. This man might have him arrested and hanged. If Bo came he would have to get away. He should try to escape and yet to where? Without a horse? Sick and in the snow? He had no choice but to stay and rest, and hope that her husband would not come home, to watch her wait and suffer. Something in him rebelled against letting this woman suffer, yet he had no choice.

About three o'clock, snow began to fall. He could just hear the faint rustle in the stillness as each flake settled on the cabin's roof. She waited. And no one came.

After Joey was asleep, she came to his bedside.

"You didn't tell him to take your horse. You couldn't have. I was always here." There was disappointment in her voice. But not with him.

"No ma'am, I didn't. But a boy needs his Pa, a Pa he can look up to." He stopped. He was about to add, "and a Pa who will accept him for what he is, have patience with infirmity, and support for weakness. A woman needs a man who takes care of her, a man whose trap lines are full and who brings meat to his family, a man who doesn't walk out whenever he pleases for whatever reason strikes him, leaving her cruelly uncertain and alone," but he held his tongue. He had defended Bo Fletcher in front of his boy, but he didn't like him. Maybe he was jealous. This woman understood him, this he could feel.

Two weeks passed with no sign of Bo. No stranger passed and stopped for a home-cooked meal, not even an Indian in the bitter cold on his way back to the reservation from town. The weather was calm, mostly overcast days with a flurry or two and the famous northerly wind, the moaning wind, that the Indians called Kissin-ey-oo-way-oo, straight out of the Arctic Circle. The nights were bitterly cold, between twenty and forty degrees below zero, tempera-tures which tested the fortitude of man and beast. Most of the game had retreated to the shelter of breaks and canyons. The buffalo, main source of winter nourishment and warmth to Indians and homesteaders, had disappeared completely a few years ago, slaughtered by mindless hide-hunters. Cattlemen, powerful barons, like the Meachums, and even foreign syndicates had requisitioned their grassland. The cattle, lacking the buffalo's dense coat, the coat for which they were hunted nearly to extinction, and suffering from a summer of brutal heat and drought, now faced the intense cold and hunger, and the winter had only just begun. The Indians, too, faced starvation. Many believed that the Great Spirit in his anger had killed the buffalo and that the Spirit, if appeased, would return the wooly beasts to their habitual range. This was their dream. For this, they made scant provision for the future. White settlers, too, without cattle of their own, lived as precariously.

Nan walked to the window and looked out. Bessie and Blazer stood tranquilly in the corral, munching the frozen edge of a haystack. Shaggy beasts, at least they had shelter and fodder. She had seen to that herself last August, when she insisted on cutting twice the prairie grass than Bo thought necessary. Good grass it was, the rich blue grama and buffalo grass native to Montana Territory. But she had not done the hunting as she had the haying, and after the elk haunch that Tom Ludlam had brought was gone, there would be no more meat. There was good supply of flour, sugar, and coffee, and she had preserved her vegetables from the garden and made jams of the wild berries that grew nearby. Still, she would have to make one trip to town when these staples ran short. She looked out at Joey, playing among the barn cats by the big door. He could not survive without meat. Where was Bo? She shook her head in dismay, having now to admit his carelessness and indifference. This land, so wildly beautiful and demanding, had broken him like a dry twig beneath a fawn's hoof. He would never come back and she would have to go on alone. She let this cruel reality surface in her consciousness now for the first time.

And there was Joey, and this strangely sensitive man, this Wendell Morgan, to provide for. She walked over to the gun rack and picked up the old Henry rifle from its slot. She would have to learn how to use it. It was heavy. The stock thumped as she lowered its weight to the floor. Carefully, she raised the gun into firing position against her shoulder and sighted down the barrel. The trigger seemed slippery and cold to the touch. Keeping the stock against her shoulder, she lowered the muzzle, staring around for some innocent practice target. There was the frying pan hanging on the wall by the hearth. She raised the gun again, aimed at the pan, and squeezed. With a shattering report, the gun suddenly boomed, smashing a hole in the frying pan, and sending splinters flying from the log wall behind. The unexpected recoil sent Nan reeling backwards onto the floor.

"What are you doing?" It was Morgan bursting in from the back room door, too surprised and startled to remember the courtesies of the sick room. He could walk now and would be leaving soon if the weather stayed clear and he could find a horse. With his good arm, he picked a dishevelled Nan up off the floor. Then he grabbed the gun, opened the magazine, and took out the rest of the cartridges. Seconds later, they heard Joey's worried voice from the yard.

"It's all right Joey...I didn't know it was loaded." Nan looked up sheepishly. "I need to learn how to use it. I guess I'm lucky it didn't ricochet."

"You mean that bastard left you two alone out here and didn't even show you how to shoot?" He'd been such an agreeable patient, the profanity surprised her. "There's wolves and Indians and outlaws...." She was staring at him now, aware of his anger, anger on her own and Joey's behalf. His eyes flared and his cheeks reddened. He was handsome when he was angry, and his arm had felt very strong. Weeks of forced silence burst forth.

He raged on, "You know, lady, this Bo of yours, he's not doin' very much to preserve his happy home! Two weeks I been here now, and I've never seen him chop wood or carry a bucket of water. Hunting, he says he's goin', but he never brought in so much as a scrawny hare. He calls me a horse thief and then sneaks outta here on my horse. Lady, I'll lay odds we'll never see him or that horse again. Why if I had a pretty wife like you and a kid as cute as him, I'd...." He was gripping her firmly by the shoulder with his good hand, a broad palm with long firm fingers. The fire in his eyes burned right through hers. And his words stung.

A tear slid down her cheek. He couldn't stand the sight of it and suddenly he turned away and let her go. Speechless, he knew he'd hurt her. How had he come here? Sixteen days ago he was a prosperous stockman, driving a small but valuable herd toward a new life in the breaks of the Beartooths. And now, his entire herd lost, he was arguing with an impoverished and deserted woman over her wayward husband. In no way could he have anticipated this. And why should he stay here with a posse of lawmen or outlaws, he didn't know which, hunting him?

"You're right. But I'm still married to him and I have my son and you to care for!" She was upset, too, that he had pinpointed her vulnerability, him a total stranger, a drifter, a suspected thief. "Calm down or you'll tear yourself open and start bleeding again."

"Me to care for!" He swallowed hard. "Lady, I ain't never been accused of not being able to take care of myself. Maybe it's high time I'll be movin' on, findin' out just where your Bo's finally hidin' out with my horse. And I just might find 'im hidin' the rest of my stock. And I'm gonna tell 'im just what I been thinking all these hours laying here. He's your husband ma'am and I'm a guest in this house, but a finer example of a skunk I've never known!" He'd said it. She would have to face it now.

He turned abruptly, grabbing his saddle and blanket roll where they were piled in the corner.

"Wait! You're not strong enough. All the nursing I've done, don't waste it! You're still hurt and without a horse, you'll freeze out there. I wish you'd stay and so does Joey...you can teach me how to shoot."

"Not strong enough!" He hadn't heard most of what she'd said.

He looked down. Blood was seeping through the shirt and dripping from his shoulder onto his blanket roll. He was so irate that he had hoisted the saddle onto his injured shoulder and not felt the pain, but the quick motion must have torn the knitting flesh. Nan put a hand on his forearm. Her fingers were cool to the touch, easing away the suffering of these last weeks. He hesitated.

CHAPTER 9

The sound of a horse galloping up and the barking of a dog interrupted them. Morgan froze. Were they coming for him?

"Halloo inside...Fletcher! Who's shootin'?" It was a strange, gruff voice. "Joey, you here? You can come out. Joker won't hurt you."

Joey was peeking out from behind the crack in the barn door. The gunshot had scared him too. The cats he had been playing with vanished under the hay at the loud report and stayed hidden from the big black mongrel, who was pawing and sniffing at the door, ready for the next game.

"He stole my hat and mittens and knocked me over last time he was here."

"What, Joker? Thought you had better manners. Now you, Joker, sit!" At the sound of his master's command, the dog returned to his side and sat.

Morgan could see the dog through a crack in the door. This was not one of his pursuers. The tightness in his throat subsided. He glared at the woman. The soft pressure of her fingertips held him immobile. What was it about her that gripped him so? Who was this man? He did not and would not put down his saddle. Nan dropped her eyes, but still held onto his arm.

She whispered, "He's our closest neighbor. He heard the shot. He's rough but he's been a boon to us both."

When the door opened, Morgan looked out at a wrinkled old man on a shaggy blue roan, no cause for a young man's jealousy. Wisps of steel grey hair had escaped his wolfskin hat, and a matted beard enveloped the lower half of his face. You could read his expression only from his intelligent blue eyes that squinted out from under folds of skin and white, shaggy brows. He had an Army greatcoat on over a worn pair of buffalo-hide leggings, probably the last pair Morgan would ever see, and he had the carcass of a deer thrown over the shoulders of his horse in front of the saddle. He made a formidable picture, wooly and unkempt. Morgan knew the type immediately, old Army scout, tough, independent. He had known many in his young days growing up at Fort Laramie. If he was friendly, then Nan Fletcher had one sure champion.

"Don't mean to disturb you ma'am, but I shot this here buck this mornin' and thought you may be able to use some meat. That young feller of yours needs good red meat to build up his strength."

"Why, thank you, Tom. Yes, we can. Joey, take Mr. Ludlam's horse and the venison into the barn. I'll do the butchering in there. Don't let it freeze."

Rifle in hand, Tom stepped up to the door and saw Morgan for the first time. Neither smiled. "Oh, Tom Ludlam, this is Wendell Morgan. Bo brought him in, shot and his horse was stolen."

Morgan nodded. Ludlam grunted a greeting at Morgan, who was still standing near the door. Their eyes met and held.

"You do the shootin' I just heard?" He directed the question straight at Morgan.

Nan watched Morgan tense under the cold appraising glare of the old pioneer. "No Tom, that was me and it was an accident. Wendy...Mr. Morgan here was going to show me how."

"Wendy, huh, funny name." He spoke only to Nan. "Where's he goin'? He don't look to me like he's plannin' to stay for dinner." And then to Morgan, "Mister, you ain't goin' nowhere without a horse or you plannin' to take mine?" Old Tom raised the butt of his rifle just by inches. Morgan's one good hand was still holding his saddle. "An' you're bleedin', man. Bleedin' men freeze easy. You botherin' her? She shoot at you? Tell you to git?" And then to Nan, "You got a reason you don't want him around?"

"Tom, please. He's a good man. He's just angry at Bo."

"Bo, huh, he here? He should do the butchering."

"He's not here, Tom. I'm worried. He's been gone more than

two weeks, ever since he brought in Mr. Morgan from the Deer Creek. Mr. Morgan here has been very helpful."

"Two weeks you say? In two weeks a man can wander far. Just how helpful were you, mister?" He was still skeptical.

Morgan spoke up. "I ain't touched her mister. Didn't you hear the lady?"

"He's right, Tom. After all, I'm a married woman."

"Well then, why don't you put that saddle down and settle and be friendly?" The beard suddenly broadened. The old man was actually smiling. Then he added, "and mebbe I can fix you something to stanch that bleedin'."

"Mister, I come to understand I'm no longer welcome in this house."

"Well, now," Tom raised the gun an inch higher. He hadn't missed her hand lying on Morgan's arm. "Appears to me she's tryin' to make you right at home."

"No, no Tom, nothing like that." She was blushing now. "It's all a mistake, him not understanding why Bo has been gone so long and Bo left on his horse. He wants to go get it back."

Tom studied the younger man. There was a awkward silence. "I'm with you there, son. Got a few prize head o' my own." Slowly he walked over to the table, leaned his rifle against it and sat down. "Set down, mister, 'an tell me about it, an' maybe the Missus will feed a starvin' ole man who came in out of the snow."

Wendy gave in reluctantly and sat down. What was it about this woman? She did calm him. He just couldn't stay angry with her. And the old man seemed crusty but kind. His arm was throbbing and he was beginning to feel very tired. He cupped his chin in his hands and rested his elbows on the table. "Son, I got somethin' in my saddle bags can fix you up right smart. At this rate you'll faint right away on us. Ma'am, I'm thinkin' the barn's warm enough so's that deer won't freeze if you get the butchering done before sundown. You can pack it all in a snow drift, just so's you keep the wolves away and remember where you stashed it."

"Good! Tom, I'll get out there as soon as I set the stew on the table. You and Wendy can help yourselves."

Tom went out and came back chewing hard. "Now, son, this here thing I'm chewin' is chokecherry root. Indians use the gum to stop bleedin' an' it'll do the job on you. Then the two of us can set down to a good meal and talk while Mrs. Fletcher butchers that buck. Then he added, "An' mebbe you can fill me in on what's goin' on around here." He took a wad of gum out from his mouth, laid back Morgan's shirt and shoved it hard against the torn and macerated flesh. Morgan almost passed out, but the pain did not last.

The two men, one young, one old, talked far into the evening. Morgan delighted in the hum of a human voice. It broke the monotony and the long, inactive days. Tom sat quietly on a crate near the bed. He'd always been a lonely sort of man; he appreciated the chance to ramble on with his captive audience. They talked some about the army and old Tom's days of scouting, but mainly about horses, in the equine language that only true horsemen know. Tom knew a fair amount about stud books and race training. He had grown up among the Amish in Pennsylvania and had watched the gentler ways of subduing a colt, ways that resembled the Indian's patient methods and not the more violent bronco-busting of the western cowboys. And old Tom had been very successful in his later years. He had trained both for riding and driving, but now he did mostly riding, although he still drove them first to a dog cart to settle them. The big yokes and harnesses were just too much for an old man to haul around. His horses were not many, about four or five at a time, and he rode each one in training himself every day. And they always found eager buyers. They could be found scattered around ranches and farms in the valleys east of the Beartooths, all bearing the LT brand. And Wendy knew that each one had brought old Tom a good price. He could remember seeing one as far south as Fort Laramie, and how his father had admired the smooth gait and balance of the dark brown gelding, a rather unprepossessing mount but superbly schooled even to voice commands. The gelding had belonged to Cappy Walsh, General Miles's old scout.

Slowly, without arousing suspicion, old Tom pried pieces of information from the younger man: the loss of his stock and the death of his father; the treacherous escape through Deer Creek Canyon in the snow; his rescue and recovery. Then Nan came in from the butchering. Morgan drowsed.

"You save those antlers ma'am. They'll make a fine hatrack for the young'un. That's a five-pointer, boy!" Maybe someday you'll be hangin' yer school bag from 'em."

Joey beamed.

The wind hummed a slow moan outside.

"Now ma'am, with your permission, I'll just lay out my bedroll over by the corner, and spend the night. Like to breakfast on some of them biscuits you're famous for. An I'll be gittin' Baldy there into the spare stall. Night's comin' on cold."

Old Tom knew the weather and he had known some young and handsome con men in his time. He was not leaving until he was sure Mrs. Fletcher and her boy were safe. He and Morgan stoked the fire and bedded down close to the hearth, Nan and Joey in the back room. The moaning wind became a shrieking howl as it rushed down from the mountains. Tom woke once to the mewing of the barn cats on the porch and Joker's scratching at the door. The animals also needed warmth tonight, more than the barn could offer. Tom opened the door a crack to let them in, briefly looking out at the sheets of frozen whiteness. The grateful animals curled up, sharing their warmth, dogs and cats together around Tom.

The next morning was cold and grey, and snow fell most of the day, but the following day was sunny. Tom led an eager old Baldy out of the barn into the snow, and yelled for Joker. When he was ready to leave, he made a last turn past the cabin and called to Morgan.

"Young feller, this is December. You stay here this winter." It sounded like a command. "She needn't count on that husband comin' home. You stay here. You hear me? I like you an' I'll make it up to you. You got a good roof and good grub and you even got you a nurse. Get well, all well, an' come spring, you come see me. You can work for me or with me, I ain't gettin' any younger. And we'll find your horse, but only if'n you stay put an' keep an eye open an' a gun handy." He tilted his weight forward ever so slightly. Old Baldy responded and walked forward. "That's a fine woman and a prize little boy. I'd stay mesself, 'cept I got stock to feed and a business to tend and I'm an old man. I never had a family, but I've seen a mite of this world and I ain't so old that I can't appreciate a fine woman, and that lady and that boy are as pure a breed a thoroughbreds as I ever knew. You stay put. An' don't you forget what I told you!" He was still shouting when the horse trotted out of earshot.

Morgan was stammering agreement. Sure he'd stay, unless a posse came galloping down on him. Where else would he go? And those two did need a man close by. What would happen come spring...or if the winter turned violent?

CHAPTER 10

Tom rode back through the brakes to the pristine box canyon that he called home. This year he was wintering only five head of horses. That was all he could support after such a dry summer, when the grass had reached only half its usual height and two of his water holes had dried up. But for the five, he was well prepared. This year he had abandoned his log hut and added a stall to the dug-out barn for himself and Joker. The dug-out was better protection, facing the south-east, and he and the mongrel would stay warmer bedding with the horses. He'd just have to keep that south face clear of snow and that stallion under control.

Gently, now, riding up to his spread, Tom stroked his horse's neck to quiet him as the animal caught the familiar smells of home. Thick shaggy dense hairs covered Baldy's neck and stuck between Tom's fingers.

"You growin' a bear's coat this year boy." The jealous dog rambled up. "Yeah, you too, Joker, only you grow a fur coat every year and shed most of it all over me."

His horses, one stallion and three mares, two of them in foal, had sought the shelter of the dug-out in the storm. Tom dismounted, unsaddled Baldy, the only gelding that he kept for riding, rubbed him down and put him away. Baldy was a pet like Joker, someone the lonely old man could talk to. Then he forked a good portion of hay to each hungry horse and sat down on his crude bunk. Joker lay his head across Tom's knee and nudged. Tom did not immediately respond and start to scratch. His mind was still at the Fletcher cabin, trying to figure what had happened there, why Bo had not yet returned when he had always returned before.

"You an' me, Joker, mebbee you an' me should take a trip to town, just do a bit of listenin' to what folks are sayin'."

The idea still rankled, like a cocklebur under a saddle pad, when at sunset he turned in, and in the morning, when he fried some biscuits. Tom was not one to let ideas rest and fester. After breakfast, he forked a few days' feed to the horses and, calling to Joker, he saddled a pretty paint mare and headed for town. Dave Lewis was hammering a hinge on his anvil when Tom Ludlam rode up. He looked up from his work briefly when he saw the familiar face and grinned.

"How do, Dave? You can attach a set of shoes to this here mare when you git the time. Better use those fancy shoes, those sharp ones of yorn, so's she don't slide on the ice."

"Expectin' a hard winter, Tom? You're the first so far this year askin' for those sharpies."

"Well, Dave, I just like to be ready. An' maybe I'll just throw a blanket over her while she's waitin'. Joker an' me will be over to the saloon."

"I'll put 'er in the livery when I'm done. Save you a trek." The burly blacksmith stopped and eyed his crusty old friend. "And where you stayin' tonight? There's a bunk here with me if you've the need."

"Obliged."

The old scout shuffled across the snow-packed street. Horses were scattered at the various hitch-rails, especially in front of the saloon, the hotel, and the restaurant. Tom scanned each one. They were all of short stature, stocky and shaggy, the hardy Indian ponies, cutting horses, and mustangs of the open range. There was one sorrel among them, but it was a gelding with no white markings, about fifteen hands high. The tall, imposing mare with white blaze and stockings that Morgan had described was not there. But then, old Tom didn't expect to find the mare quite so easily.

He climbed the steps to the saloon, swung the doors wide, and entered. Joker clung to his side. Two men made room for them at the end of the bar. Tom nodded a greeting - he was acquainted with most men in town, although friendly with very few. One loyal friend was Dave Lewis, who did all the shoeing and some of the doctoring for Tom's horses. And the loyalty was mutual. Tom supplied Dave with fresh meat, moonshine (from a still he wouldn't admit to but everybody knew he ran), and an extra horse when needed. Still, old Tom and his dog were a town fixture, cantankerous, rough, sometimes even smelly and dirty or drunk, but at the same time honest and proud. Civilization was racing ahead of the old-timer. The West and Red Lodge with it was filling up with newcomers. There was even talk that a spur of the Northern Pacific would be heading toward Red Lodge. The Crow Indians now remained on their shrinking reservation. No more roaming with the buffalo - there were no more buffalo. The marauding Sioux were quiet. There was no more need for army scouts. Still, for all his gruffness, Tom held the town's curiosity and respect.

The bartender drew a beer from the barrel and pushed it across in front of Tom. Tom nodded, picked it up, and crossed to a corner table where he could quietly observe the door and the comings and goings at the bar. There was a poker game in progress, the green-shaded dealer and two mustachioed players intent on their cards. Two of Rose's girls were leaning against the wall on the other side of the room. Tom remembered the pretty one with the thick auburn hair. She was slimmer than the other girls here and probably younger. Tom remembered having seen her before and wondering what an attractive girl like her was doing in that profession.

"Money," he thought, "they all do it for the money, and for the fancy clothes and the lazy life. But this girl was really pretty, with wide-set green eyes and a milky complexion, and tall, must have been cut from some fine bloodlines." He always described his women in terms of horses and meant no disrespect. It was just his peculiar habit of speech. But he was thinking that this one, - Amelia, he even remembered her name - should have found herself a husband by this time, like Nan Fletcher. Yet Nan Fletcher's husband was missing and there weren't very many ways a woman alone could make as good a living as this on the frontier. Would Nan Fletcher ever stoop to this? The very thought appalled him. Yet she could not continue on the homestead by herself, and with Joey, too, and him not well. Old Tom worried about Nan Fletcher and whiled away the afternoon watching the pretty bargirl.

Several men saluted Amelia, but none seemed to claim her and she didn't pursue their attentions. Tom suddenly realized she was waiting for someone, and it must have been someone with influential friends to make these tough cowhands stand aside.

CHAPTER 11

About five o'clock, the doors quietly swung back and two tall cowboys strutted in. Tom recognized the one for Dancer Meachum; the other one he did not know, but he was as tall as Dancer with dark, hard eyes, and a pearl-handled Colt tied down at his left hip. The pearl handle faced forward, ready for a quick and easy draw. Tom knew the type - gunhand - and he'd heard Big Harv had been hiring some sharpshooters.

Amelia stepped right up to Dancer, who hugged her like a bear right there for all to see. Tom understood - she belonged to a Meachum. She was spoken for.

Tom easily overheard their conversation. Dancer was a showman true to the Meachum clan, like his brother George, and talked resonantly in his deep baritone for all to hear.

"Amy, we got to find a nice girl for Bill here. He's been mournin' his friend nigh on two weeks now, an' I told him that was enough." Hendl devoured an eyeful of Amelia's ample bust. "Now I told 'im you'd know just the girl."

Amelia eyed Hendl. "You a hell raiser, just like your friend Dancer here? Lotsa gals like to meet you." She winked over her shoulder at three barroom beauties and they all converged on an eager Bill Hendl. This way she could have Dancer Meachum to herself.

Tom Ludlam just sat and watched and listened.

Bill Hendl moved up to the bar with his bevy of companions,

and the bartender shoved a bottle at them. There were many advantages to working for the Meachums.

"We all glad to make your acquaintance, mister. You're a big brave man. I seen what you can do with a gun." Melly was talking, she was always talking, making inane conversation, thoughtlessly and brazenly flattering every tall, tough man.

Bill Hendl had not been much to town, not to Red Lodge. They had always headed for Helena, a longer ride, but Grady had a brother there working a gold mine. Now he accepted Melly's obvious fawning, and basked in it.

"You seen the shootin'? Fool rustler, ridin' in here on that fancy horse. Thought we wouldn't know 'im. Ya can't never miss a horse like that. An' then 'im drawin' a gun!"

"But you showed 'im!" Melly had a loud voice. The poker players frowned their annoyance at the disturbance but did nothing more in the face of the gunman. Tom Ludlam sat and listened.

The conversation at the bar droned on, increasing in volume with each shot of whiskey. Old Tom was getting restless. He still hadn't heard just who it was got shot and the description of the horse fit Morgan's. Talking quietly to Joker, they crossed the barroom inconspicuously and walked out.

Back at the blacksmith shop, Dave Lewis was still hammering when they strode up.

"You ready fur eatin', Dave? I take you over to Auntie's."

"Right with you, Tom. I'd like that."

Over a hot meal, the story unfolded. Bo Fletcher, a newcomer of sorts, a homesteader from out in the breaks of the Beartooths (a place over east of Deer Creek Canyon) had come in here riding a very smart red horse. What Fletcher was doing with that horse, nobody knew. He'd always been a brooding man and hadn't made very many friends in town. His wife on the other hand, had befriended Aunt Bess, of Auntie's restaurant, and sold her cream and fresh vegetables. She was a hard-working, handsome woman, younger than him by maybe ten years. They had a little boy. Fletcher had been around about two years, since the opening of the reservation lands, and always had trouble scraping up whatever he needed for simple supplies. He always rode a scraggly old bay with a stripe down the middle of her face. Dave had shoed his horse. He clearly wasn't making a success of homesteading, and the Meachums said he'd stolen the mare. They'd been trailing him on the other side of Deer Creek when he shot Grady and young Tag Meachum from ambush and escaped through Deer Creek Canyon. Young Meachum lived; Grady didn't. Bill Hendl, Grady's saddle pal and another Meachum gun, spotted the stolen horse at the hitch rail right here in Red Lodge a few days later and went gunnin' for Fletcher. Hendl was quicker.

"So Fletcher's dead." Tom stated the obvious.

"Right, Tom. They wrapped up the body and put it in a snowdrift like they do with all a them that dies in the winter. Come the Chinook, when it thaws and they can dig a hole deep enough, they'll bury 'im."

"Ain't nobody tol' his wife and kid?"

"That I can't say, Tom. I reckon Sheriff Walsh or the parson or the undertaker rode out to see 'er and the kid, but you know how it is, snow an' cold an' that's a long ride...an' then he shot a Meachum. Them's the boss outfit around these parts. Do right by their men. Had a proper Bible readin' for Grady and planted 'im under a carved headstone in th' churchyard." Then he added, "Shame about the wife and kid."

Tom Ludlam studied his hands. He had what he had come for. Bo Fletcher wasn't coming home again this time. Nan Fletcher and her boy had lost their man for good and he, Tom Ludlam, would have to bear the news. Even now the old Indian fighter could feel his throat swell up and close, like when the noose snaps tight at a hanging.

Finally, he broke the silence. "And the horse, where's the horse?"

"Can't say that neither, Tom. Reckon the Meachums took her. A fine animal like that don't go uncared for. They didn't leave her tied to no hitchin' post, I can tell you that."

Tom Ludlam saw to a pauper's funeral for Fletcher and rode out the next morning. He couldn't face the widow. He went straight home and didn't stop at the Fletcher place. Men died, old men, young men, family men and loners, he'd seen it all before. What bothered him was that this woman deserved better. He cursed himself for being born fifty years too soon.

CHAPTER 12

George Meachum sat pensively in the drawing room of his new house in downtown Billings. A cheroot poked out beneath his impeccably waxed moustache. It was December 9th. Jay Compton of the Northern Pacific Railroad was expected at eight, and George sat quietly reviewing a railroad progress report in preparation for their meeting. A carafe and two brandy snifters rested on a silver tray on the Pembroke table at his right hand. Meachum cattle would be shipped at a reduced rate in exchange for mining and lumbering rights on various portions of the vast Meachum holdings. The two men would discuss the preliminary agreement this evening.

George, for all his good looks and social poise, was an intelligent and shrewd man. He knew the eastern businessmen coveted the copper deposits of Anaconda and the gold of Virginia City, to the north and west. He knew about the wild successes of William A. Clark and Marcus Daly, and had followed carefully the careers of both men. Henry Villard's Northern Pacific Railroad had skirted Red Lodge about seventy miles to the north in search of the fastest route to these riches. Billings, on the Yellowstone River, was the cattle railhead with pens, chutes, and loading platforms that stretched for a quarter mile. Billings was booming. From Billings, cattle went east to the burgeoning cities, but also west to feed the miners. George Meachum had similar ambitions. He had neither gold nor copper. He had cattle and coal.

George had no intention of relinquishing Meachum coal too cheaply. He would push for low shipping rates, but he would delay any lease or entitlement until the Northern Pacific agreed to construct a spur from Billings to Red Lodge. They'd already extended the tracks as far as Laurel. He had to move them just a little farther, dangle a bigger carrot in front of their engines. George was a good businessman. The graciousness and amicability he displayed on the outside concealed a basic distrust of Yankees, the same Yankees who had driven the Meachums from their Kentucky holdings when George was twelve years old. A branch line would not only benefit the Meachums financially and facilitate shipping cattle and coal, but would contribute to the overall economic prosperity of the entire area. It would bring immigrants and social organization to what had been, until four years ago, the domain of the Absaroka or Crow Indians. Red Lodge would boom. George knew, too, that as the local resident who had promoted the Red Lodge spur, he would experience an explosion of popularity with the new residents who would greatly outnumber the old. And he would contrive to remain in the public eye, as Montana grew inevitably from territory to statehood. Then, with his reputation and Meachum money behind him, he would run for office.

He sat immobile when the doorbell chimed and listened quietly while Ling, in his chopped English, disposed of Compton's snow boots and greatcoat.

"Mista Jay Compton, sir."

Compton marched confidently forward, rubbing his cold hands together to warm them before shaking hands. Of military bearing, he had a ruddy complexion, thick brown hair, and side whiskers, amply salted with white. George Meachum was taller and younger. Majestically, he folded his papers and stood. Both gripped palms firmly, each measuring in a handshake and first appraising glance, the breadth and width of the other man.

"Mr. Compton, a distinct pleasure to meet you sir. I hope you've found Montana hospitality sufficient." George had the first words.

"For a New Yorker, sir, it's overwhelming. It's the weather that's disconcerting."

The big, handsome son of the Confederate cattle rancher offered Compton a chair and then brandy. "This is the best available in Montana...by boat from France via New Orleans, St. Louis, and our great Missouri River."

"The Northern Pacific will see to it that you get more where that came from."

"I do hope so sir, but I'm more interested in shipping Montana's beef back east."

Compton sat up. This man was something more than the ingenuous frontier type with whom he had regularly dealt. He accepted his drink with uneasy reserve. A negotiator by trade, he should keep each side thinking they had profited most, while always eking out an ample commission for himself.

"The trade will go both ways. It always does. And that has proved profitable for all. You've no doubt studied the Union Pacific and the experience of the eastern roads.

"True. But can you tackle our Montana winters? This has been a nasty winter so far, heavy snow followed by that abominable November thaw. Mud up to our knees. Cattle were standing in six inches of muck before it froze over again. We lost some. We'll be haying more before it's over, but we'll survive. What's a railroad do in the mud and the ice?"

Compton sat up and leaned forward. "We plow and shovel. We keep the tracks clear...but haying? I thought the open range provided fodder enough for even very large herds."

George sensed the lapse and snickered. "You've been visiting gold settlements. In good years, yes, and we've had a number of very good years. I only hope they will continue, but I remember some fearful winters years ago, storms that blew straight off the glaciers...but I'm digressing. You haven't come all this way to hear me moan over a winter storm. You're building a railroad. Can you handle, have you handled a winter like this?"

"Meachum, these storms you speak of could cause schedule irregularities, derailments or even blockages. But we, too, will survive." Then he added, "Please, I'll find our mutual business easier to discuss if you'll call me Jay."

"Of course, and I'm George." He beamed a smile worthy of Montana's friendly best.

Both men were relaxing now; both conscious of the inherent strengths of their respective positions; both ready to spar for some minute advantage, yet knowing full well that he would have to surrender some ground. George wanted to ship cattle now, enough cattle to thin the Meachum herds substantially, without arousing the suspicions of the Circle C and the Niobrara Cattle Company, two very large, British-owned competitors. Fewer cattle meant less

Meachum exposure to the vagaries of winter, less effort for the Meachum cowhands, some of whom, George knew, had little practical experience with animals. He intended to speak to Harv about that. And sending the steers to market now meant an easier spring roundup and extra money to fill out the herds when the weather improved - if he could find a buyer. Harv would have to get his boys out in the cold to cut some steers for shipment now. They wouldn't like that. And if Compton and the Northern Pacific were to prospect for coal, those gunmen would have to go.

"And now, Mr. Meachum...George, if we could get down to business. You've heard I suppose that the directors of the Northern Pacific are considering building a spur down to Red Lodge, a laborious and expensive project, worthwhile only if assured of substantial shipping revenue from the area in question." Compton paused.

"I've heard, yes, and I'm assuming the coal you're referring to lies underneath my range."

"That is our first concern. Whose range is it? Only four years ago it was Indian land. Territorial law recognizes your customary range. But my directors want to know not only if you run cattle there but if you own it outright. Do you?" He did not flinch. "Can you prove title to your holdings?"

Deliberately, George reached for his sheaf of papers on the table at his elbow. He drew out a yellowed document. "This is the deed to our original 3,000 acres - signed by the Territorial Governor, T.F. Meagher, and dated 1866. Beyond that I have deeds to six more sections, each filed in the name of one of us six Meachum brothers, two half-sections each. We used the Desert Land Act to our benefit. Then there's an adjacent ranch acquired through marriage. My wife, sir, holds title to those two thousand acres. As for the Indian portion, the Meachum ranch holds deeds to five sections in and around the city of Red Lodge, acquired by purchase from various owners. Our relations with the Crows are excellent and we hold the agency's contract for supplying beef to the Indians. You may examine the papers. They are in order." He reached across the table and handed the papers to Compton.

Silently, Compton examined them. Finally, he looked up.

"You've done your homework, George. That's ample acreage. Shall we proceed?" He looked up at his companion with a newborn respect. "You received the letter from Mr. Villard, our chairman? And another from Mr. Hauser?"

"I did, sir. The one where he refers to a possible contract, your railroad for my coal. Tell me, sir...Jay, if Red Lodge gets a railhead, how does the Meachum ranch stand to profit?"

"We pay you for all coal extracted."

"And who does the extraction? I'm a rancher. I know my land and my business, and that's cattle and horses. I'm as good a rancher as my father before me and my grandfather before him. But I'm not a miner." He paused and lifted an eyebrow. "I would be interested, however, in leasing the mineral rights underneath my range."

"I see." Compton had envisioned persuading the rancher to try his hand at mining, assuring him all the time of a steady market for his coal, and watching him struggle with the cruel challenges of ownership and management. For the uninitiated, a first attempt was usually doomed. When the mines faltered, the Northern Pacific would step in and buy the whole operation at bargain rates.

Compton continued, "The directors might be interested in establishing a mining company, as a subsidiary of course, if they can be assured of enough lumber and certainly enough water. That is, if they can foresee a bright and profitable future for their investment. We all do want to profit after all. This is dependent upon our own proper survey of the land." He stopped. There was a lull.

"I see no problem with that. We can ride out tomorrow and show you evidence of all you'd need, the coal, timber and lumber. It's all there. It should take us about a week to inspect all of it."

Compton lifted an eyebrow. He was not eager to brave a Montana winter. "I'd like that, to see at first hand what we're talking about." Compton would be at a disadvantage on Meachum's home range but he was curious and George Meachum was frank and open.

"It'll be a long cold ride. I'll pick you up at the hotel tomorrow at eight. Agreed?"

"Agreed."

They shook hands again, this time more warmly. They would leave Billings not tomorrow, but Friday, for the ranch headquarters and make day trips from there. Compton would see not only the ranch proper, but the site of the future railhead, now the hamlet of Red Lodge. And then he had other reasons for accepting George's invitation. A substantial portion of his own net worth was invested in common shares of the Circle C. He would appraise the competition and the relative value of his own common stock.

CHAPTER 13

Days were short in December. Friday, the third, dawned grey but not too cold. George arrived at the Rex Hotel across from the new Northern Pacific Depot shortly before eight o'clock. The big stone station, its platforms and loading chutes, the sparkling new brick hotel, and the expense involved in building them etched into his brain. The Northern Pacific controlled money. He could afford to drive a hard bargain.

George rode a handsome black horse and led a lumbering bay for Compton and one stocky pack horse. He wore a huge stockman's coat, slit in the back, that hung on either side of his mount down to his ankles, a beaver hat, fur side in, and scuffed, laced lumberman's boots. He dismounted, subtly but gracefully slipped a piece of silver to the doorman, and walked tall, rough, and handsome into the hotel. The dapper railroad executives and their finely-dressed ladies stared. Compton arrived in the lobby dressed in his latest winter riding habit, breeches, Melton coat, and polished field boots.

"Top hat and overcoat is the best I can do. I'll probably freeze."

George laughed. The squint lines at the edges of his eyes tilted upwards, lending him an amused but encouraging expression. Here was a man who inspired the confidence of his fellows. "Can't let you do that." He handed Compton a coat and boots identical to his own. Compton stripped off his own coat and boots and donned the new ones right there in the lobby, while the surprised ladies gleefully oogled at the sight of the rippling muscles beneath his shirt, then, remembering themselves, gasped their shock behind his back.

"You'll do...come on. We take the train as far as Laurel and then ride the rest of the way." They exited laughing.

The icy Yellowstone had thawed and flowed swiftly. The black ribbon of the main channel tossed aside whole trees and blocks of ice which now lined the already slippery banks. The train bridged the Yellowstone and cruised south along the floodplain. Progress was slow. They sat back leisurely in their seats. Compton noticed some scrawny, forlorn cattle.

"I hear your cattle are thriving. Why do you want to ship?"

"Right now they're fine, yes, but the winter has only started. We had a very dry summer. Not much good grass under that snow and we didn't take in as much hay..." he was about to stop, then weighed his thoughts carefully and decided he could gain more by telling Compton plainly. "The way I see it - and this is just a feeling I have - we're in for a very hard winter...." He didn't rush. His mouth was still working, his cheek ticking. Compton did not interrupt. "The old timers around here and I have an Indian friend...that's what they tell me...look at the signs, the hair coat on these horses...cottonwoods were brown in August."

Compton was thinking of the Circle C. "What about the other cattlemen? Don't they see the same things? What do they think?"

"Other cattlemen? Most of the owners are back east or in London sitting behind their desks...except for Wibaux and he knows. He's already sold, raised his cash. Some smaller ranchers and grangers'll be fine. They shelter and feed. The others, they've got some good foremen, but they don't listen to them. All they look at is their balance sheets and profit margins. Look out there. You can see for yourself, the range is over-grazed and over-stocked. Least that's what I think, and I'll put my money on it."

Compton looked. All he saw was wet and white. He was quiet after that. They were climbing to the top of the great sandstone rimrocks southwest of the booming new town of Billings. The tracks were steep and slippery. They were about three-quarters of the way up. From here, the view was awesome. The valley of the Yellowstone stretched out before them, the town like a tiny insect on a still pond. Lowly hills sloped away from the sandstone rimrocks to where they swallowed the great snaking river in their folds, dwarfing cattle, homesteads, huge trees, the black thread of railroad, and even the town and the river itself. All was bathed in eerie white. To the easterner it seemed that this vast land could feed millions of cattle for centuries to come.

Laurel was crowded and bustling. They led their horses off the flatbed car and mounted up for the long, cold ride home to the M-bar. Mud sucked at the horses' hooves, yet patches of ice still lined the deep wagon ruts in the trail. George drew his Winchester from its scabbard and held it across the pommel of his saddle. Desperate men on the lonely trail would kill for the horses alone, and they were passing temptingly close to the Crow Reservation. The Crows, or Absarokas, had always been friendly to the whites, but the government had repaid their friendship only scantily and had grabbed piece after piece of their homeland, continually shrinking their reservation. Now, with no more buffalo, they would steal to provide for their families. The Crows were master horse thieves. They loved good horses, and George Meachum always rode the best.

They topped out on the rim. A new vista spread out before them and the angry river was left behind. The rolling prairie was cut by the abrupt rise of the Beartooth Plateau. There were still miles of grasslands to cross, but now huge jagged peaks threatened like the sharpened canines of the enormous carnivore. Jay Compton had never been a religious man, but he suddenly shuddered. Where was he going, alone, with this virtual stranger, a business acquaintance, and under what hazard?

"My God!" It had slipped out. He hoped Meachum had not heard. But George Meachum had heard, and as if he had read the other man's thought, gestured at the vastness with a sweep of his Winchester.

"It's big all right, but not that big. We'll get there before dark with an hour to spare. It's beautiful, this country, and cold, but I've been ridin' over it for twenty years. Wouldn't trade it for any other. They'll send a rider out to meet us."

Jay Compton hoped so with all his heart.

They sent two riders out, Slim and Dancer Meachum. Still far off, they spotted each other across the snowfields. Dancer made a striking silhouette in his black cowman's coat, waving his great cowboy hat and spurring his big sorrel into a gallop.

"Dammit, Dancer, slow down!" They could just make out the words. It was Slim worrying about the horse. Animals that overheated too much in the cold, could cool down too quickly and die.

Jay Compton watched as the younger Meachum reined in alongside his brother, leaned over his saddle and enveloped him in a bear hug. George pushed him off, but couldn't help grinning at his exuberance.

"George, you been away too long. You be with us for Christmas? Git that wife a yours down here for the holidays. We need a woman at the ranch...and some younguns. You get her pregnant yet? Who's this you're bringing?"

"Jay Compton, this is my kid brother, Dan, known to all as Dancer Meachum...for obvious reasons. He can't sit still." Dancer rode up alongside Compton and shook hands heartily.

"Welcome, welcome, good to have a new face at the house even if it isn't female."

"Jay's here on business, came down to see the place. Works for the Northern Pacific and wants to know if we have coal on our land. Treat him with respect."

"Hey, George, I'm a prince, you know that!" He looked at Compton apologetically, "Chivalrous, that's what the ladies say I am, a fine word...chivalrous," and he rolled it again liquidly over his tongue, "chivalrous...looked it up in my brother Tag's dictionary. Just you ask Amy."

"Well, you bring that chivalry home from the saloon...and tell the boys the same goes for them. You're all on good behavior, including Harv." Then he added to Compton, "My brother, Harvey, runs the place. Sometimes he hires some rough hands, but then, this is rough country."

"I understand." Compton snickered. He was enjoying himself in spite of the cold.

Slim rode up to George quietly. The grizzled old puncher knew his place. "Mr. Meachum, sir, glad you're here. I'll lead that pack horse fer ya." George threw the lead shank over Slim's saddlehorn. "An' you'll be glad to hear we got your horse back."

George Meachum hesitated a moment, trying to sort the sense out of what he had heard.

"My horse, Slim, what horse? I'm not missing any horses." George knew what he owned, especially the horses. He had learned long ago from his father, the colonel, how to keep the records of the sires and dams, all the vital statistics in the stud books. He knew it all by heart.

"Sir, the horse that Dancer's ridin', big red mare with a white blaze," Mr. Harv said it was yorn. And the other eight head, all prime stock."

George twisted around in his saddle to look at the big sorrel horse. "Slim, I never saw that horse before. Hope you didn't go to too much trouble." It was a flip remark, but Slim's reply was serious.

"Trouble? No sir...three men dead, one wounded."

George Meachum arrived a worried man. Compton went to his room. George confronted his brother.

"Heard you've been acquiring new horses, Harv."

"Oh, the horses. Slim tell you? Nine prime head. Young feller and an old geezer, rustlers, cut your herd, was pushin' 'em south along the river headin' for Deer Creek Canyon. But we stopped 'em. Only that young feller could shoot. Clipped Tag and killed a good hand, fella named Grady, from Texas, but we got the old man and we got all the horses back, 'cept for that fancy sorrel with the blaze face the young buck was ridin'. But Hendl caught up with him in town, recognized the horse straight off and settled the score...a homesteader named Bo Fletcher, no account farmer about ten miles west a town. Wasn't makin' a decent livin' so's I guess he thought that horseflesh would put some money in his pocket. He won't be botherin' us no more."

"Harv, they're not my horses."

Harv's bass voice bellowed, "Hold on, George, the guy's broke, a loser, has a measly little homestead on two quarter-sections over by Rock Creek, west fork, a dirty shack and barn, a cow, an overworked wife and a sickly kid. Had to run trap lines to keep 'em all fed. They'll sell out to the M-bar when they get poor enough. Where'd he get a horse like that? He didn't buy it...you'll see it, the one Hendl took a likin' to. She's out at the hitch rail now."

"I already saw 'er. Dancer rode 'er out to meet us." He glared at his massive brother. "Harv, I got papers for every head I own and I know them by heart, every single one. Besides, they each have a notched ear and I don't see any notch on that sorrel's ear."

"Calm down, little brother. I was doin' you a favor. It's winter an' that notch is covered by two inches a hair. Go out and feel her. It's there."

"The ear's smooth, Harv. It's not my horse." The last three words were clipped. The brown eyes narrowed. Stark lines carved out the handsome but determined square jaw and straight brow. When George Meachum got angry, his left cheek started to tick as it was ticking now. "Three men dead, Harv. Three men and for something that's not ours. You're gettin' trigger-happy, Harv, too cocksure of yourself. Now you take those horses back, I don't care how. And you tell your men that the shootin' is over as long as I'm around."

"All right, all right. But we're the ones do the work around here, sloggin' through the mud and freezin' cold, while you sit around on your throne in the big city." Harv tucked his thumbs into the loops of his Levi's and stretched to his full height. "An' remember these are my men. I hired 'em and I'll fire 'em. The Meachums done just fine while I'm in charge. We held our range, even added some." George had a good idea how.

He was not intimidated. "You jealous, Harv? Think I sit around eatin' bonbons and beddin' that wench of a wife y'all picked out for me. Well, Harv, think again. I'm the one who plans for a future of this outfit. You're gonna have to deal with people, Harv, and I don't mean deal bullets from a pat hand. They hang men for that. You start stealin' other people's horses, they'll shoot you for a thief, Meachum or not. The big city's boomin', Harv, and it's comin' here, to your mud and snow, with family folks and laws, Harv. The railroad's gonna bring 'em. The Indians tried to stop 'em ten years ago and look what it got them. It's comin' and I'm not going to watch you and your gunmen shoot folks full of holes and die doing it. I want my ranch and I want my good name. I'm tryin' to make some plans for the future, Harv, for all our futures. Why do you think I brought this Compton out here? We need friends in the right places, Harv, friends, not widows and children aching for revenge. I didn't come here to lecture. Where's this Hendl? I want to talk to him."

"Over in the bunkhouse washing up." The words spat out from between clenched teeth.

CHAPTER 14

George marched across the yard to the bunkhouse. It was quiet inside.

He didn't knock. He stuck his head, Stetson and all, through the door. Only four cowboys were there, Slim, Bill Hendl, and a new man, young fellow with sleepy blue eyes, named Al. Hendl was rinsing his face and hands in the sink, and he hadn't taken off his gun to wash up.

"Bill Hendl, I'm George Meachum and I'd like to see you outside a minute."

Hendl finished wiping his hands defiantly and walked outside into the dusk.

"George, you say, didn't know there was a George in this outfit. Where you been?"

"I handle the shipping and business end of this operation, Hendl. My brothers, Harv and Mose, usually handle the day to day ranch work. They do the hirin' and the firin', decide how many cattle to run on which range, and I usually leave 'em alone."

Hendl lifted his dark eyebrows and looked his opponent straight in the eye. "Usually?"

George continued, "Most times, how they operate has little to do with what I do. The cattle arrive fattened and on time at the railhead in Billings and I have no complaints. But my last shipment didn't look so good. Then I began hearing stories about shooting and thieving and how some of the old herders in this outfit were bein' replaced by guns like you."

The Texan caught the insult and stiffened. His hand rested lightly on his belt only a few inches from the handle of his Colt.

"Now, Hendl," George continued, "I hear you killed a man over a horse. You made me your excuse, said you thought the horse was mine. Now you've been ridin' that horse. I don't appreciate being made a party to a shooting."

"Mista, I follow my orders. Your own brother would a' shot the sucker quicker than I did. An' that murderin' sodbuster killed my pard. I evened things up."

He was turning on his heel to walk defiantly back to the house.

"Hendl, I'm sorry about your partner. You all acted too hastily, not knowin' whose horse it was. Now, I like my men to think before they shoot. You come up to the house and collect your pay. Then you get your gear and get off this ranch!"

Hendl was incredulous. He looked snidely at aristocratic George Meachum and snickered. George stood not three feet away. Suddenly, his broad palm shot forward in a sideways swing and slapped Hendl right across the cheek.

"I'm the boss around here. Now pack up, get your pay and get out!"

The range between men was only a few feet, too close for fair gunplay, but the quick temper that made Hendl the dangerous gunman he was, flared once more from simple habit. Hendl turned to go back into the bunkhouse. It was a feint. As he turned to his right, masking his gun hand from view, he drew.

George Meachum saw the gun coming up and dove straight down on the gunman's arm. Hendl fired, still on the upswing as the force of George Meachum's body hit his legs. They gave way. The shot went wild past the bunkhouse door. Men ducked for cover. George came up and grabbed Hendl's gun hand with his two hands, slamming it against the solid door jamb. Hendl screamed in pain. The gun fell to the floor. George stooped to pick it up, removed the other five bullets, and offered it back to Hendl, butt first.

"Take it and leave."

Not a whimper or protest escaped Bill Hendl. With his left hand, he took his gun and holstered it. Then, wrapping his smashed right hand in his bandanna, he headed for the main house and Harv.

The other cowboys, attracted by the noise of combat, had come to the door and a few had even left their hot meal to watch a good fight. Most had arrived too late to know what it was all about.

But they witnessed Hendl humiliated, as he holstered his empty gun, turned on his heel, and stalked away. Murphy, the other Texan, scowled. Hendl ached for revenge.

The conversation that night in the cowboys' mess, the room out back of the cookhouse, was subdued. The old cowpunchers collected at one end of the long wooden table, the gunmen at the other. Sometimes Mose joined them. Most of the old-timers had seen George Meachum in action before and were quietly enjoying the results of the fight. The gunmen were talking.

"He was fast, I'm tellin' you, Bill just didn't see 'im."

"Aw, Bill Hendl's no fool, he saw 'im but he just thinks ever'body's gonna go for a gun like hisself. That there George feller, he's smart as they come. If'n he can shoot a gun as fast as he can fight, he's a tough man. An' he's a Meachum all right, a real scrapper. He'll probably wrap that thar' railroad feller up like a Christmas present, all tied up and bowed."

"Wonder what big Harv is thinkin'?" This from Murphy. He continued. "He's thinkin' this here George needs hobblin'. He's been given a mite too much rein, an' his schoolin' and big city ways kinda swelled his head." There was snickering all around. "As for myself, I'm gonna tread a little lighter around George and Big Harv. Wait 'til I see which one is really the foreman of this here outfit, or if maybe they both are."

They all nodded and one thoughtful cowboy added, "Yeah, we just mind our manners and be nice and agreeable to 'em both."

"Gonna be a dull winter."

CHAPTER 15

George came in to dinner and took his place at one end of the table, across from Dancer. Harv was at the head. Jay Compton sat at Harv Meachum's right, Mose on Harv's left. Gabe sat between Compton and George; Tag between Dancer and Mose. George knew immediately that Harv had engineered the seating. George would have to talk across his brother Gabe in order to communicate with Compton at all. He snatched what little initiative he could by introducing Compton all around, hoping all the while that he had befriended him enough already to dispel any wrong impressions his unscrupulous brothers might make.

Once seated, Harv led right off, "This is an occasion, Mr. Compton, Jay, if I may. All six of us Meachums haven't been together like this since Christmas before last."

Compton blended right in, "I'm delighted then, Mr. Meachum...Harv, if the business I have to conduct got you all together, and I'm glad to have things on a first name basis, I might add.

"That's how we do it, friendly-like, first names, nicknames, we take a man as he comes, no frills, and there's many a man just wants to start over again so's he takes a new handle out here. It's a big country, easy to get lost in. Meachum holdings are spread out. But we each of us tend to our own. Sometimes we don't see folks or even family for months at a time, or even years. Tag there went east to school. And of course, you know George now lives in Billings with his wife, and sees to our prospects there. We all mind our own business." The implication that George was out of his bounds here on the home ranch was not lost. Big Harv spoke at his eloquent best tonight. It disgusted George. He hoped Compton would have intelligence enough to sort the truth from the bluster.

It was Tag who broke the tension. Although he was still weak from his wounds, his mind was perceptive and he delighted in the opportunity for interesting dinner conversation.

"Tell us, Jay, how you find the territory. It's hard to believe a New Yorker would enjoy it, especially in the dead of winter. Billings is booming, I hear, and you've been to Helena."

"Tag, I'm a businessman, but then so are your brothers. I came out here as an agent for the railroad. And then, I don't mind telling you all that I've a few dollars of my own invested, and that George, as I'm sure all you men will, has given me some very astute advice on the conduct of my own affairs."

They all looked back quizzically.

"Maybe that's why you make me feel so much at home. I have some investments in cattle southeast of here and your brother has warned me of the hardships of wintering a herd. I intend to sell my interests now and perhaps buy in again in the spring when the price falls." He was smiling and added congenially, "Just like you Meachums."

Harv arched a brow. "George, you didn't mention selling any beef to me."

"Haven't had a chance to talk to you, Harv," and he outlined the plan to round up as many head as possible during the present thaw and ship east, now, before Christmas.

Harv, listened, frowning. Compton apologized for speaking out of turn, but George dismissed the remark.

"It's all right, Jay, we're all businessmen together and we all want to turn a dollar." He eyed Harv.

"Yeah, we can mount a roundup now." Harv knew that the winter would be harsh and had also thought of shipping, but had been too busy chasing the horse thieves.

He turned to Compton, "You won't be seeing cattle ranching at its best, but you can learn a lot if you come along on a winter roundup. See the land hereabouts too, and see where you can lay your road."

"Jay hasn't promised any railroad yet, Harv. He's here to see if there's coal enough around to make building it worthwhile."

Harv smiled. "Coal, that what you want? I got tons of it. Costs like hell to get it shipped out. We'll see it tomorrow too."

Before George had a chance to regain Compton's attention, there was a loud rap at the door, and Slim Halloway was waving for him to come outside. George got up quietly, leaving Compton and all his negotiations in the hands of his unprincipled brother.

Slim squinted at the darkness, his narrow eyes and blistered lips flat and emotionless. "Thought you'd want to know, Mr. Meachum, but that feller you licked, Bill Hendl, he lit out all right, just like you told him, smashed hand and all. An' he took that big red mare there's been all the killin' over."

George looked at him silently, comprehending.

Slim continued softly, "I figure he's gonna have to see a doctor."

George smiled. "Slim, you're right. Think we should go after him?"

"Mr. Meachum, you want an end to this, so's that Mr. Compton won't git the wrong impression? Appears to me we got to git that red horse back to her rightful owner, and them other horses too. And there's the widow woman - man Hendl shot had a wife an' kid."

George Meachum's jaw tensed. The tic just below the left eye was throbbing again now. Slim continued.

"You didn't know that? Lots you don't know, lots happened while you been away in town. Harv's been hasslin' all the sodbusters. Hell, that's what got you a wife. Ask him what happened to her first husband."

"Damn...Slim, leave my wife out of this. Go saddle up...and pack some grub and some blankets. Maybe we can catch him before he gets clean out of the territory."

Dave Lewis was working late by the dim light of his forge. It was warmer here in the forge than in his damp shack down by the creek on these cold nights, and he liked his work. He was hammering a new handle for a fryin pan when a man rode up. Dave looked up. Not too many riders came in from the cold at this hour.

"Howdy...can I help you mister?"

The reply was slow to come, and it came out in a throaty grumble. "Horse is lathered...can you throw a blanket over 'er and cool 'er down? I'll be back in 'bout an hour." He flipped a coin Dave's way. It caught the flame from the forge, flickered, and fell at his feet. Dave stooped over and picked it up.

"Sure, I never turn down a fair wage."

The man dismounted slowly. He seemed to be holding a bundle close against him which he carefully raised above the saddle horn. Against the background of night, Dave could not see his face. The whole picture, horse and rider, was but a vague silhouette. He picked up a rein and led the animal indoors. When he came back to the forge, he looked at the coin. It was pure gold.

Still nursing his wounded hand, Hendl walked from the smithy straight down Main Street toward the Elkhead Saloon, then turned down an alley and doubled back to Doc Zilka's house. He rapped loudly on the kitchen door.

Not twenty minutes later, Slim and George Meachum rode into town. They rode straight up to Doc Zilka's house and dismounted. George handed his reins to Slim, who stayed outside with the horses. He knocked on the cottage door and from within, a muffled voice grumbled.

"I'm coming, I'm coming. What is it this time? You folks only get sick in the middle of the night?"

"George Meachum, Doc, come to see if you've been working on one of my men."

"Oh, Mr. Meachum, sorry to keep you waiting." He flung the door wide. His eyes were red-rimmed and coffee from a tin mug in his left hand slopped over the edge and onto the floor.

"One of our men - he was one of our men until tonight - I fired 'im and he rode off on a Meachum horse. Had a busted hand and I thought he might stop to see you."

"Come in here." Doc led the way to the front room that he used as a dispensary. He opened the door and gestured toward a form on a sagging couch. "That him?"

Bill Hendl was slumped clumsily on the couch, his bandaged hand lying across his chest, sound asleep.

"Had to likker him up some before he would sit still so I could paste his hand back together. What you want him for?"

"I don't want him, Doc, I just want his horse."

"Came to my door nigh onto midnight. Woke me up. Fell asleep over my desk like a cat on a velvet cushion. Out all day deliverin'...that's babies, not grub. Should have been in bed like most normal folks...and he comes snortin' in here like a bull in a herd a cows in heat, wavin' that bleedin' hand like a cavalry flag in front of Injuns and tellin' me my own job. I'd have liked to send him packin' except for that big gun of his and my big old soft heart. That and I'm a coward. I can't send a wounded man away and on foot in this kinda weather in the middle of the night. Not even a snake like him rattlin' his tail!"

"Well, he didn't get to town on foot. He got to town on a stolen horse." George turned to go. Then he added, "Thanks Doc. How long's that liquor going to last?"

"Mornin', and then he's gonna have himself a drummin' head for a while. Don't reckon he'll do much ridin' for a day or two. But I'll get him out of my house, I can tell you that. Maybe Rose McCartle'll take him in."

The Doc shut the door behind him and George turned to Slim.

"Check the liveries, Slim. That mare is here in town."

CHAPTER 16

Late morning, December 11th, George Meachum, Jay Compton, and Slim Halloway rode up to the Fletcher homestead. After weeks of enforced isolation and worry, with the only visitor old Tom Ludlam, the three horsemen created a not unwelcome surprise. Joey, in his favorite place, the barn, ran to the door for a better look at the three strangers. Nan picked up the Winchester and stood it behind the sill, out of sight but at hand, before opening the door. Only Wendy Morgan, the memory of his gunfight still raw, clung to the shadows. His wounds had healed; his strength was rapidly returning; but scars remained etched on his memory. Fear of recognition and arrest had bored its way into the deep core of his brain.

Three men, two of them young, strong, and well-appointed, each with a rifle in the scabbard and a revolver at the hip, the other one old and weathered, with the self-assurance that only years of survival can give, these three men could well be a posse. They were all clothed in heavy coats and carried food but no bedrolls. And they were all well-mounted on long-legged, sturdy horses. Morgan had been quietly forking hay down from the loft when he saw the men ride in. He was backing further into the back crevices of the barn. The envelope of darkness concealed him entirely from the men outside, who squinted from the glare of the snow. Joey called to him.

"It's your horse, Wen!"

Wendy Morgan stabbed the pitchfork into the hay and

quietly crept to the edge of the loft. He had not been seen. He signalled Joey for silence. Outside they could hear voices. Nan was talking.

"State your name and business, and you'll be welcome," Her words rang clear and even in the brittle cold air. She stood tall in the doorway, her soft brown hair waving gently in the wind, framing her oval face.

"George Meachum, ma'am. I'm returning your horse." He tipped his hat to her and held out the lead rope.

The square jaw was set, the brown eyes doleful, penetrating, the blond hair glistening with a tinge of sweat. His eyes held hers for an instant. Quickly she looked away at the horse. He continued to stare. It was Wendy's horse, the same bright sorrel that she had bedded down that night Bo had brought Wendy in, the same blaze-faced sorrel Bo had ridden away. The mare stood quietly. Her winter coat had filled in and masked the sleek body, but she had been carefully groomed and fed. Questions flooded Nan's mind. Was this urbane and handsome man who was speaking to her, was this George Meachum? Of the M-bar? How did he come by the mare? Homesteaders feared the M-bar riders. She knew the rumors by heart, tales of theft and murder, never proven, never doubted. There was only the one powerful cattle clan by that name in Montana. She stood silent, acutely conscious of her vulnerability, of this man's intense stare, and of the rifle within her reach.

The handsome stranger kept talking. "She's a good horse ma'am - you should be glad to get her back." The sight of the horse, the vision of Bo riding away, and the rich fluid bass of this stranger's voice held back her words.

His voice, like a steady drum roll, continued.

"If she were mine, ma'am, I'd have offered a reward. She's that nice. And quiet too, you could ride her yourself." This time, he hesitated long enough to let her gain confidence. "And the others, too, ma'am, my men are out rounding them up. Three of them in foal. They'll make the start of a fine herd come spring."

"Others?" she had finally answered. "What others?"

"They're my horses, mister." The deep, steady voice rose out from the barn. Its heavy door creaked on its hinges and Wendell Morgan stepped out into the glare. He was unarmed. Still, George Meachum thought he read a challenge in his flanking movement.

"I have papers to claim the mare, mister, and the others too, that you're talking about."

George Meachum ignored him and looked back at the woman. "May I step down, ma'am? If you own the horses, I will see to it that you get them." She was staring at the Winchester in his scabbard. He recognized her fear. "This is a wild country. We go everywhere armed, but we mean no harm. My colleague and I are well-known in these parts. May I present Mr. Jay Compton of the Northern Pacific. Slim here has been with me for years, I can vouch for him, too, and so would the good people of Red Lodge. And you, I'm assuming, are Mrs. Bolen Fletcher."

Hearing Bo's full first name jarred her. It had not been used since they had left Cedarville, Iowa. Hearing it now in his absence, pained. That these were important men, that they were her neighbors in this wild land, that they had come for an urgent reason bearing news of Bo, this she sensed innately, and George Meachum's courtesy was very convincing.

"If I may step down..." George continued disarmingly.

"Yes, I'm Nan Fletcher...yes, of course gentlemen...Joey come help with the horses."

Morgan stood there, aghast that she could be so unsuspecting as to ask two armed men, two complete strangers, into her home on their word alone. They were dismounting now. How he wished he had not left his Colt in the house.

Joey, answering his mother's summons, tripped coming out of the barn and tumbled into the snow. George Meachum watched the little boy struggle to his feet again, pushing himself up with hand over hand on his skinny thighs, pants wet with slush, bracing his knees and arching his shoulders backwards for support, but he said nothing. On the frontier, everyone struggled. It was just that this boy had his own peculiar struggle. He handed his reins to Joey without question. Compton gave his to Slim.

"I'm good with animals, sir. They like me." Joey spoke right up to Slim and grabbed the mare's lead rope. That made two horses each. The boy would be one to reckon with. He neither demanded nor wanted help. Slim grunted. Squinting through the glittering sunlight, he was watching the movements of the man by the barn. Hadn't they met before?

Wendy Morgan walked past Slim and Joey and followed the men up the wet path to the door. Three men, there were three men left of the five who had run off with his horses. Three or four. Five began the chase. One, he knew, he had shot in the body, probably killed from a painful gut wound. That left four. And another one was hurt badly, some fool kid who didn't know enough to keep his head down. That left three. And now these three show up with his horse and seem to know what happened to the rest of his herd. Wendell Morgan tread carefully that morning.

CHAPTER 17

Nan's welcome was spontaneous. She offered them seats at the big gate-leg table that had survived the covered wagon trip west from Iowa and that they used for work and meals. Its surface was littered with the morning's bread-makings, which she deftly whisked away, and poured each a cup of steaming black coffee. The whole cabin smelled richly of freshly baked bread and brewed coffee. Compton sat gratefully - he was not used to long rides, inhaling all the warmth of the humble home - but George Meachum waited, standing stiffly, until Nan was there. He held out a chair for her, then sat down himself. Wendy Morgan entered warily. Morgan sifted nervously through his bedroll in the corner behind the door, gathering the registry papers for each of his horses. He noted the rifle that Nan had quietly left there, all the while painfully aware of the courtesies that George Meachum was showering on Nan. Then he, too, pulled up a chair.

Nan spoke first, "Mr. Meachum, before we go any further, you have to understand that I am not the rightful owner of that horse. She really does belong to Wendy...to Mr. Morgan, here."

George Meachum took his time. He looked quietly from Nan Fletcher to Wendy Morgan. Did she already know her husband was dead and was this his replacement? George Meachum was no prude. The frontier was wild, women scarce and in need of protection, and many were fickle as a sun shower on mountain dew. Was this man here because of a kindness? He certainly looked honest, but deeds, not appearances, were the judge of a man. Or was he a parasite, extorting the price of his help from a lonely female and a small boy?

The rancher-would-be-politician opted for tact.

"Ma'am, Mrs. Fletcher, if I may explain." Nan nodded. "The last person seen riding that horse was your husband, Bolen Fletcher. Since this homestead is filed in his name, I...we here, and Tim Walsh, who you know as our town sheriff...thought it was your horse." He glanced openly at Morgan seated to his right.

"Mr. Meachum, I must do the explaining." She looked across the table at Morgan, still confused. She had never seen any of these men before, yet how did they know that Morgan was not her husband? And now she must explain how and why she and Joey were living under the same roof with this virile and rugged intruder. She was blushing.

"Gentlemen, you must understand, he...Mr. Morgan here, is a guest in this house. He came to our door bleeding and unconscious, riding that horse. It was my husband, Bo Fletcher - we haven't called him Bolen in years - who brought him in, in such condition I hate to tell. He was half dead from bullet wounds and exposure. Without that horse, he would have died in the Deer Creek. Miraculously, he recovered. Mr. Morgan owes his life to that horse. Shortly afterwards Bo, my husband...rode off...borrowed...that mare there for a trip to town. It was not his horse. It was never his horse and he took it without permission...without even asking." She bowed her head, ashamed. "He never came back..." Then she looked up gratefully at Morgan. "This man has stayed with us, has helped me keep the place together ever since he has recovered. I'm sure he has the papers he speaks of. I've no reason not to believe him. So, you see, the horse does belong to him, and probably the other horses too. He would have died if that horse had not brought him through the Deer Creek in the November storm. He's been very kind. I was hoping he would stay with Joey and me through the winter, or at least until Bo, my husband returns."

"Mrs. Fletcher," George was looking across the table at Morgan. His cheek was ticking. Morgan thumbed the small pile of papers in front of him, his dark blue eyes bleak, cheeks sucked in, a deep crevice carved out between arched brows. He began again, "Mrs. Fletcher, for your sake I'm glad you have found some help," and he nodded at Morgan. "A woman alone, on a double section, you see...your husband, Bo Fletcher, is dead."

Steam rattled the lid as the coffee boiled over on the stove. Wendy Morgan let the corners of his papers fall.

Nan just looked up at George Meachum blankly, and the initial moment passed.

Then she almost whispered, "How?... Was he sick? Did he leave word for us?... No, I guess he's been wanting to leave us all these years, what with poor Joey and...the farm work...he...he...just couldn't do here... and two quarter sections are so small, hardly feed one cow..." Her voice just trailed away.

"Mrs. Fletcher," George Meachum's melodious voice cracked, "he was shot."

Nan Fletcher stared straight ahead, her blue eyes were dry, comprehending. So this was the end. Hadn't it been coming for so long? It wasn't like she had imagined. Not the grand finale she had imagined on her wedding day. It was more like sinking, slowly, inevitably into a bog, inch by inch, piece by piece, limb by limb, choking, surrendering to the relentless elements, until there was nothing left, no family, no hopes, no love. Except for Joey. For Joey, she could not give up.

"Did he suffer?" she countered.

George Meachum grimaced, "No, he didn't suffer. He was probably dead when he hit the floor. It was a gun duel, at the Elkhead Saloon. The man who shot him accused him of murdering his partner."

"Bo, murder...no...Bo would not kill a man." Nan rose from her chair. "He was a religious man, or was, back in Iowa. Out here he didn't go to church, but he believed. No, he would not shoot a man...gentlemen, will you excuse me." She turned and left, to be alone in the back room. The lid on the coffeepot rattled away and steam hissed on the wet coals.

Morgan got up and moved the pot to the table. A horse whinnied in the stillness.

George Meachum faced Wendell Morgan. "Those the papers?"

"These are the papers. Ohio and Missouri registries," and he slid the pile toward George. "The mare's are on top. All her markings are listed in detail. I had eight others, stolen at the head of Deer Creek Canyon, last November 12th. Their health histories are there too and all their markings noted..." Then he added, "The thieves, they shot and killed my father. I survived."

"I'm sorry. Your horse was at the livery in town. I brought her from there. The others, so I've been advised, have been mixed in with my herd near Bearcreek. I don't know how they got there," - this was true until now, but George Meachum was going to find out - "I live in Billings and I haven't been around lately. My man, Slim, told me of the extra horses, someone trying to hide them out until spring...probably drove them into my herd, thought I wouldn't notice, and I wouldn't have, except that I've come home for a spell and I know my stock...just like you know yours. They'll be here tomorrow." He got up to leave and offered his hand to Morgan. Wen Morgan reached out and shook it, dumbfounded. "Please offer Mrs. Fletcher my condolences...and if there's any way I can help..."

"Of course."

Compton was already walking toward the door and Meachum had pushed out his chair and stood up when Morgan called out, "Meachum, there is a way you can help. We can't feed eight more horses here. Not through the winter. Not without buying grass."

Meachum stopped. Morgan continued. "We cut hay enough for three or maybe four, but with a milk cow, we just can't feed 'em all. Whatever grass is still left on the pasture is either covered with slush or so mildewed and worn that its nourishment is gone."

"Look, Morgan, I'll help where I can, but my stock will suffer too. We're in this together, all us stockmen. I need all the grass I have and your horses have been feasting off of my range for how long I don't know." He was simply stating the obvious. "But I'll ask around town, see if maybe Dave Lewis has some surplus. And if I were you, I'd pray for a mild winter."

"Thanks."

"And Morgan, I don't want to see the widow suffer. I'll see if I can find some extra feed."

Wendy Morgan watched the three men ride out and walked out toward the barn. The news about Bo Fletcher made him sorry for the woman, but secretly glad. She'd find another man, no doubt about that. That he could possibly be that other man crossed his mind for the first time, to his great surprise. He'd been with girls at the post, gone to the socials, even courted one. It hadn't worked. She wanted him to go back east, and he'd been saddled with grief and a degree of anger ever since. Now time had dulled all that. What few others there were had always flirted with the soldiers, never with him. It didn't seem to trouble him, the lack of female companionship. It was just a fact of life on the western frontier. This past month was the first time he had ever lived in a woman's home, however humble, with the smell of freshly baked biscuits in the air, ruffled curtains at the windows, and dried cornflowers on the table, the first time since his mother died when he was six years old. He should probably go to Nan now, give her sympathy in her grief, yet he did not share that grief, and shied from the emotions the grief would summon.

And now he had been found. The news of his whereabouts would travel back to town and quite possibly back to the men who had ambushed him in the first place, and the man who had killed Bo Fletcher in an act of revenge. When would he learn he had shot the wrong man?

His boots sank into the wet snow melt as he crossed the yard and cold feet woke him from his thoughts. A faint voice carried from the barn. Joey and his cats were talking to the mare.

Joey - the thought struck like a sledgehammer. Joey would have to be told. And there he was, right in front of him, leaning on the partition, grinning and talking to the mare. He looked back as Wendy walked in. "She's real glad to be back with her own, I can tell. We weren't her own for very long, but we're mighty glad to have her."

Wendy tousled the boy's hair and put his arm around his shoulder. "Come on, sit down. There's something I have to tell you."

The grin disappeared and Wendy led the boy to a pile of hay between the mare's and Blazer's stalls. He sat down and motioned Joey to sit beside him. How to tell a small boy his father was dead? How to be gentle, not brutal, and still face reality? Morgan gritted his teeth and looked at Joey sideways. "Joey, those men who brought my horse in, they didn't just bring the horse. They knew what happened to your father."

The young face started to brighten, the corners of the small mouth to smile, but when he saw the furrowed brow and iron stare of the man, Joey eyes widened and the corners of his mouth turned down.

"He's all right, isn't he? When is he coming home?"

There was no answer, just a tightening of the man's jaw and an audible swallow.

"He is coming home, isn't he?"

Wendy Morgan put his arm around the boy and hugged him to him. "No, Joey, he's not." The boy's worried stare solidified. The small mouth gaped. "He's dead, Joey." A tear began its slow and painful journey down one cheek. Then the floods began in earnest.

These were the two shadowy figures in the hay, amid the cats and cobwebs, dusty harnesses and slanting shadows of the barnboards when Nan stepped through the door. To Wendy Morgan, the sight of her lithe figure silhouetted against the shining sunlight stirred all his latent emotions. He wanted to reach out to her, to hug her to him as he had hugged her boy. And there she was, so quiet that Joey had not even heard her enter.

"Does Joey know? Did you tell him?" Her voice rasped like dried corn in the grinding.

"Yes...yes...I'm sorry." He took his hands from the boy. "I should have left it for you."

"No, this past month, you've befriended him. He trusts you. He loves you. He'll get over the grief quickly. You'll see. He's young." She looked down, unable to meet Morgan's piercing blue eyes and sighed. "His own father only ignored him...and me."

At this, Morgan lifted the boy from the cushion of hay. Joey went to his mother. Morgan stood by, embarrassed.

Nan was the first to break away, with the easy excuse of preparing dinner. But she couldn't look Morgan straight in the eye.

CHAPTER 18

The next day, Wendy Morgan checked the fencing on the corral. Then he saddled the mare and with Joey in front in the saddle, rode around the back meadow to check footing and forage in the pasture. He filled in one deep rabbit hole. The nest had not been occupied recently, but the builder had left a six-inch vertical tunnel that could snap a horse's leg.

The grass on the pasture was wet but not rotted. The weather was still warm for December. A real Chinook, the thawing and warming wind, was blowing. Wendy and Joey rode back laughing. He lifted the boy down and set him on the porch. It had been a good ride, good for Joey and good for him to be back on his own horse.

"Tell your Ma, I'm riding back a piece into the foothills. Pay a visit to your old friends Tom and Joker."

He turned the mare and loped out of the yard before Joey had a chance to ask to go along.

Tom lived about five miles up the creek in a sod-roofed cabin about ten feet square, tucked back in the valley against a wall of limestone, which formed the rear wall of the cabin. It was crude, but the site was excellent with ample forage and protection from the northwest wind. Tom had built a shelter for his horses in one of the larger undercuts in the limestone, but today they were out roaming the meadow. They were all scruffy and wind blown, but seemed to be healthy and grazed peacefully.

The mare clopped tranquilly along, reaching eagerly forward with each stride, glad for the freedom after the livery stall, and glad to have a familiar rider on her back. Morgan's heart lightened with the sunshine that spattered the snow between deep clumps of spruce and glanced in silver streaks off the boulders. The north fork of Rock Creek was flowing strongly where he had to cross it twice. The trail led him upstream between groves of aspen and then fir, climbing continually until he finally arrived at a small feeder stream by a beautiful meadow, where he let the horse drink. There had been a good thaw even here. The horse gratefully stretched her long, regal neck to the fresh mountain water and as eagerly as she had bent low, her head came quickly up, ears pricked. Wen could hear only the collision of water and rocks, but the mare had caught something else, and his senses immediately sharpened. Then he smelled it, homemade whiskey.

There was a sudden crashing in the brush off to his right. He reached for his Colt. A prairie chicken took flight, squawking alarm. Suddenly, a black form broke from the brush, nose tight to the ground, intent on its scent.

"Joker, you come out to welcome me?"

The dog kept right on, intent on his hunt.

"Ho there, Wendy! That you?" The old scout had crept up on him, more silent than a bobcat stalking a gopher.

Morgan spun around. "Tom, you old fox, you scared me. I must be lettin' my guard down after that accident."

"Naw, it was Joker. He makes for a good diversion. Always gets a feller lookin' his way while I check up on 'em. Man's home is his relaxin' place and I only wants to relax with me friends...I was tendin' to the still. You come share a jug," and he held out his huge palm. "How's that fine lady and the lad? See you got your horse back." He waited for Wendy to explain.

"Handsome dude, said his name was George Meachum, brought her back and says he's sendin' the rest of my horses." He stopped, the remainder of his news was nothing Tom would be eager to hear. Tom looked up at him. His eyes were squinting; his brows were furrowed; his lips seemed to be working, chewing nervously.

"Guess you already heard the news...from the look a you."

"You mean about Fletcher? I know he's dead."

"Figured. How she doin'?"

"All right I guess. She's got the boy, and she's a doer. Keeps busy all the while and that's good for grievin'. She'll get by, but she'll need some help."

"She always did. That why you come to me?"

Wendell Morgan grinned from ear to ear. "Tom, you knew it all along didn't you? You knew I'd come to you."

"An you knew I'd he'p 'er." Sheepishly, he added, "Don't you go tellin' 'er about no still now. Never drink in front of the ladies anyways."

The next morning, Wendy Morgan saddled the mare a second time. He gave Nan instructions for handling the horses that George Meachum would deliver and set out again for Tom Ludlam's. Together, they would ride back into the mountains, to some hidden flats where the nourishing grasses blew mostly clear of snow and still stood tall and ready for cutting. No other white man had ever penetrated so far back toward the mountains except maybe one of the *metis*, the half-French, half-Indians who lived wild and independent lives and who now had escaped back across the Canadian border. Here was where old Tom Ludlam had his reserve, where there was ample feed for the taking. They took two spare horses. "We gonna need 'em," Tom explained, "Them's company fer ole Baldy there. One fer the hayin' an' one fer me jugs." Tom's mouth was working. "Sides, keeps me ar-ther-i-tis happy."

They rode up a narrow game trail, past two waterfalls, switching back around boulders larger than houses, and tracing the west fork of Rock Creek almost back to its source. They rode past huge sentinel pine trees, aspen groves, Engelman spruce, and Douglas fir, some alive, some great ghosts of trees, blasted by the volts of summer storms or burst open by the freezing temperatures of past winters. They rode past crystal lakes beneath a plateau of grey granite. The snow-melt sparkled in the slanting winter light and streaked the rocky slopes with silver. A man could live up here in the crevices beneath the overhangs if he had to, like the Indians had before. Soon they emerged into a fair-sized meadow that the Indians called *Itsa Bots Sots*, "very good place" in the Crow language. And a beautiful place it was, fringed by towering pines with a good sized stream winding down to the larger creek. Wen could imagine it in summer, its green grass streaked with the purple and golds and pinks and blues of the mountain wildflowers. And there was a great grey boulder that jutted halfway out into the creek, perfect for fishing and dreaming. You could see the trout as they swam by. Yes, a man could live here all alone with his thoughts. He would bring Joey back here in the summer.

But now, even in December, there was a stand of grass in the meadow, good grass, that still stood high, brushed clear of snow by the wind, and trampled only lightly by one or two lonely whitetail deer. The two men went about building a travois from two straight pine trunks and cutting and loading the hay. It was grueling work. They filled the one sledge, then built another for the second horse, and loaded that heavily too. Then they started down.

"You lead, Wen. That mare a yorn will outwalk my Baldy ever'time. We just ain't as young as we used to be. Only look out for yer footing. Trail gets slippery, starts to freeze up when the sun goes down."

Wen smiled. He'd been up and down mountains too, and the old man knew it, but still he insisted on treating him like a kid.

They got back to the Fletcher place about dusk and still had the stacking to do, piling the hay in huge humps alongside the barn. Nan had hot biscuits and beef stew on the table when they finally came in. Tom slept with them that night.

Next day was bright and clear again, and the next and the one after that. And each day they made another trip to the Indian meadows where the sun warmed the south face of Whitetail Mountain, opposite the plateau where the silvery water ran.

On the fourth day, while Nan was alone with Joey, George Meachum came again. It was December 16th, nearing Christmas. With him were Slim and two hardened M-bar cowhands driving the other eight horses. They drove them right into the corral and slammed shut the gate. What with the new haystacks and the extra horses, the corral had shrunk.

Nan watched from the porch. George Meachum cut a masculine figure. She watched him wheel his big paint behind the last of the horses, stretch out a long arm, and swing the gate open. His men drove in the horses. Then he swung his leg over the cantle, dismounted, and slid the bar, closing the gate, all in the fluid and graceful motion of a finely coordinated athlete. He walked leisurely over toward the house.

"Ma'am, there they are. Tell Morgan to check them against his papers." The new and more spirited animals quickly subdued old Blazer, nipping and pushing, and effectively excluding him from the hay. "And you may want to cut out that old pet if you want him to eat. Where's Morgan?"

"Mr. Morgan isn't here, now. He and Tom Ludlam went up in the brakes to cut hay." She was amazed at how easily she trusted this man. "That's where those stacks came from. You know Tom Ludlam?"

"He's a smart man, ma'am." It was unclear whether he meant Morgan or Ludlam. "You'll need it all, that hay. How'd he know where to look?"

"He didn't. Tom Ludlam did."

Slim rode alongside and interrupted. "Mr. Meachum, we'll ride back by town if that's all right with you."

George waved assent. He was still looking at Nan, and now Joey had poked a head around the door.

"Ma'am, you have a cup of coffee for a thirsty cowman?"

"But of course, I'm sorry. Your men are welcome too."

"Ma'am, my men are more interested in Elkhead liquor than in your kind hospitality." The men had already turned their horses and were jogging toward town.

Nan blushed. George walked airily up to the door, smiled, pushed it back and held it open for her. Nervously, she walked in. He took off his hat. Joey popped up from a seat near the fire.

"You come for dinner mister?" Joey loved visitors.

George Meachum's handsome face laughed. "I haven't been invited, young man."

"You can stay, please. Tom always does and Mom always has enough."

"He misses the menfolk. They've been away these past few days cutting hay and he's lonesome."

"I understand. If you want me, I'd appreciate a good meal. Fine young man you have there..."

CHAPTER 19

The way down was steep in spots. Wendy could feel his horse lean its weight and push his hocks under him. The big travois and its load of hay rocked with each jerky step. Wen kept the pace slow, lest the bulk and the weighty load topple them all. Tom Ludlam followed about six lengths behind, the pack horses on lead ropes behind him. Joker ranged about fifty yards to the side of the trail, leaping happily among the rocks. It was just past one o'clock but already the shadows were deepening. Suddenly, Tom pulled up.

"Hold on there, got to get me something."

At this, he dismounted, ground hitched his horse, and jumped off. He had taken out his knife and headed for a three-foot spruce sapling about ten feet up the slope.

"We goin' to have Christmas fixin's for that young'un."

As he stooped to cut the sapling, a ugly growl sounded from the woods. Wen's horse shot forward down the trail. The two pack animals turned and scooted back up. Tom's horse, with the trail in front blocked and the big travois load and pack horses behind, reared. The travois toppled sideways and slid off the trail, toppling the horse over backward and dragging it downslope on its back across the slippery snow until it wedged against a giant deadfall. Old Baldy screamed his fear. His legs, tangled in the harness, flayed the cold clear air, unable to free himself from the bulky load. The deadfall stopped his skid but wedged old Baldy into the crevice between it and the mountainslope.

Tom Ludlam, for once, wasn't looking at his horse. He stood frozen in his tracks, knife in hand, staring straight uphill at a big female grizzly. His rifle was on his saddle, underneath old Baldy, but he carried a Colt in his belt.

Wen stopped the mare where she had lunged, about fifty yards down the trail, but he could not turn animal and travois in the narrow path. He was out of sight of the bear and Tom, and downwind. Carefully, he dismounted. Then he untied the mare from the heavy load and ground-hitched her. The mare twitched nervously, but did not run.

"At least you'll be able to get out of this girl."

He lifted his rifle from its scabbard and started back up through the heavy evergreen growth. Tom was still standing stock still. And the bear stood facing him.

"Morgan, don't move, stay where you are."

Wendy Morgan aimed his big rifle at the bear's head and froze. Grizzlies were unpredictable. Some would charge; some would take a good sniff and leave peacefully. There was no telling, but a grizzly provoked was a formidable opponent even for a man with a rifle. And a female grizzly with cubs was the fiercest. So far, there was no sign of cubs. Only a bullet in the brain or heart would stop a grizzly for sure. Wen had heard many a tale of grizzlies shot five, six times or more, who kept coming, one swipe of their tremendous paw enough to kill a man or maim him for life. He looked down the sights of his Winchester into the eyes of the bear. If he had to, he would make his shot count, but he held his fire. Tom stood; the bear stood; only the doomed horse kicked and struggled.

"Hold your fire." The bear had turned his head to look curiously at the horse. She was sniffling, shuffling, then as suddenly as she had appeared, she turned and lumbered back into the forest from which she had come.

Wen Morgan let down his rifle barrel slowly. Tom still stood where he was, but his muscles had relaxed. He stooped over and finished cutting his sapling. Joker bounded back from the woods.

"Got to see to that horse." Together they started down over the slippery, rocky slope. The horse was pinned, hind legs wrapped in the harness straps.

"If we can free those legs, maybe he can get them under 'im and pull 'imself out. But watch those hooves, he'll kick like a jackass when he knows they're loose."

"Settle 'im down a bit first." Wen was quietly approaching her head, trying to calm the frantic animal, but Tom had already gone behind, knife in hand. He started to cut the tough cowhide that coiled around the legs. He was bent, arms outstretched and tugging at the harness, intent on the effort when the horse jerked, snapping the strap and letting fly with a wicked hoof just underneath Tom's raised left arm. The hoof slammed into the side of his rib cage. He gasped and pitched over into the snow.

Wendy was there in an instant, pulling him out of reach of the flying hooves.

"I'm all right, I'm all right. Just can't take my own advice."

"That was a mean kick."

Wendy slogged down to cut the second trace, and kept well out of range of the flashing hooves. Still the horse could not get his feet under him. But old Tom was on his feet again. The two men knew they could not leave the horse - you did not leave an animal to suffer, prey to the buzzards and wolves and bears. Both were loathe to shoot him, but Tom had raised his rifle. The horse was exhausting himself, sweating fiercely. His thick winter coat was soaked through. In this state, the cold could kill him as easily a bullet.

"Take the travois poles and maybe we can wedge him up."

By this time, the horse was winded and spent. They pushed the poles under him from over the top of the deadfall, and pushed down using the sturdy poles like a lever. Morgan watched Tom grimace, whether with the strain of the effort or with a broken rib he could not tell. The animal rocked and grunted. Old Baldy was cast, legs useless, upon his back. They stuffed their hay under him to give him leverage. They pushed and tried again. On the third try, as if with his last effort, Baldy twisted his haunches, caught his rear hooves on solid ground and rolled. He was up and trembling, badly bruised and cut.

Wendy ran his hands over the terrified animal, over his shoulders and rump and up and down each leg. He was especially careful of the ankles and hocks.

"He's cut up a bit, but nothing broken...and nothing cut too deep. Let's get a blanket on 'im before he freezes. Take my bedroll." The horse tentatively put one hoof out in front of the other, trying what strength he had left. Slowly, the two men scrambled to get him back on the trail.

"How you doin'?" Wendy suddenly noticed that Tom was breathing in short sticky gasps.

"You go ahead. Take the pack animals and your load. Joker an' me'll give ole Baldy a rest and be along a mite later."

"You crazy old man? We'll wait and we all go down together. I don't leave a horse or man alone in the mountains even if he is an ornery old critter who kicks and screams. A youngster like me may never find you again." And he grinned. "Besides, I wouldn't separate your ar-ther-i-tis from your jug." Tom tried a laugh and frowned. Wendy passed him the jug.

CHAPTER 20

Dusk was lowering over the valley as George rode down over the bench and back to the Meachum Ranch. The slant rays of the setting sun cast an orange sheen on the eastern hills. He could see all the ranch buildings like sugar cookies on a tray, spread before him, glistening with a layer of frost. It would be dark soon. His horse snaked warily down the icy trail in short jerky steps with hocks tucked well underneath, carefully balancing himself and his rider with each separate step. It had been a long ride.

Thoughts of Nan, Wendy, and the peculiar little boy invaded his mind. How different their life was from the turmoil he was seeing at the ranch. He remembered the better days he had known, beginning with his roots on the Missouri farm. He was ten years old when they had left Kentucky for good. The farm outside of St. Joe was his first real memory of home and even that was vague. Most of all he remembered the horses, the big brown stallion, and his herd of docile mares. He could remember sitting on the fence in the south corner pasture, waiting for the Pony Express riders to gallop by. He and Dan would imagine themselves to be the hard-bitten, dusty men, setting out on their pounding relays across scorching desert and frigid mountain. How he wished he could ride like that. Maybe this was the source of his great love for horses. But that was about all he did remember of Missouri. The next summer the whole family, the Colonel, his six boys, old Jerry and Ma Simpson had trailed out and headed for Montana and a new home.

George remembered that journey. Every day had brought a new horizon and new elements of wonder to the life of an impressionable sixteen-year-old: prairie dogs, buffalo wallows, the first river crossing. During this passage, he met his first Indian, an old Pawnee come to beg food. Then there was that first summer, when all of them lived in one tent, with the horses herded or hobbled nearby.

That was the summer of building. He remembered the trips into the forest on the mountain slopes to select logs for the ranch house. Only tall and strong trees would do. Then they had to be trailed out to the ranch site one by one, hewn and notched to form the corners and beams, and hoisted into place. He remembered the walls rising, the chinking and the daubing to keep out the eternal prairie wind, and the day they were finished. He remembered cutting sections of sod for the roof. That first winter they had all lived under that roof and it had even harbored them when the temperature sank to thirty below. A log cabin was snug in the real cold. It was only after the thaw and the persistent spring rains that it began to leak little streams of muddy water. The dampness was almost worse than the cold and it persisted until the dry winds of summer aired everything out.

George thought of Nan Fletcher now. How would her tiny family fare this winter? He would not have liked to go back to those days of struggle. That old ranch house, added on to and re-roofed, had now become the bunkhouse, and a new and much larger house was the family dwelling and command post of the M-bar. And there was a calving barn and a large horse barn and corrals and fenced pastures. His was a proud, imposing home. The Fletchers' pride was not so evident.

He rode quietly into the yard. A lone cowboy was just lighting a lantern to cross the yard. It was not Fat Willie, whom George had respected as lord of the horse stable since his teens. This man was too thin. Willie would never have lighted a match so close to the barns and haystacks. Fire was a huge danger out here to man and beast alike, and once started, there was never sufficient water to quench the blaze quickly, especially a blaze fed by the dry logs. The cowboy reached the bunkhouse where the dim glow of oil lamps shone. Voices raised a hello. The cowboy was expected.

Not so George Meachum. He dismounted in front of the darkening horse barn and led his mount inside. Gently, he unsaddled and unbridled his mount and tied him in the aisle with a pile of hay.

No one had saved a stall for him. Then he, too, strolled somberly toward the house, alone.

He washed up at the stand in the hall and then joined his brothers, who were assembled at dinner.

"George, where've you been? Slim and the boys got back hours ago and from the looks of them, they'd been to town." It was Compton who was genuinely glad to see him.

He spotted Tag at one end of the table to Harv's left. His youngest brother was pushing back his chair, standing. "Hey George, I was wondering when you'd be here." Tag had walked across the room and had a hand on his shoulder, motioning him to a seat between himself and Gabe. He stared a moment at Tag. Tag was stooped and pale.

"I've been workin', countin' my herd." They all knew that meant the horse herd.

Harv spoke, "Good roast beef here. Set and eat." The words tumbled sullenly from beneath his moustache.

"I already ate, thanks."

"Well, sit down anyway." Harv was gruff, but seemed disposed to forget their disagreements for the time being.

Compton was in high spirits and seated at big Harv's right. He chimed in. "Harv's been showing me some real sign of coal out on the south range today. You've already some fair diggings."

"Gabe's doings. He knows where to look."

"And we saw that man you punched, out by the mine."

"Hendl? What's he want at the mine?"

Mose interrupted Compton. "Came to talk to Gabe. He's fretting, still has a burr under 'is blanket... He's mad about his horse. Not too many foremen would turn a puncher out without a horse."

"I paid his wages. He didn't need his horse to earn his keep." George did not like the gist of the conversation.

His implication was not lost on Harv. "George, I hired Hendl and he came in on a horse. You want him gone, he'll go on a horse."

"Not that horse. She's not his horse."

"No, She's your horse, brother." The suggestion of a smile curled one end of Harv's hairy lip. "I know. You want her for breeding. Give you some mighty fine colts. You ain't the Colonel's son for nothin'."

"It's not my horse either." George's tone was escalating. He was fast losing patience. "You asked where I'd been. I was returning that horse to its rightful owner, man name of Wendell Morgan over at the Fletcher homestead." George's cheek was ticking.

Harv's smile vanished and the hard straight lines in his face returned. "The Fletcher homestead?"

"You gave 'er to some greasy hoe-wielder!" Mose interrupted, almost shouting. "You gave away that mare to some no account farmer, probably underfeed 'er and work 'er like an ox. Kill 'er 'fore spring buds a poppin'."

"Morgan showed me breeding papers and a bill of sale. He raised her from a filly." George was answering Mose but looking directly at Harv. He threw his napkin onto his plate, disgusted. He got up from the table and bounded through the nearest exit door. It led to the porch and the cold night wind bit into his face like clusters of tiny icicles. Tonight, it felt refreshing.

Inside, he heard Mose snicker through his beard. "Fletcher homestead. That'd be the widow Fletcher. I seen 'er about town. Right smart piece a skirt. But that mare's a high price to pay for a lay." They all laughed. The tick in George's cheek pounded brutally.

Then Harv's voice bellowed almost congenially, "Surprised, Jay? Prairie's a big spread and women come scarce. A man gets mighty lonesome." Jay Compton did not reply. Harv added glibly, "Dan can take Hendl a horse tomorrow. Tell 'im we can probably use 'im again come spring. See if he's got enough to tide 'im over."

George felt the bile rise in his throat and every nerve tense with anger. He was turning to go back in, punching mad, enraged enough to smash the truth into Mose's brain, even take on blustering Harv. Tag intercepted him.

"Easy George." Tag had one hand on each of his shoulders and stood between him and the door. And behind Tag was Jay Compton. His torso filled the doorway. His face was grey and inscrutable.

"Leave it alone. They really mean no harm. Rough boys in a rough country. That's all."

George focused his eyes on his little brother. Tag was ghostly pale, his blond hair hung limp and dry, and his left shoulder hunched forward, giving him a crooked look like an old arthritic miner George once knew.

And there was Jay Compton, dapper and urbane, witness to the family feud. That wasn't the way George Meachum had envisioned the visit. But then, home was not what he had expected. He'd been away too long. They'd married him off to that vixen and he'd been fool enough to go along. Oh, it might have worked. He had wanted children and family, but she wanted no part of babies, too messy and too loud, too many creases in her velvet cushions and fingerprints on her sterling, too many pounds to bloat her corsetted waist. The brothers Meachum had put him well out to pasture behind the iron fence and manicured lawn in his gleaming gingerbread house. With another woman, it might have worked. With her, never.

"Sorry, Jay." He was regaining control.

They went back in by the hall, and on up to bed. And George Meachum made a decision that night as he lay sleepless, staring at the beams and quenching his smoldering resentment. He wasn't going back. Not to featherbed and soft-breasted wife, not to china plates and crystal, not to imported brandy and social prestige. Maybe, just maybe, he could clean the Meachum slate right here. He would hold his head up high again.

CHAPTER 21

Next morning, December 17th, George came down to breakfast late. Dance and Harv had gone off with some of the hands to start a herd toward Laurel and the railhead. Compton had gone along and would probably trail with them, and continue all the way to Billings and then home for Christmas. They had about four hundred head, not many, but they would probably roust out a couple of hundred more en route. Mose and Gabe had gone into town with a horse for Hendl. Tag and George rode out together to check the horse herd.

Slim and the Indian had close-herded the horses in a wide grassland, rimmed by sandstone outcroppings, called Boulder Basin. Here the horses would winter sheltered from the cold north wind and fed on windswept grasses. From the rim, the two men could see the old cowhand sitting a big-boned hairy grey on the left flank and the Indian walking his piebald pony quietly along the right. The brown and white horses grazed peacefully, pawing the snow to uncover the grass. George noticed stacks of fresh-cut hay, stored under the rim, out of the weather. Slim and the Indian had been busy.

George looked fondly toward the old man. "Tag, you ever want advice, you listen to that old-timer. He knows his horses and he knows ranching, knows where the good grass is and which way the wind's gonna blow tomorrow."

Tag nodded absent-mindedly, "I owe my life to 'im."

The younger man's voice was so soft, George was not sure he was supposed to have heard. He gave his brother time to collect his meandering thoughts.

Tag was glaring off into the distant hills over the heads of the herd and riders. "He saved my life." The horses' hooves were the only intrusion as they clopped evenly through the frozen silence. Tag's gaze focused straight ahead at a shining point in the distant peaks. His words spilled out in a sort of choking hiss. George was hearing a great confidence. "When Harv was chasin' those horses...I mean the day Grady was shot...I was with them. So were Slim and that Indian. We chased 'em, two men, eight prime horses." He hung his head. Again the silence, its only punctuation the steady hoofbeats. "Harv shot one, killed him from the way he fell. I'm not proud of that...thought about it for a long time...." He looked up at George. "You listenin'? I thought you should know... "

"You know I'm listenin'." George tugged the brim of his hat hard down over his face. The story finally started to flow.

And Tag continued, "The other man couldn't hold the horses and shoot at the same time, all alone. We had him holed up in some rocks the other side of Deer Creek. We got the horses, but then he winged me and took off through Deer Creek Canyon." He stopped to catch his breath, so long that George wondered if he had finished. But Tag did continue. "I was hurtin' and cold. They propped me against a tree. Must've passed out there...then, Slim and that Indian was nursin' me back."

"Harv left you there alone? Wounded, on the mountain?" No man left a friend, much less a brother, alone in the wilderness, prey to the wolves and the vultures.

"He sent Slim back, and that Indian there, Bull, Slim calls him."

They were nearing the herd now and Slim was riding up alongside.

"They're all here Mr. Meachum and in as good condition as me and Bull can do." Slim took his time, chewed, and spat a long stripe of brown tobacco juice onto the pristine snow. "They got their coats growed in thick as the bear cubs an' we got hay stashed under the overhang just like last year."

"Expecting cold weather, Slim?" The mercury had already hit ten below that morning, but then the air had rapidly warmed.

Slim bit off another chew, munched and rolled it into his cheek. "Well, Mr. Meachum, I don't know much, but this Chinook comes and goes. Lots a folks git their hopes up...like them dumb animals a yorn, thinkin' its spring in December...but that old Indian there tole me he saw a white owl settin' about dusk near Rock Creek, up the crags of a big ole cottonwood tree."

"A white owl?"

"That's the way he told it. It was white and it was an owl. Now, I didn't see it, but these Indians been here for generations and generations more 'n any of us an' I believe him." He paused again for effect, never rushing, collecting every strand of his memory, as if the good Lord's revelations depended on him. "And Bull says it's a bad omen, that the last time he saw one was when he was a young brave and he was coming back from a raid on the Sioux. Twenty horses, some of them buffalo runners, they'd stolen..." Slim was building his story now, like men do who spend lots of time alone and suddenly sense they have an eager audience. "Bull there was comin' in from that raid, waitin' for the hoopla like the redskins allays do for VIC-tor-i-ous warriors." Slim had a peculiar habit of punching first syllables and chopping important words into staccato bits. "He was a hero, Bull was. An he was all ready to buy himself a bride. But coming near to the camp, all he heard was wailin'. An' all he smelt was soot and ashes. Half the village, his sweetheart, and all his folks were dead, murdered by them yellow-bellied Pecunies while the warriors were away. Shoot a man in the back them Pec-cu-nies would."

"He told you all that?" There was no stopping Slim once he got a good story rolling and George had never heard the Indian speak of himself or his people. He was curious.

"He told me that's what happened the day after he saw that owl the first time, that he finished that day by building the burial platforms for every member of his family an' the girl he'd forever love. He rode away that night from that ghost place - that's what he calls it now - an' he swore revenge, but by this time the buffalo were scarce and the whites had taken over most of the water holes and river crossings. He chased them painted faces as far as the Musselshell River, where his horse gave out." Slim stopped.

George stared for a moment at the Indian who, sensing he was watched, reined his horse behind a big sandstone block. Tag cocked his head at Slim. Slim wasn't finished.

"That owl, I'd like to have seen it, Slim."

"Mr. Meachum, he's got his ways an' I have mine. I believe in every word that Indian says. But you got to unnerstand Indians.

They believe in signs." And now old Slim was talking down to his employers much as he did when they were youngsters on his knee, for their greater edification. "And now he says he seen that owl and dreamed of calves dyin' and wolves howlin'. Them's the dreams he been havin'." Slim's jaws rotated around the wad of tobacco. "Yeah, I think we're in for a bad time. Too many cattle, too dry a summer, grass didn't grow and what did is all et up."

"You sure you got enough hay stashed?" George knew the question was rhetorical.

"Much as we're gonna get this year.... Bull, he showed me where to get it. Back in the foothills. He allays knowed."

"Maybe we should ask him where to find more hay for the cows."

"He wouldn't know about that." Again, Slim stopped. He tongued the wad from one cheek to the other and started some serious chewing.

"What's the count now, Slim?"

"Fifty-two head, two stallions, fourteen yearlings, and nine two-year-olds. The rest is all brood mares except for a couple a geldings we keep for ridin'. Oh an' that little black mountain horse. That's Bull's when he heads for the mountains."

"He go often?"

"Only when he thinks the soldiers is after 'im or the law. He's careful 'bout them. He was runnin' from them fust time I seen 'im. Rode up to the ole ranch house lookin' like the wooliest savage you ever did see, but yer ole man knew what was up. Bluecoats was a chasin' 'im sure. Smart, yer ole man. An he let that Injun hole up in the barn an' in all his southland eloquence he explained to the good Sergeant that no Injun had 'ppeared anywheres near the M-bar. The soldier boys would a hanged 'im for bein' off a the reservation or plugged 'im full a holes or both. Naw, he only goes away now if'n he thinks the law is after 'im and sometimes to do his dreamin'. Goes to the mountain to dream and allays comes back lookin' like his hide's saggin' off'n his bones. Fastin' that's what he tole me he does. An' he has visions." George nodded and didn't question further.

On the way home, Tag and George rode side by side. "How long that Indian been with us, George?"

"Long time, since the buffalo disappeared. He's a good man with a horse, the best. Disappears from time to time, like Slim says. Goes back to the reservation and to his squaw, if he has one, or back into the mountains, but he's always here when you need him. Pa earned his loyalty all right. Saved him from the army boys - Pa never liked bluecoats anyway, being a Jeff Davis man. Bull won't work cattle though." This time it was Tag's turn to listen, and his brother rambled on. "Slim told me about that once too. Seems long ago, an old chief had a dream. He saw all the millions of buffalo stampeding down a big hole...every last one, right down into the gullet of the earth. And then he saw the earth vomit back herds of spotted buffalo." He was talking like Slim, almost biblically.

"Cattle."

"Yeah, cattle...white man's buffalo. And they devoured the range grasses that once fed the buffalo. That part's sure come true." He looked over at his young brother. "You remember the buffalo, Tag, how they used to play havoc with those first herds we had? Charge the herd and the steers would cut and run. I think that's why Dad moved the cattle in closer to the mountains, fewer buffalo here."

"I was just a kid." And George noticed that youth had vanished from this man. He was hunched, gaunt, and had sharp lines etched in his face. Tag had felt pain. He had aged.

As they neared the ranch, George Meachum was again riding down into the valley, this time with Tag, just as he had ridden twenty-four hours earlier, alone. He saw the same low-slung buildings, the same corrals glistening quiet and white beneath the snow, the same corkscrews of smoke twisting gently skyward from the chimneys. He thought again of Nan, of Joe, and the simple tranquillity of their poor cabin. He thought of the tall Crow lodges and the same smoke of homefires twisting gently from them, too. And he thought of the slurs and accusations of his own brothers at last evening's meal. Hendl, he'd have to find Hendl. But he'd have to leave Tag home.

They rode into the yard and Tag dismounted. George sat his horse.

"You comin' or goin'?" Tag interrupted the reverie.

"Me? Got some business in town. Got to do it myself."

CHAPTER 22

Town was alive that afternoon. The sun shone brightly and the warming wind had brought temperatures up to thirty-five degrees. Men and beasts were enjoying the thaw. Chairs were out on boardwalks, hats and gloves were off, dogs were barking and cats were sunning themselves or eagerly sniffing out the mice. Homesteaders' wagons lined the streets and shops were buzzing. Many had come in from the outlying ranches, trusting their herds to the warmth of what they were certain would be the mildest winter in ten years - especially after last year's freeze. And Christmas was coming.

George headed for the Elkhead Saloon and Rose McCartle. Heads turned, fingers pointed like witching sticks, some nodded a greeting, and others whispered the rumors of Meachum debauchery behind his back. He was well known in town. Tall and imposing, he had been like a feudal lord to Red Lodge until eighteen months ago, when he had officially moved to Billings. Even Rose, "the Rose" to most of the boys, gave him her heartiest welcome, a wet kiss on his clean shaven cheek and a bear hug. But nobody paid her much attention. Their dalliance had begun and ended years ago. Rumor was he'd almost married her. Almost was a flimsy word, two superlatives that, when joined, lost all their meaning. He thought of his own marriage. How much happier he might have been with Rose. They were simply good friends now, although her way of showing friendship was a bit more demonstrative than proper

Victorian behavior allowed. She took a bottle from the bar and led him to a back corner table. He poured out two whiskeys, sipped and rolled the yellow fluid around in his mouth before swallowing. She only touched the bitter liquid to her tongue.

"You been away too long." The perennial opener, the same greeting she gave his brothers.

"I'm back now." It was a simple statement. There was no immediate pressure to talk. They'd known each other a long time. George stretched his long legs comfortably under the table, hunched his broad shoulders, and leaned forward on his elbows. His right hand cupped the shot glass; his left lay flat, fingers splayed. His hat lay on the chair to his left. Rose sat close on his right. Together they watched every breed of plainsman enter or depart through the swinging doors. The Rose always sat against the wall, facing the room, in constant vigil of her patrons. George had chosen the chair against the wall for another reason. A man should always be careful of what or who was behind him. Now he was staring grimly and intently at the door. He rocked his chair all the way back to lean against the wall and took another swallow. The burning sensation in his throat soothed. Rose did not intrude, but waited. Many a man had come here troubled, depressed or just plain worn out, and she had learned to let whiskey and talk ease them out of it.

Finally, he looked over her way. "You want to know why I came?"

She met his gaze and nodded.

"Looking for a man, tall, dark, shot down that sodbuster, Fletcher. Maybe he left town, maybe he didn't. He probably came in here. He's a drinker."

"I remember. I saw it happen right over there. Bloodstain is still on the floor. He's been here. Why?" She was inquisitive, this one, and he smothered a chuckle.

"Used to work for us. I fired 'im. I want him gone. He's a hired gun. Used to be cattlemen had to hold on to their range, protect it, keep it clean for their brand. Now, too many ploughmen moving in with families and laws. Last few years, too many cattle crowding in, too many fenced off water holes. Things are changing, Rose..." He stopped, wondering if he should explain further. Would she understand? He changed the subject. "Lookin' to bring the railroad down from Billings. Sam Hauser's backin' it."

Rose groaned inwardly. The railroad to Red Lodge. It had already passed by sixty miles to the north. Why did intelligent men always confess their wildest dreams to call girls? What kind of insane hopes was this fine man harboring? She'd heard it before, from the miners who knew their vein was thinning and went bust in their last wild excesses of spending, from the cattlemen who know rustlers and harsh weather were constantly reducing their herds. They were always buying more steers. She listened incredulously, though patiently. "We'd be the central railhead for all the outfits south to the Shoshone, and east to the Rosebud." Rose listened but kept her eyes glued to the wall, her face inscrutable. News was bad, she knew, so bad the newspapers openly mocked the ranchers. What was it she'd read? She'd forgotten exactly. Something about fat Texas cattle munching figs and bananas. She hadn't seen any fat cattle this year, or any figs or bananas either.

His voice droned on, "We get the railroad. The railroad gets our coal contracts. Put us on the map permanently." He lifted his eyes and looked across at her. "Statehood's been a long time comin, Rose." He hesitated. "Can I trust you to keep quiet?"

"I'd never betray you, you know that."

Silence. He still drew back. "When Montana becomes a state, Rose, I'm going to run for Congress. Gettin' my house in order now."

Finally, she looked back at him, but the words stuck in her throat. Railroads and coal and Congress were the farthest things from her mind. Those mournful brown eyes and the rich bass voice worked their charm on her. She should have roped him and tied him years ago. She swallowed the whiskey. He'd be a good man to speak for the territory. But ever the pragmatist, she added, "And just what do you want me to do?"

"Do?" He hesitated. The question brought him back to the present. This was a women accustomed to "do" for a man, yet a woman with a highly developed business sense, and a stark realist. She'd asked that question of other men with differing results.

"Do?" he repeated. "Tell me about Bill Hendl. When did you see him last?"

"I didn't lay him, if that's what you mean."

Just then, one of the bargirls screamed, not just the shrill yelp of a puppy at play, but the piercing howl of physical pain. Rose was instantly on her feet and the burly bartender with her.

"Let her be, mister." This from the bartender-bouncer.

A pretty girl, very young in comparison to the others, cowered back at one end of the bar.

"Hey, no harm done. I just twistin' 'er arm a bit, persuadin' her to come wi' me upstairs an' she don't seem to ken." His voice was oily, it was so sweet. But his eyes shone from pure scorn.

"Back off then. That one there is taken."

"Don't see no other fellers cuttin' in on me." The cowboy had been drinking.

"Don't you know Amy's mista Dan Meachum's girl?"

"Wal," and the cowboy looked haughtily at the girl, "now you just call your mista Dan Meachum an' see if he can come take care a you. An' if he ain't here, mista Reb Jenks, that's me," and he swept his arm back in a mocking bow, swiping Amy a mean blow in the stomach, "Reb Jenks, he take care a you in good southern style, a whole sight better than your mista Dan Meachum."

The girl regained her breath, grimaced, pursed her lips, and spat. The soggy mass landed squarely on Jenks' moustache. He couldn't just wipe it off. Enraged, he lunged at her but the bartender's hefty arm blocked his path like an iron pipe. It slid up his chest and locked around his neck like a vise. The other fist gripped Jenks' arm and pushed it backwards to near breaking. Then Jenks was shoved summarily out the swinging door.

Rose came back to George's table, leading a shaken Amy.

Amy sat and gaped at the handsome rancher. Here was an older, more serious, confident, and very handsome version of Dancer. The physical resemblance was striking, same thick blond hair and brown eyes, same firm jawline and sensuous mouth. But Dancer was thinner somehow, narrower, more relaxed and playful, and of course younger, than this quiet imposing presence seated before her. She felt like a dirty little street urchin scooped out of the gutter and led into the presence of her prince.

"Amy, you've met George Meachum before." It was an offhand remark from Rose, even casual.

"No...ma'am."

"I'm George Meachum, Amy." The prince was holding out his hand.

Amy took it weakly while the Rose went on, to George. "Sorry, thought you knew each other. Amy's Dancer's girl."

"So I heard... How long you two been seein' each other?"

"'Bout a year."

George nodded silently.

"Your brother's been good to me."

"I'd expect him to be, to a pretty girl like you."

The compliment unnerved her and she blushed prettily. Conversation came to a halt.

Rose pushed things along. "Dancer has a reserve on Amy, and most of the men come in here know it and leave 'er alone. But there's always an occasional drifter wants to rob the nest. That and we got a crowd tonight. More and more cowhands comin' up from the south."

"Think he'll be back?" George cocked an eyebrow at Rose.

Rose shrugged. "And if he does, she's sittin' here with you. She's taken..." And she added with a smirk. "Think you can handle her?"

He smiled. "If I can handle him, you mean. You're a wise woman, Rose."

"Now, if you'll excuse me, I have other guests to entertain." George chuckled. Women, even whores, all pretended to perfect manners. He watched the Rose sweep away in taffeta skirts and decolletage, across the smokey room. She was still a good-looking woman.

Amy studied her hands, held together firmly on the table.

"Drink?" George offered.

"Please." Amy fingered her glass.

The conversation reached another hiatus. Both sipped slowly.

"Where'd you meet Dance?"

"Here, 'bout a month after I came... I wasn't liking it very much...I mean the work..." her face was scarlet. "Never enough of us girls to go around, specially after roundup. And some a them cowboys never seen a woman in months... Dance came along and he was good to me... gentle...and rumor just kind of happened that I was his girl...Rose understood, she's treated me fair. So I'm kinda on retainer for Dancer. Thought he'd be in tonight."

"He's in Laurel, maybe went on to Billings. We sent a herd up yesterday."

"Oh."

"He should be back for Christmas. You have any family? Where you from?"

"I was raised in New Orleans." That explained her easy drawl. "Grew up with my Granny and my Pappy. But they died from the fever when I was ten. Then I lived with my Daddy 'bout a year 'til he put me in school. A convent, it was, with nuns and all. How I hated that!" She laughed.

"You came from a convent, here?" It was a bit much even for George Meachum.

"Yeah." She giggled now.

George was laughing at the bizarre circumstances that form a life on the frontier.

"Just 'bout. Couple a months on a paddle wheeler with my Daddy. Then he disappeared. He always told me to come to his old friend Rose McCartle if something happened, and he left me just money enough for the stage ride.... So here I am. I think Daddy and Rose had something together on a time." She shrugged. "No matter, Rose's been good to me. You come from a fine old family of the South, too, least that's what Dan told me."

"You could say that." George was smiling now, not paying much attention to Amy, musing at the wiles of women, of Rose in particular, curious about her colorful past and her matchmaking with his brother and this little waif. How he could read the Rose's mind! But then, Amy was a perky and friendly little thing. He was laughing inwardly and enjoying himself. And she really seemed to like Dance.

Amy prattled on about Dan and all the exaggerated things he had told her about the Meachum heritage, all the old Colonel's inventions and aspirations to glory. For a whore, she was entirely too gullible. But as he watched her, it occurred to him that those bright eyes, trusting now after the resolution of the Jenks episode, and that gently humming soprano voice, flowing now without the pauses born from the fear of imminent physical harm, that this girl just possibly might be in love with Dancer, his little brother Dancer, who all his life had tagged along at his bigger brothers' heels. Lucky Dancer.

"Well, look, you can drink with me tonight. But I am Dancer's brother and I'm not here to pay your wages." It occurred to him that he ought to have used his marriage as an excuse, but that it really didn't matter. He held out his glass, "Cheers!" he said, "May you bet the limit on every whirl, kid." And he echoed his thoughts, "Lucky Dan!"

Amy smiled, clicking her glass to his, "To brother Dan." When she smiled, she was even beautiful.

CHAPTER 23

It was getting late. Darkness had fallen, but George had not forsaken the thought of getting back to the M-bar for the night. He walked Amy down to Auntie Nell's. Her easy conversation and a hearty steak dinner relaxed him further and when he walked her back to the Elkhead, their footsteps tapped lightly on the boardwalk. He held back the swinging door for her and it swung wide.

"One more before you go."

He nodded, "O.K., one to ride home on."

As they walked through the smoke and between the gambling tables, George felt a hundred eyes directed at him, like a hundred little pricks on the back of his neck. They came up to the bar and George recognized the surly Mose and Gabe, who quietly nodded and elbowed a space for them, staring all the while at Amy. This would give them something else to think of besides him and the Fletcher woman. And just beyond them, gripping his shot and squinting darkly and sourly sideways, stood Bill Hendl.

George addressed his brothers in a way to dispel all doubt. "You know Dancer's best girl, Amy? Amy, my brothers Moses and Gabriel." The formality masked any feelings of hostility for the time being, but George sensed that his time in town need not be prolonged any further. To take on Hendl here, in front of his brothers in a crowded barroom, would only expose the family dissent. He ignored Hendl. Mose and Gabe duly nodded to Amy, Mose almost bowing. Even the meanest of the Meachum boys was ingrained with

120

good plantation manners in front of the ladies. "Ma'am, 'tis my greatest pleasure." Mose even produced a rare smile through the tufts of his beard.

"Amy had a little unpleasantry with a rowdy puncher, stranger in town, didn't know how we Meachums treat our women. And, of course, Dan being in Billings, I stepped in."

Mose nodded. Gabe followed suit and in his most flattering, sugary baritone added, "We'all do the same, ma'am. You have any little troubles, you can always call a Meachum. I'm sure Dance told you that." The Meachum boys, so different in temperament and sensibilities, hung tightly together when the affront was from an outsider. Amy, now, was one of their own, and George knew that Mose and Gabe would spring to her defense should the need arise and Reb Jenks return. As for himself, it was time to go home. Hendl's drunken stare from the end of the bar only reminded him more urgently.

He brushed back the thick strands of golden hair with his hand, set his hat firmly on his head and slapped a silver coin on the bar.

"I'm headin' back home. You boys all have another on me!" It was a peace gesture toward Bill Hendl, a truce for the time being.

George Meachum picked up his horse at Dave Lewis's livery and blacksmith shop and started down the trail for the M-bar, a tired and shadowy figure on a plain brown horse. In summer, he would have blended quietly into the background of prairie and outcrop, but now in winter, the dark horse and rider etched a stark silhouette against the moonlit snow. The night was somber, the moon and its light having retreated behind a curtain of thickening clouds. George was tired. He probably should have waited until morning to ride home. He would have waited if he'd been with any other girl except his brother's, and if he had not still been nagged by thoughts of that poor farmer's wife, Nan, and her kid, and that Morgan and his horses. He could have gone to the lonely hotel, a not very appetizing prospect of dirty sheets, bedbugs, and dormitory privacy, as were many of the west's pioneer establishments. But he had a good horse, a clean bed waiting for him, and his more cantankerous brothers had gone to Billings. Tonight, tomorrow, he and Tag could relax. He was adept, like most cowboys, at sleeping in the saddle to the even rhythm and sway of his horse. So he picked up the horse at Dave Lewis' livery and blacksmith shop and started down the trail for the M-bar.

He thought of Hendl, the Texan, he should have taken care of that little matter this afternoon, but to do so in front of Mose and Gabe would have aired the family linen for the whole town to see. It wasn't that he was afraid of Hendl. He'd already bested him, but George did have a sense of time and place. He swung round in the saddle now and looked back at his trail. Had he heard a horseman behind him? Some extra sense, some vibration on the night wind seemed to warn him. George Meachum trusted his instincts. Bleeker's Rock was just ahead, the same Bleeker's Rock where the mysterious stranger had ambushed Harv and shot Tag. He did not slow his horse's even march. To do so would announce his warning as clearly as any cavalry bugle. He did loosen the flap of his holster and draw his rifle from its boot on the saddle. And so, with one hand on the reins and one on the trigger, George Meachum approached Bleeker's Rock. The horse walked evenly onward. George strained his ears to hear any and every extra sound. An owl hooted. No Indians near here anymore. It was a real owl, maybe the white owl. Then he heard a scratching. A mouse? Too small. A squirrel? Again, he heard it, like a roll of tiny pebbles scraping against the smoother surface of rock. He tried to increase his horse's gait little by little so the quickening rhythm would not be detected. His eyes searched the darkness. Bleeker's Rock loomed near his right now. Again the scratching, and George Meachum thought he heard a rifle cock. He dug his spurs into the horse's flanks. The animal shot forward with a surge of power like a charger in the medieval lists. A shot rang out from behind the rock, but wide in back of its mark. George had lunged forward the instant before the shooting. He turned, swinging the rifle barrel behind him, trying to find a target in the darkness from the back of his lunging horse. There was nothing. A moment sooner, and he might have seen the flame from the discharge. As it was, he could only trust to his hearing, and that was muffled by the thundering clatter of the racing horse.

Recklessly, he let the horse gallop onward across the slippery frozen ruts of the icy trail. He only slowed when the trail turned downward at the rim of the valley and he could see the flickering lights of the oil lamps through the canvas windows and smell the smoldering cottonwood logs of the evening's hearth fires. His poor horse was lathered from nose to tail. The animal had saved his life. Now wet and winded, he could easily get chilled. The temperature was dropping fast. George dismounted and threw his tarp over his horse. He walked him down the valley slope, out of the wind, and into the stable. Miraculously, Willie was still there, walking a colicky mare.

"You there, ain't no place for late boys in here." Willie's voice squeaked irritation.

"It's me, Willie. Been ridin' fast and hard. Somebody tried to plant me up by Bleeker's Rock. Horse is winded bad."

Willie's throat gurgled. "Yeah, mista George," Fat Willie remembered many a night when George had been courting one or another of the area beauties, many a night later than this. Willie minded his animals, but he had little patience for George's supposed carousings. "Wa'al, mista George, you go turn Brownie there out in the corral. Take his stall, if'n ye ken. I'm busy."

There was nothing to do with Willie in such a mood, so George, tired and sore from a tail-slapping ride, set about the stable work himself. That meant he had to walk his horse until he dried or he took the chance of seeing the animal founder and sicken. So he walked back and forth in the steps of Fat Willie, monotonously up and down the aisle between the stalls. As the animal's breathing slowed and he cooled down, so did George Meachum's anxieties. Gradually, rational thought and common sense replaced impulse. Hendl, it could only be Hendl. Hendl, the drunken gunslinger who held a grudge; Hendl, to whom his brother Mose had given a horse and his brother Gabe a new job at his infant mine; Hendl, who had tried to draw on him once and failed, and who had seen him leave the Elkhead. Hendl was cowardly enough to shoot from ambush, especially with his smashed hand. His days of fast draws were over.

Dawn was breaking when George finally crept into bed. The next morning, December 18th, it started to snow.

CHAPTER 24

Wendy Morgan wrapped himself in an old buffalo robe and prepared to brave the blizzard. Snowflakes swirled into furious eddies as they blasted against the door. The temperature had fallen to thirty below. It had been snowing since just before dawn. He had to get the horses into the shelter of the barn. The prospect of leaving the warm hearth fire in the snug cabin was not at all inviting, and he had to cover every inch of skin to avoid the whitening numbness that was frostbite. Now he knew why Tom Ludlam insisted that he stay: no woman and boy alone could have coped with this kind of ferocity. Nan opened the door for him and he stepped out. Visibility was limited to a few feet. He had heard stories of men, camped in storms not fifty yards from the shelter of a stage station or barn, who shivered through whole nights thinking they were lost. And wasn't it the Hartley brothers, two young and robust men, who had starved and frozen in their very own cabin for lack of fuel!

Thanks to Tom Ludlam, they were ready, with a good supply of split logs stored inside and kept dry and free of snow, and a good supply of meat and grain. Chickens and cats had moved in with the family. It was crowded, but snug. The chickens' eggs were a precious source of protein and cats were their front line protection against an invasion of starving rodents. Wendy wondered how the wild animals fared in such conditions. God had prepared them. But what about the range cattle, wild though they behaved, newly imported from the milder climes of Texas? They didn't have the heavy coat or fat layer that nature had evolved in her native species.

Nan had wisely conserved the fruits and berries of the previous harvest, and ground the grain, and very wisely strung a rope the short distance from cabin to barn in anticipation of just the kind of gale Morgan faced now.

As he stepped onto their narrow porch, the wind hit him. It was enough to flatten a weaker man. He held the rope firmly to keep his balance and reached the quiet stable quickly and safely, then edged along the barn wall and corral fence to the gate. There stood the horses, all eight of them, their heads tucked down to their knees and their rumps turned to the driving snow. Only two rope halters hung by the gate. He would have to lead them two at a time, taking no chances of letting some follow freely. They were not yet used to their new home and might bolt and run in the storm. Wen knew each one well. He had raised them, and he was not about to lose them now. Two by two, like Noah to his ark, he brought them into the barn. It was crowded here, too, and the animals nipped and stomped. Two horses for each box, Blazer and the cow in the third, and four horses tied in the aisle. They all quieted when he forked them a little hay. Bless old Tom for the hay. And that damn dog.

Where was Tom Ludlam now? How was he doing after the accident on the mountain? Wendy thought he had cracked a rib, maybe several. Have to ride over there after the storm - if the valley is clear. Have to invite him over for Christmas dinner. Tom would like that. No man should be alone for Christmas. He chuckled at the thought of Joey's scrawny Christmas tree. And Joker, he'd have to come along too.

He forked more hay to all the horses and stroked the mare's sinuous neck. It was bitter cold in the barn, but the horses and the cow munched peacefully. With good feed and protection from the Arctic wind, they would survive. He braced himself for the trip back across the yard. Opening the big door a crack, he squeezed through just as the gale tore it from his hands, slamming it shut. With his right hand he lunged for the rope, caught it as the wind wrenched his body around. Sharp pain blinded him and he fell. On hands and knees, he groped for the lifeline, found it, and struggled back the way he had come. How long had he been gone?

Nan was waiting, at the door. When she heard his rumbling steps on the porch, she let the door fly and the snow rush inside. He was hurting again. She sensed it as he stumbled in. Joey shut the door. The cold, the blizzard, the wind, the struggle to survive, all melted into a haze of warmth. They clung to each other.

And Wendell Morgan ached in his heart, not the sort of ache that comes from the sudden stress on an old wound. It was the ache of a man for a beautiful woman. Yet he could not form words to soothe his pain.

"Horses are safe."

"Yes...and you, your bullet wound, it's still sore." And she smiled and led him to the chair by the fire. "Maybe I should look at the scar." She laid her hand on his arm.

"No, it's fine." He was forcing a smile and inwardly denouncing his own self-doubts. What could he say to this woman? He wanted to say that he would stay with her and her son for the rest of the winter, that in the spring he would leave them, but that he had come to care deeply about them even now, and that he wanted to take her to bed. She wanted him too. This he could sense. They were both afraid. What would they say to the boy? And he had nothing, no land, no money, only a string of horses that were the envy of every thief. He had lost them once already and almost lost his life. He thought about Old Tom, even he had more.

Tom Ludlam felt the blizzard coming. "Joint disease" he called it. "Arthritis," Doc Zilka called it. Nothing he could do about it. Every year his knees, shoulders, hips, and the back of his neck started to ache with the coming of December. Each year it was getting worse, especially worse before an approaching storm, when the air pressure was dropping. And this year he had broken a couple of ribs and had to strap himself up for that. He didn't feel too well, but he was ready for the storm. His aches and pains had warned him.

Now he watched the coals settle in the bottom of his hearth. This year, he wouldn't be going hunting. He'd be a long time settin' alone like this, longer than ever before. He just couldn't quite keep up like he used to, not even with Joker. Joker was a young dog. This year Tom had thinned his stock, delivering most of his yearlings and two-year-olds to Dave Lewis for sale. He'd only kept old Baldy, who was ailing like himself, and three other mares and his stallion, and they were snug in the dugout stable - safe that is, until the mares came into season with the spring and he'd have to find separate quarters for the stallion, or he'd have a tiger in a tea kettle. By then, all his aches would have eased, snow would have melted and he could turn the stallion out.

He lifted himself slowly off his chair, walked to the door and opened it a crack. It was getting colder by the hour. His bones never lied.

"Joker, you devil, you come." His old voice was still loud enough.

The shaggy black beast lumbered out of the blackness, jaws gripping a fat grey squirrel.

"You too fast for 'em, huh boy...come on in. He'll make a good stew and I'll give you some too." He scratched the mongrel's ears. Joker hadn't gotten as many treks this year either. They spent all their time fetching enough hay and after that, the exertion of an elk hunt would have exhausted him completely. Had to have some strength left to face winter emergencies. They were inevitable.

Joker tramped in and took his usual place in front of the fire.

Old Tom talked to the dog as he talked to the horses and as he talked to himself. It was a peculiar habit from so many years of living alone.

"You come in quick tonight, boy. Gonna snow isn't it. You can smell it an' I can feel it."

The dog stared back, yawned and settled his snout on the hearth. Tom took out his hunting knife, skinned and cleaned the squirrel and slid it into the large iron pot suspended over the fire.

"'T ain't beefsteak, boy, but it's a meal. Time was, I et better and I et worse."

Together, they ate and fell asleep. Tom awoke to Joker's wet black nose nudging his chin and a long pink tongue slurping his cheek. It was the tongue that woke him, like a splash of ice water in the frigid temperatures inside the cabin. The fire that had burned brightly the night before and that had exuded a penetrating warmth, now had burned to embers. Tom immediately got up and stirred it, adding extra logs. The flames picked up but it would be a while before they warmed the air. Then he walked to the door to let Joker out. The door swung inward and when he pulled it, snow blew in. It was already piled about a foot against the door.

"I knew it was a comin'," Tom mumbled to himself. Joker had already bounded out, a frolicking black whirl in the thickening snow.

CHAPTER 25

Harv and Dancer Meachum had arrived at the loading pens in Billings on the afternoon of the seventeenth. Immediately, they contacted the buyer Harv had contracted and made the official sale: 620 head. They crossed the street to the glistening new King's Hotel, booked rooms, had a hot bath and a shave, and headed out to spend what was left of their evening on the town. A wild and eager town it was.

And an incongruous pair of Meachum brothers they were. Big Harv, all six feet four inches of him, the wide chest and stomach hanging out over his silver buckle, the Colt strapped to his heavy thigh, ten gallon Stetson adding another three inches to his height, spent the evening with a whiskey bottle and a deck of cards right there in the hotel lobby. No one challenged him. They left him alone. Dancer, lithe, agile, and ten years his junior, donned a black cutaway, string tie, and planter's porkpie, tucked his share of the receipts of sale into his breast pocket, and strutted off with a whistle and a grin to woo the ladies and see the sights of bustling downtown Billings. No riverboat gambler was better dressed. No one would have suspected that he was newly arrived from the trail. Harv frowned when he saw Dan's "dude outfit," as he called it, but the younger man had become inured to his disapproval years ago. Dan simply went his own carefree way. Never had the older man entrusted the younger brother with any important responsibility, just as now Harv withheld the greater portion of their proceeds from the spendthrift fingers of his little brother.

As Dancer Meachum picked his way across the crunchy frosted street - it had gotten much colder - it occurred to him that he had not been to Billings since his brother, George's wedding day. And it occurred to him that Mrs. George Meachum, the former Brenda Crowley, was languishing all alone in her big, new, as yet still empty Victorian house. So Dancer Meachum avowed then and there to pay a call on his sister-in-law, Mrs. George P. Meachum.

Finding the house was no problem, a discreet inquiry from an all-knowing barkeep, a two-block stroll, and he was pushing open the iron gate and knocking at the glass panelled door. All the while his mind was whirling at the sight of such luxury. Even greater was his surprise when a pigtailed Chinaman answered. He hadn't known his brother was a Chink-lover. In Red Lodge, they ran them out of town. Yellow buggers only good for blasting the insides out of mountain ranges and blowing themselves to hellfire in little pieces. Such were the cruel prejudices Dancer Meachum had been taught.

But Ling ushered him promptly and courteously into the hall and from thence into a spacious salon.

"Would Missa kinly sit comfortable while he go tell Missa Meachum you here."

Dancer nodded, took off his hat and laid it gently on an emerald green satin pillow.

Ten minutes later, Dan Meachum was still waiting. But he had relaxed in the same deep cushioned gentlemen's chair that was his brother's favorite.

Ling came back with a bottle of brandy, two glasses, and a cigar on a silver platter. "Was there anything missa needs?"

"No, thank you." Dancer shook his head and poured himself a glass of brandy, smiling. He was fast beginning to appreciate his brother George's style. He walked aimlessly about the room, drumming his fingers on the mahogany mantel, fingering the silver candlesticks and crystal vase on the sideboard, stroking a marble table-top and a shiny ebony piano. He ran a finger across the keys. The piano was in tune. It was hard to comprehend that all this belonged to a Meachum and to his brother.

And ten minutes later, after the cigar was lit and the glass of brandy settled leisurely on the nerves, Mrs. George Meachum made her entry.

"Dan Meachum, what a charming surprise! And just tell me all about what brings you to Billings this fine evening." The accent was southern, maybe authentic. No mention of George, not even a simple query about when he would be back.

"Ma'am," Dan was deferential, "we made a cattle drive, ma'am."

"No bother this 'ma'am,' I'm your sister now," she interrupted brazenly. "You call me Brenda. Now, what's all this about a cattle drive? In this weather? It's winter!"

"Last one this year, ma'am."

"You should have told me you were comin'. Why you-all must be hungry and Ling hasn't got a bite in the larder. I was retirin' early."

How Dancer could possibly have told her he was coming, he could not imagine. He had never met a woman quite like this one before. He launched into a description of the drive, of George's reasons, of big Harv and Jay Compton. At the mention of Compton, she paid attention.

"Mr. Compton, you say, of the Northern Pacific. He was here the other day to see my husband. What a charming gentleman! Don't tell me he's in town?"

"Yes, ma'am. Matter of fact, I'm due to meet him at the National in about an hour." The National was the biggest hotel in town.

And so it was that the trio, Mr. Jay Compton of the Northern Pacific, Mr. Daniel Meachum of the M-bar, and Mrs. George Meachum, hostess and social climber, dined together until midnight at the National on the evening of December 17th. Dan Meachum never remembered inviting her to come. He had never intended spending the whole evening with his sister-in law.

Nor had he ever seen so many different utensils at one place for dinner in his life. There were two knives and three spoons to the right of his plate, dinner and dessert fork to the left, and above his plate to the left of his four glasses lay another spoon, a small, three-pronged fork, and a larger fork. Then there was the water goblet, the claret glass, a taller wine glass for white wine, and a special wide one for champagne. Never had he tasted champagne. The bill of fare was longer than the Laramie Daily Boomerang. The meal itself proceeded through a bevy of dishes from hors d'oeuvres to after dinner liqueur. Dan Meachum picked up one fork and one knife pushing the superfluous silverware out of his way. Brenda Meachum's jaw dropped. He ate every morsel. The food was delicious. And she pretended he wasn't there.

Compton was hungry too, after the long ride back, but was too polite to let Brenda Meachum's prattle go unanswered. As the conversation bounced between the two of them, Dan enjoyed one of the best feeds he'd ever had. And his young mind absorbed it all, from the fringed, brocaded curtains to the last drop of brandy in his snifter. He listened to the bits of social banter going on around him and heartily shook the hands of Compton's acquaintances who came to their table to pay respects. It was Daniel Meachum's blooding to civilized society despite his horrified in-law.

He slept well that night in spite of the snores and grumblings that penetrated the paper-thin walls. Harv, too, was content after doubling his profits at the blackjack table. Nothing George need know about. He could afford to pay gunman's wages. He could afford Bill Hendl when he needed him.

On the morning of the 18th, when the two of them woke, snow was falling thickly. It was not a day to travel. Dan welcomed the excuse to stay, but Harv was restless. And during the day, more and more cowboys and stockman drifted in to join them, unable to keep watch over their cattle in the deepening snow. And the cattle drifted before the gale, seeking whatever brakes and canyons they could find.

Bill Hendl drifted too. He clapped his hands together on his way back to town. He was cursing his sour luck. Not like him to miss a clean shot even in the dark. The night had been very dark, clouds settling in and covering the moon, but the reflection of starlight on the snow gave faint light. Usually, he had good night vision. The hand George had smashed was still sore and stiff with the cold. He wiggled his fingers for warmth. The blood pounded in his temples. He'd been drinking. It was colder than he could ever remember, but then he was used to Texas, and Texas is to Montana in the winter like bananas are to icicles. He'd head back to Texas except for the Rangers. In Texas, he was a wanted man, him and Murph and Jenks. He wondered when Jenks was going to show up. They catch him and it was life in the pen or the end of the rope, and he had no intention of getting planted in Boot Hill too soon. Besides, Harv Meachum paid well. Reb Jenks would ride in soon to replace Grady. He clapped his hands some more, blew on his fingers and put his gloves back on. Weather was just too damn cold for this outdoor stuff. There had to be a warmer way of evening the score with George Meachum, one more comfortably suited to the temperature. Grady would have known what to do. He missed Grady. He unhitched the nag Mose had brought him, snapping the reins cruelly. He needed a better, faster horse. That mare now, she was a fine mount. He remembered well his departure from the M-bar, the swift long and even strides of the superior horse. The choppy little jog of his present mount only irritated him more.

Now he headed back toward Red Lodge. A shot of whiskey in his gut would warm him fast. What he really needed on a night like this was a flask. It was a cold ride back to town.

For the second time that night he swaggered through the Elkhead doors. He stood just inside the door shaking the trail dust from his hat and heavy sheepskin coat, a dark hulk of a man. People would know he'd been gone. And George Meachum would hear of it for certain - Mose and Gabe were still there. Let them tell him. Let him know it was Bill Hendl had taken a shot at him and was out to kill him. Let him writhe a little under his fancy white dude's collar. "Fear," he liked the silky sound of the word. George Meachum would fear him, Hendl, the toughest man in the outfit. The failed ambush irked him, but it had not shaken his confidence. He'd make his mark. But his hand was sore and his trigger finger cramped from the cold.

The bartender put out a bottle of whiskey when he saw Hendl approach and turned his back to wipe another glass with a dirty towel.

Hendl leaned casually over the bar rail and pulled off his gloves. Again, he clapped his cold hands together and poured himself a drink.

Rose watched from her table, fingering an empty glass. Hendl was a hard drinker and had proved it. He was a dead shot and had proved that too. The combination needed careful watching, like George had said. She signalled Melly to tend to Bill Hendl. A little female distraction always helped to divert his kind from the bottle and the gun.

Melly promptly rubbed up against Hendl at the bar.

"You come back to Red Lodge, big boy," she cooed.

Hendl smiled. He had just acquired a pocketful of cash from Mose Meachum. The whiskey snaking down from his throat had warmed him, while his frustrations were fading fast.

"Yeah, Melly, and I'm buyin'." He poured her a drink, then ran a finger down her cleavage and across the low-cut top of her gown. Rose watched. Melly performed on cue.

They moved off to a nearby table and soon were climbing the stairs to new delights. Hendl, it turned out, was a disappointing lover, too fast, too soon, and he fell asleep like a hibernating bear right after. He snored and it was cold in the room. Melly dressed and went back downstairs.

The crowd should have been thinning by now, but the cold had driven more and more men in from the mining camps and the ranges, even from the squatters' huts nearby. It was warmer where men collected in groups and warmer where lust and liquor boiled the blood. Besides, the Rose's place never really closed, even when dawn was fast approaching. There was a perpetual poker game, always an ongoing blackjack game, and, most popular among the patrons, a large green pool table, not to mention the best stocked bar within a hundred and sixty miles. Fortunes ebbed and flowed as much on the game of pool as on the game of poker. Bookies circulated through the crowd, quoting odds and collecting money. And, of course, the Rose and her girls earned a hefty profit.

Mose and Gabe watched the pool players now from the edge of the table. They'd paid Bill Hendl, delivered the horse, and told him to stick with the M-bar, that his job was still waiting, pending the departure of George Meachum for Billings, come spring. Come sooner than that, they hoped. They resented George. Gabe had tried his hand at pool earlier and had lost. He always did better, as did Mose, when he bet on someone else, like his brother Harv. Harv was the family ace at this game. They had seen Bill Hendl enter for the second time and seen him strike his pose by the entrance. He looked like he belonged in one of those travelling melodramas, pruning and peacocking like that. Gunmen were a flamboyant breed - they all loved a little swagger. Hendl was no different from the rest and he'd be around come spring, or, if he ran out of money, sooner. If he kept a running account with the ladies, he'd run out of money very soon.

Mose walked to the door and looked out. Too late and too cold to start for the M-bar tonight. He walked back over to his brother. "I ain't goin' home in the dark. Wait 'til mornin'." He was leaning back, putting his feet up on the table, and stirring the ashes in his pipe. He was thinking of George, who had headed home earlier. He'd sleep comfortably tonight. "It's cold and snow's comin'."

Gabe spoke. "George's gettin' in the way."

"You mean with that tough, Hendl?" Mose grumbled through his beard never even opening an eye. "Yeah, Hendl an' the others...an' the cattle drive an' all them fancy horses. An' now he

says they ain't his. Harv don't like it much. Can't say I do neither."
Gabe stared intently at his older brother.

"I was thinkin' the same." Mose still hadn't moved, but he sensed the envy and resentment in his brother's voice. He felt the same. "You stick to yer minin'," he had pushed the brim of his hat back above his eyes and was scrutinizing his younger brother carefully, "You ain't thinkin' a mustering out, are you?"

"Nah." It was abrupt, final. There was a long pause.

"I'm gonna catch me a few winks 'fore the sun comes up." And Mose leaned back, put his feet definitively up on the table and pulled his hat down over his eyes. The subject was closed.

Gabe pulled out a chair and sat restlessly down beside his older brother, watching the clientele go in and out, until one cowboy entered, took off a huge Texas Stetson and showered the floor with a circle of snow.

"Damn!" Gabe cursed. He got up and looked out the door at the beginnings of a blizzard. "Damn!" he muttered again, grabbed his coat and pushed his way out the door and across the street to the hotel.

CHAPTER 26

The day had been so pleasant, Slim would have untied his bedroll out in the open, until the Indian kicked it, grumbling about the lumps in the ground, the wind in his face, wet ground. Finally, he laid it out back under the overhang simply to escape Bull's constant needling. They bedded comfortably under the sheltering rocks on a soft mattress of stored hay and picketed their mounts nearby. Slim lay awake, his head resting against the soft sheepskin lining on the underside of his saddle. The Indian had finally fallen off to sleep and ceased his interminable hassling. Slim didn't remember Bull ever acting like that before. Bull was usually silent, and Slim Halloway liked him like that. He was silent, except when he snored and grumbled in his sleep, in the language of his people. If he said something intelligible, Slim had no idea what it was. The two men, so different in culture and race, had developed a quiet cohesiveness, never intruding on one another's privacy, yet each fully respectful and helpful in their work. Tonight's episode was a new role for Bull. Slim wasn't sure he liked it much.

Trouble was, from back under this overhang, you couldn't see the horses from your bunk. If they started to wander during the night, it would be morning before anyone knew it, and it would take some long, hard and cold riding to round them up and bring them back. No question, it was more comfortable, but warmer? Without a fire? Bull was adamant that they avoid *kissin-ey-oo-way-o* even without a fire, and that the horses would find them in the morning. Slim wondered if the old Indian had been dreaming again.

The old man shivered. He felt the cold invade first his old toes and the tips of his fingers and nose. It would have been warmer with a campfire, out a ways, where you could keep an eye on the horses. No fire, not back here near the hay. He looked over at the Indian. You could hardly see him, bundled down as he was deep into the hay, on such a dark night as this. But you could hear him snore, softly, steadily. And every so often you could hear a rustling on the ground, the scrape of pebble on pebble, stick upon stick, as a horse got up or lay down. Slim rubbed his eyes. No moon, no stars, he really couldn't see at all, just hear. And he was cold. Finally, he wiggled farther down into the hay and dozed off.

He awoke suddenly to the sound of breaking sticks and rasping pebbles. It was the horses, pushing in closer toward the rocks. And then he heard it - the wild and insistent howl of the north wind as it rushed out of the Arctic, over their cutbank, and out onto the sweep of plains. As dawn crept in, slowly, ever so slowly from black to grey, he could finally focus on huge crystals of white pouring out of the sky. He barely saw the horses huddled in close. He blinked, not fully comprehending, then slowly began to understand. A blizzard, this was a vicious blizzard, knocking out with one swift blow all the balminess of yesterday, all the casual attraction of sleeping under the stars, all the overblown hopes of an easy winter on the plains. If Slim had bedded in the open, his fire would have blown out and the horses would have tramped right over him in their frantic rush to shelter. And if he hadn't awakened, he would be nearly frozen by now or at least suffering from a touch of frostbite, him with his poor old circulation. Bull was right. He knew. And Mr. George was right, cutting out those horses. He wondered where that sodbuster family would get the extra feed. And that kid. Tough on a scrawny kid, a storm like this. He shook his head.

Joey felt the cold too. His little wasted muscles stiffened when the temperature went down. It was very difficult for him to walk through the deepening snow, not only to pick his feet up that much higher, but to pick them up with the heavy-soled lumberman's boots that he wore outside in this kind of weather. The walkway was rutted and slippery. So he stayed inside. He missed seeing the horses, but it was for his mother and Morgan now to care for the larger stock. His mother donned an old pair of buckskin breeches for the stable work, and she and Wendy filled the day cleaning out the barn, bringing in the hay, and generally soothing and calming the nervous horses, who were used to running free. Wendy struggled to keep a walkway clear, but you could have raked it every hour and still it clogged with drifts. He cursed Bo Fletcher for not having the foresight to attach the stable to the living quarters for just this kind of emergency. So Joey was left for most of the day to tend the fire and mind the house alone, and he turned to the cats and chickens for company.

It snowed all that day, and the next, and the next - three days. It did not even occur to them to measure the fall. The three of them were consumed by the necessity to survive, and mere survival required Herculean efforts. They fell into bed each night aching and sore. And Joey had assumed many of the household tasks. But survive they did, trudging through the blinding snow, walking the restless horses, milking and haying and plugging every crack in the stable walls with more snow. Watering the horses was especially difficult. The water in the barn barrels had long since frozen solid and provided only a lick. The brook and the well had frozen too, so that their only source was the snow itself, which had to be collected in buckets, melted at the hearth fire in the cabin, and quickly transported to the stable for drinking before it refroze. Every time he had to cross the narrow yard in the blizzard, Wendy Morgan cursed the oversights of Bolen Fletcher again and again. It was grueling work. And Nan worked steadily by his side.

If this had been his homestead, Wendy would have done things differently. Experience at Fort Laramie had taught him that. The buildings should be connected or, at the very least, the paths leading to them should be sheltered from the northerly blasts. The door to the barn opened out, and the path of its swing needed constant cleaning lest it freeze open or, worse, freeze shut and block access to the animals within. Come spring, Morgan would reverse the hinges so it opened inward.

And the horses, without their daily exercise, were playful. He and Nan had to watch where they walked to avoid a nip here and a stomp there. And it was dirty in the barn in spite of their diligent efforts to clean out the droppings. But the warm manure made a good skid-free lining for the walkway to the house. Nan hated the smell. Wen laughed at her.

CHAPTER 27

Finally, on the fourth day, Joey awoke to a ray of sun gleaming through the only window.

He woke them all, bounded to the door and threw it wide open. The three of them danced into a laughing huddle, twirling round and round in the light and warmth and lifting Joey right off his feet. And Wen Morgan planted a big soft kiss on Nan Fletcher's mouth.

Three days later, it was Christmas Eve. The horses were out to pasture again, kicking and frolicking their way through the airy snow. The temperature had risen and Nan was outside dressed in skirt and shawl, trying to brush snow from the wagon. Wen saw her from his lookout in the barn and burst out laughing. He went out to help.

"You want to go somewhere?" He still did not understand this woman.

"Tomorrow, yes. It's Christmas. Joey and I will go to church."

He stood immobile, trying to digest what she had just said.

"There's three feet of snow out there!" She did puzzle him.

"We always go to church on Christmas Day." She wasn't insistent or argumentative, only stating a fact. To her it was simple.

He was speechless. "You need a sled, not a wagon."

"I don't have a sled."

He tried to explain what to him was obvious. "That's a one-horse dray. You'd kill a horse makin' him pull that wagon and cut a path through snow this deep."

She looked blankly back at him. "Then we'll ride."

"You only have two saddles."

"Two saddles, Joey and me." As a second thought she added, "You want to come?"

"Yes, please." There was a pause. Wendy Morgan felt a wrench in his heart. He had not been included. Yet he could not let these two wander off alone. "Joe and me will ride double." He neglected to say that one of those saddles and all of the able-bodied horses belonged to him, not her. And he would have to show his face in Red Lodge.

"Wonderful!" She knocked the snow from her skirts, smiled, and walked back to the house. Wendy Morgan stood there by the wagon, baffled. Why hadn't she asked him outright to take her to church on Christmas Day? She must have thought he'd refuse. It was a needless and dangerous trip as far as he was concerned, after all they had been through. Yes, he would have refused. So she had inveigled her way around his better judgement. It was the first time Wendell Morgan had ever been the victim of a feminine ruse. It rankled.

Christmas morning, Wendy rose early to saddle the horses for the grueling trip to town and church. The ride itself would probably take two hours - riding through deep snow was like riding through sand. The prayer service was at eleven. They would eat in town before coming home again.

He saddled two horses, a perky little dark bay for Nan, and his trusted red mare with the four white stockings. She, he knew, would not shy or stumble with Joey aboard. They wrapped Joey in the old buffalo robe, tied his hat on firmly, and put a scarf over his face. Wendy lifted him gently into the saddle, easing his legs apart. The scrawny little legs did not unfold easily around the contours of the horse, but cramped stiffly at the knee and hip. Wendy had to pull his little legs down to reach the top of the stirrups. It was Joe's first ride on horseback all the way to town. He had always ridden in the wagon before. He was nervous.

"We'll tie you in with me right behind," Wendy smiled broadly at the boy as he laced a thong around each leg. "You'll do fine...sit tall!"

He lifted Nan to the saddle. She was a bundle of skirts and petticoats with the buckskins underneath for warmth, her right leg hooked high over the saddle horn in improvised English sidesaddle style - ladies did not ride astride or wear pants. He laughed as she smoothed out the pleats and slid himself up behind Joey's saddle. Neither one would ride in great comfort.

The going was not as slow as he expected. The snow parted like soft fluff before the mare's graceful forelegs. She strode out as she always did, in the long steps that devoured the miles. Nan's bay had to jog occasionally to keep up.

To Joey, the ride to town proved one of the most exhilarating events in his young life. He would remember this Christmas like no other. He was riding a fine horse and he sat proud in the saddle, a huge grin all over his face. Gradually, he relaxed to the swing and sway of the horse, but Wen noticed his little legs extended only partially. He just did not have the full arc of normal motion in his hips. Wen wondered if Nan had noticed. She must have. She was his mother.

They pulled up quietly in front of Dave Lewis's livery, only a short walk from the church near the edge of town. Wen lifted Joey carefully down, unsaddled and bedded the horses.

Dave Lewis stepped out to help. "Ma'am, sorry to hear about your husband. If there's anything I can do...."

"Thank you, Mr. Lewis. I appreciate that and I'll remember. Have you met Wendy Morgan? He's been a great help to us this winter."

"Heard Tom Ludlam speak of you." They shook hands and met each other's gaze. "Merry Christmas!"

"Thanks." Wen nodded genially and added, "Merry Christmas!"

"Come along, Joey, off to prayers."

Lewis watched from the livery door, noting the handsome and lithe stranger who was carefully swinging Joey over the worst drifts, steering him around the lesser ones, and guiding Nan by the elbow. A casual bystander would have thought he was her husband and the boy's father. Lewis knew otherwise.

The church was filling fast when they entered. The room echoed with the greetings, gossip, and general clamor of people who lived apart for long periods at a time, and who brimmed over with enthusiasm on seeing friends and neighbors. She had not been to town since Bo's death. Several people nodded condolences to Nan as they shuffled into a rear pew.

Wendy recognized only George Meachum in a front pew. With him were three others, well-dressed, and almost as tall: more Meachum brothers. The resemblance was obvious, but George, with his expanse of shoulders and blond hair gleaming hatless in the candle light, was clearly the most imposing. Two of them, Wendy had not seen before, but as he looked at the shortest and youngest one, the set of his head and hunch of his shoulder blades, the color and cut of the red-brown hair along the back of his neck, vivid images of that day at Deer Creek came flooding back. Wendy Morgan knew he had shot that man. He hadn't killed him and hadn't wanted to kill him. He felt a relief and then a fear - he had shot another man, too, that day, and that man was not here.

The sermon and the singing swelled around him, but Wendell Morgan was not listening. He was staring dully at the back of Tag Meachum. Nan must have noticed. She reached over and handed him a hymn book. He began to mouth the words.

The service over, they all poured out into the sunshine. There were the usual compliments to Parson Bowden and more chatter. Wendy Morgan felt himself the subject of polite curiosity and nothing more, until George Meachum approached with the shorter brother to wish them well, and Morgan felt the grip of apprehension in his throat.

"Mrs. Nan Fletcher, I'd like you to meet my younger brother, Taggert Meachum, Tag, as we call him."

"A pleasure, Mr. Meachum." Her eyes twinkled and the lilt was back in her voice now that she was back with people. Wendy Morgan stood stiffly, facing the man he had shot.

"And young Joe Fletcher and Wendell Morgan." George Meachum's melodious voice droned on. Tag smiled, "It's my pleasure." He winked at Joey and stared hard at Morgan. But there were no accusations.

"You all gonna have Christmas dinner out here in the ice an' snow?" the gruff voice grumbled from behind them. It was Tom Ludlam.

"Tom, you come to church too?" Nan was laughing now. "Didn't know you knew how to pray."

And introductions were made all over again.

Finally, the little group broke up. The Meachums headed to the hotel, for their Christmas feast. The Fletcher-Morgan group

sought out simpler fare at Aunt Nellie's Restaurant and Bakery. But
before they went their separate ways, George Meachum stopped
Wendell Morgan.

"Like to speak to you, Morgan, before you leave town. I know
I'm not a favorite of yours, but we have a common interest. It's about
the boy. You can find me at the Hotel."

The request irked Morgan all through dinner. It had not
been a pleasant day for him. Too many uncertainties to face and yet
once faced, they seemed to shrink and melt away. Except Joey was
truly sick. Morgan didn't know how sick, but he knew exactly what
George Meachum meant "about the boy." But Joey was none of
George Meachum's damn business. He would see George for Joey's
sake, because Meachum had the connections and money that he
didn't have, that Nan didn't have, but that might be able to help
somehow. Still, the idea of accepting help from George Meachum
repelled him. He was a proud man. He had an alternative. He could
leave.

After dessert was served, he excused himself and walked
deliberately over to the Hotel. The Meachum clan was seated at a
prominent table, easy to find. George saw him coming and got up
motioning to a chair in the lobby.

"Morgan, glad you came."

Wendy nodded, "Like you said, it's about the boy. I like that
boy. That's why I'm here."

"I know. Look, Nan Fletcher is a fine woman, but I don't have
to tell you that," he arched an eyebrow, recognizing he was looking
straight into the eyes of his rival. Morgan stared right back, eye to
eye, fighting down a fierce feeling of possession, or was it jealousy?

George continued, "You can tell me what the problem is.
Why can't that boy walk like most boys his age? He doesn't run. He's
so small. You see him every day. How old is he anyway?"

At this question, George stopped. Wendell Morgan mustered some fragile words from among his chaotic feelings.

"Six. He'll be seven in March, March the twenty-fourth."
Wendy's voice almost cracked, but no trace of his intense emotions
spilled onto his face. He stuck to the facts and continued evenly. "He
doesn't move normally. His legs are weak".

Meachum sensed the tension between them. "I know that.
Look this isn't easy for me either...you don't like me...I don't
particularly like you. I admit I'm attracted to Nan Fletcher. If I were
single, I'd take you on." Meachum didn't lie. Morgan felt his jaws

clamp tightly and his fists clench. "She's both damn pretty and she's got some crust. She raisin' that poor kid against all the odds. If he were a calf, he'd probably have been shot as a runt...as a poddy should." At this, a white fury swept over Morgan's handsome face. George saw his nostrils flare and lips stiffen, but he persisted brutally, "You don't like what I'm saying, but I'm just stating the truth and you know it, or you would've plunged your fist into my face five minutes ago. You're livin' with 'em. Now why don't you simmer down and listen intelligently to what I'm saying."

"You're a rich meddlin' bastard!" The last three words sizzled from Wendy Morgan's lips.

"Listen to me!" George felt like seizing Morgan by the collar and shaking reality into him. "I'm trying to help. Take that boy to a doctor. You hear me? I'm tellin' you I'll pay the bills and you don't even have to tell 'er." George's cultivated speech was slipping back into his old vernacular. "Tell 'er it's your money; you can be 'er hero."

"I don't take charity."

"I ain't offerin' it to you. But that kid can't make it on his own out here without charity, and you know it."

It was true. Joey could not live out his life on the homestead. He had not enough strength to perform even the elementary chores: chop wood for fuel, trudge the woods to check a trap line, swing a scythe to cut the hay or maintain his balance on a horse.

"You want me to take him to a doctor? That all?" Wendy had seen the bungling of some army doctors at Laramie.

"That and get him some schooling...so's maybe he can have a future here in town, teaching or clerking, who knows, where he can be with people who can stand by him, and be independent, and have a little pride," George's frustration was mounting too, "Goddammit, so maybe he can walk!"

The anger was evaporating. They would always be rivals, but this was a more consuming problem. "I'll do what I can."

"That's all I ask. Get through the winter as best you can. They need anything, I want to know. Come spring, take that kid to Doc Zilka."

Morgan nodded and grudgingly offered Meachum his hand. They shook. Just as Wendy turned to leave, George addressed his back. "You planning to marry her?" He couldn't see Morgan's face but he could hear the answer, and sense the challenge.

"That...is none of your goddamn business!"

When he got back to Nellie's, dessert was finished. Nan was sitting there with Joey on her lap, smiling at him from beneath those frothy brown curls. He could picture himself being married to this woman, in a nice ranch house, with fenced pastures all around and flowers blooming in boxes beneath the windows, and Joey sitting on his knee. But not now, not this way. He was penniless. He said very little during the rest of the meal, trying all the while to suppress his emotions.

"Time to go, if you want to be 'ome afore dark." Tom was ever practical. Together, they walked across to the livery. Tom went for the horses while Wen assembled the tack. He came back, ashen-faced, with only one horse. It was Nan's little bay. The sorrel mare was gone.

CHAPTER 28

A tear slid down Nan Fletcher's cheek
and froze as it reached the edge of her lip. It had been such a
beautiful day, the church, the singing, the first dinner she didn't
have to cook and scramble for all year, Wendy Morgan's strong arm
lightening her step along the way. She used to get so lonely when
Bo was gone and delighted so in Wendy Morgan's quiet companionship. Now he was gone. He had stayed behind to search for his horse.
She clung to Joey, perched before her in the saddle. The little bay
trod slowly down the snowy trail, her nose buried in the tail of Tom
Ludlam's brown mare. Tom, too, was huddled and silent. Even Joey,
perky and curious when Wendy had tied him in the saddle, had
stopped talking. The red rays of the setting sun slanted across the
snowy pasture and glowed rosy against the weathered boards of the
cabin and barn. They were coming home. There were cats to feed,
a cow to milk and horses to hay, a fire to kindle and a kettle to boil.
Old Tom could use Morgan's bunk. He would stay the night. Then
she would be on her own.

Wendy Morgan had stayed in town. He had rushed back
grimly to Nellie's and flung open the door. Dave Lewis was still at
dinner, wiping the last drop of gravy from his beard. Morgan burst
in on him, no longer the congenial escort of the pretty widow, Mrs.
Fletcher.

"Lewis, you move the mare? She's not in her stall."

Dave Lewis dropped the napkin and blinked back at him.
"You say that again, boy."

"My mare, the sorrel with the white stockinged forelegs, she's gone!"

"Calm down, boy. You look in the other boxes? I was full up today, ever'body comin' in for a holiday."

"I looked. You have any helpers might have turned her out?"

Lewis pursed his lips and heaved a sigh. This Morgan might be a friend of old Tom Ludlam's, a handsome chap, and kind and attentive to the Fletcher woman, but he was wet behind the ears if he couldn't find his own horse. Grudgingly, he got up from the table.

"You keep it hot Nellie, I'll be right back."

And he walked out the door and across the street with Morgan in the lead.

They walked slowly down the aisle of the stable. It was dark inside and steamy from the breath of the animals, many of whom were doubled up in stalls meant for one.

"Where's Tom? He check with you? I seen 'im dine with you."

"He left with Nan and the boy, leading them home. We got stock to feed and no money to start renting out space in a hotel." They were walking down the aisle. Dave eyed each animal carefully with the outwardly careless yet penetrating gaze of the old-time horse trader. He knew every animal. They reached the end of the aisle.

Lewis stopped and worked his palm over his whiskers. Dave Lewis was still skeptical of this stranger. "You sure you didn't move her? Mares you know...mares is temperamental, don't allays take to crowding in with th'others. Let's look outside." Dave still wasn't worried. He had never lost a horse yet. Horse thieves operated on the open range where the pickings were easier, not here in town. He turned and shuffled back through the stable doors.

Only two scruffy nags were tied to the corral fence waiting to come in.

"Not yours, huh?"

"Not mine." Wendy's frustration and anger were mounting.

Lewis, nonplussed, looked back at him blankly. "I don't unnerstand it. Never happened afore." He put a conciliatory palm on Morgan's shoulder. "Look, you go check the rest of the stables in town, that'd be Doc Zilka's and the one down there by the new schoolhouse. She'll turn up and we'll have you on your way."

Morgan simply grunted agreement, turned and started up the street. He was getting only perfunctory help from the casual

Lewis. When he got out of sight, Lewis shrugged and went back to Nellie's to finish his dinner. It was still warm.

Morgan knocked at the Doctor's door and asked if he could look in the barn. "Go right ahead, young man," was the prompt reply of the good Doctor over the voices of his Christmas guests, and Wendy Morgan noted how trusting he was - that as a doctor, he was probably immune to the vagaries of horse thieves. The Doctor treated criminals and honest men alike. His services were valued by the most ruthless outlaw. The mare was not in his barn.

An inquiry pointed out the schoolhouse down the street. This was not the typical red building with the belfry in front. Red Lodge had just embarked on its first educational effort and classes were held in Greg Burdett's vacant cabin. Burdett was a miner who died last year from the ravages of demon rum. Wendy Morgan found the cabin about a hundred yards back behind the Elkhead Saloon with a rundown stable in between.

Night had fallen swiftly, as it does in the foothills, and the stable's interior was black. Morgan struck a match and entered. In the third stall, he found his horse. For a moment, incredulous, he stood back and gaped. She stood in a bed of clean straw, threw up her head and pricked her ears when she saw him. Relieved, he slipped a halter over her ears and led her back down the alley and up the street to Lewis's Livery.

Lewis had finished dinner and was watering his boarders before turning in.

"Now there, I see you found 'er." He was still too casual.

"Over by the schoolhouse, someone had led her there and settled her in just like she belonged." He looked inquisitively, almost accusingly at Lewis.

"T'warn't me!" Lewis' face was innocent, expressionless, and Wendy believed him. "You want you should bunk in with me tonight? Ole Tom allays does when he's 'bout town. Or you can hole up in the loft if'n yer worried 'bout yer mare."

"Obliged. Think I will. Too late to start back now." And Morgan thought again of Nan and Joe and the soft cackle of the hearth fire and the steady simmer of the kettle. Nostalgia? Homesickness? He laughed at himself. He missed the simple cabin. It had been home for him for the last two months, and for all its simplicity it was more of a home and a happier one than he'd ever had. He missed it. He missed her.

Dave Lewis finished his chores and left for his lodgings. Wendy Morgan spread his bedroll on a cushion of hay just above his horse. It would be a cold night, with only the breath of the horses to warm the frigid air. Wendy Morgan couldn't sleep. Finally, he got up, brushed off the hay, slapped his hands together for warmth, put his hat on, and jumped down. The horses munched quietly. You could hear them breathe in the cold silence. He needed someplace to warm up, so he headed down the street to the Elkhead.

When he pushed through the door, Rose spotted him immediately. The deep, dark blue eyes in the long, oval face, the vaguely Roman, aristocratic nose, the broad shoulders sculpting down to the lithe waist and hips, the long graceful legs, this man could cause quite a stir with the girls, and Rose didn't want any more Reb Jenks. He took off his hat, a good sign, she thought, of a man brought up to manners. His hair was dark brown, rich and wavy. He was as tall as George Meachum, or almost, and younger, a fine specimen of manhood. His hands were clean but he was dressed rather shabbily, she thought, and he seemed to favor his left side. No easy riches here. Physical effort had built those shoulders. He didn't seem to know anybody and walked slowly, carefully toward the bar. The Rose followed.

A bartender approached - there were several for the holiday. "Mista, you drinkin'?"

"No more 'an a dollar's worth. That's all I have."

The bartender nodded and poured.

Morgan stroked his shot with the palm of his hand before taking a swallow. "Gentle hands, calloused hands," thought Rose. She watched his throat when he swallowed, the working of the sinews in the line of the neck where it squared off with the jawbone.

"Who are you?" She intruded upon his thoughts with aplomb, even daring.

"I beg your pardon?" Wendy turned abruptly to see a tall middle-aged woman in sedate black silk staring him down. There were crow's feet at the edges of her eyes and thick brown hair streaked silver over her brow, piled profusely on the top of her head and anchored with a bone clip. The effect was commanding.

Her second offering was more congenial but not less direct. "I'm Rose McCartle. This is my place. Who are you?"

"Wendell Morgan...folks call me Wendy. You always check the prospects first before you assign the girls?" He was ahead of her this one, a perceptive man. He had a wry, handsome smile and had lifted one eyebrow.

She smiled. They understood each other. "Keep my girls happy, makes a better business. You lookin' for one?"

"Me? I can't afford one...after this drink, I'll be broke. Got to sleep in the livery loft. That what you want for your girls, Rose McCartle?" His manner was disarming, calling her by her complete name.

"They'll be disappointed."

Wen shrugged and smiled back at her. "I know."

She cocked an eyebrow. "Have another on the house."

His smile widened, "Thanks, I did come in here to warm up, one way or another."

Rose probed a little further. "I haven't seen you. You been here before?"

"No." He left her hanging.

She waited.

"This is my first time to Red Lodge. Would've been here sooner, except I was delayed on the way. Set me back by about two months."

Rose had heard this kind of cowboy understatement before and knew how he must have been delayed. "Gun trouble? You look strong enough now. You came through better than many a man I know." She wasn't going to mention his favoring his left. Men liked a woman to play to their strengths.

"Except they robbed me of just about everything I owned."

"You watch your back, you'll succeed. A lot of men start from scratch out here and you seem smarter than most."

Morgan basked in this kind of compliment. It was nice to be with a free-talking woman. Women were so scarce and some were such prudes. They talked on, just friendly banter. Finally, curious, he questioned her gently.

"Why you wasting the whole evening on me when you know I'm not gonna pay?" He said it good-naturedly, with a teasing twinkle in his eye. "I'm not lookin' for a bed."

"And I'm not either."

A far-away look momentarily clouded her face, the look of someone who had loved deeply once and lost, and who had remembered vividly that she had never loved that deeply again. Seeing her, he was sorry he'd probed.

But she continued, "I've had my time. Now it's their turn and I just play the mama and smooth the feathers when they get ruffled."

A sixth sense prompted him, "And I remind you, don't I?"

She smiled back knowingly, dolefully, and nodded. She was still quite beautiful. "Wendy Morgan, new man in town, you're gonna get to know us all right quick...yeah, in a way, you're very good looking and you do remind me. Who stuck you with a name like Wendy anyway?" She was smiling again.

They talked on into the evening, each comfortable knowing there need be no bedtime, just an evening's camaraderie. The Rose offered him a bunk in her office as an alternative to a pile of hay over at Dave Lewis's place and he accepted, knowing there were no conditions attached. Rose McCartle, he knew, would probably be up all night. Finally, he excused himself and went back to the stable to check his horse and to collect his bedroll before turning in.

CHAPTER 29

$\mathbf{H}$e was approaching the livery quietly, when he heard a rustling from within, not the sustained shufflings of the animals, but a sharp squeak of hard leather. His muscles tensed. He crept silently, carefully forward. The door was open, not usual in the winter at this hour of the night. Lewis must have closed up and gone off long ago. Wendy Morgan crept up to the edge of the jamb. There were two men in the aisle. One held a lantern, the other a bridle. They were saddling a horse. The horse stood cross-tied between two upright log partitions. The light from the lantern gleamed red on the horse's flank. Morgan rubbed his eyes and looked again adjusting his night vision to the glow. It was a red flank, and white, yes, white on the forelegs. It was his horse!

Morgan let his vision clear, pulled the gun from his holster and, cocking it, stepped into the doorway. Two men, one dark and brooding, the other skinny, slightly stooped and menacing, stood framed in the light of the lantern. They heard the click of the gun and froze. To them, Morgan was but a vague and hovering blackness in the darkness of the doorway. He clearly held the advantage.

"Easy, Bill. We ain't alone." This from the skinny one who held the lantern with one hand and the horse's halter with the other.

The taller man who was tightening the cinch on the near side of the horse, looked up. The bridle's ear-piece and reins were draped over his left arm, but when he let go the cinch, his right hand was free. He looked over his shoulder. The form in the doorway was a fuzzy black blur.

"That's my horse. Now get the hell out!" An angry Morgan almost spat the words. These two must've taken the mare this afternoon, and he had walked all over town to find her. And Nan and old Tom would have to struggle with two homesteads and some twelve-odd head to feed. He raised his voice. "You hear me! I don't repeat a command! I grew up in the army..."

The taller man still stood immobile, looking back, waiting. His words were menacing, "You must be a dead shot, mister. You miss an' she's a dead horse!"

At this, the tall man dove straight under the shining white forelegs as his right hand flashed for the Colt in his belt. It was the desperate move of a crazy man or a drunk. The mare, terrified by the abrupt motion, reared backwards, snapping the tie ropes loose and tearing one log partition right out of its shallow footing. The huge log careened into the path of the shorter man, knocking him, lantern and all, backwards to the floor. But it missed the gunman, who rolled free. Horses screamed and kicked. In the confusion, the gunman fired a wild shot that slammed into the solid door. Morgan, too, leaped back from the flying partition, and rolled to the floor. The man fired again, closer this time, but he was aiming into the darkness, firing blind, listening for Morgan's position and narrowing his aim toward an amorphous human shadow. He fired again.

The fallen lantern had kindled a small pile of straw, and Morgan could see his target clearly. He held his fire, took aim steadily, and then fired. The bullet thudded against bone and the gunman winced. Morgan had hit his mark, but the man had not given up. Frantically, he held on to the gun and fired a fourth time. Again, Morgan fired back, a deadly body aim, this time just left of center. The man fell backward, motionless. His companion had fled.

In the few seconds of shooting, the straw had fueled orange flames that licked up the barnboards. Morgan lunged forward, ripping a blanket from a frightened animal, beat down the flames, and threw the blanket over the budding fire. The boards were green, the night air was damp, and so was the blanket, with animal sweat. The flames smoldered and went out. Wen Morgan picked up the lantern and struck a match to the remaining oil cautiously. He walked up to the man on the floor. Blood was pouring out from beneath his shirt. He was dead. Wendy then held out a hand to his trembling horse and untied her from the dislodged partition.

Six shots had been fired. The smell of smoke was still on the air. The shots and the screams of the horses had brought the townspeople on the run with buckets and blankets. They arrived to find a melee of frightened animals, the fire a smoldering heap, and a dead man on the floor in a pool of blood.

Wendy Morgan looked up as the first two men entered. He recognized Dave Lewis's ashen face. A fire for him would mean total disaster in his overcrowded livery barn. But he had kept his dirt floor swept clean, and this diligence had kept the fire from spreading. Still, one stall was in shambles, pulled apart by the mare's brutal heave backwards, and all the horses stamped and weaved nervously.

Morgan stammered, "Sorry, Lewis..."

Dave Lewis was in shock, staring from the broken walls to the horses, to the dead fire, to the dead man. The man with him put a hand on his shoulder. "It's all right, Dave. Could've been worse. The stock is fine, just unnerved a mite." It was the Doctor's grumbling voice. He patted Lewis's back gently, sighed, and walked over to where the dead man lay, gun still in hand.

"Bring that light here, son."

A small crowd was gathering in the doorway around Lewis and the Doctor motioned them to stand back. Morgan walked over with the lantern and turned the flame higher.

"Somebody fetch Tim Walsh." Walsh was the sheriff. "Anybody else got another lantern? We could use more light."

Two men walked over with their lanterns. "Sheriff's outta town, Doc. Went to see 'is sister in Bozeman." The light fell on an ugly red scar across the back of the gunman's hand, then on his gaping face. In death, defiance was smoothed from the black, glassy eyes, the tough frown erased. But the fingers still gripped the gun.

"Shot in the femur and chest. Chest wound killed 'im. Busted the aorta." The Doctor was grumbling to himself. "Walsh's never here when you need 'im!"

Then in a quiet monotone, he addressed Morgan, "Who are you, son, and what happened?"

"Wendell Morgan," he stopped then started again. "Folks call me Wendy Morgan, from Laramie, Wyoming, but I been out at the Fletcher place for nigh on two and a half months. They'll vouch for me, and Tom Ludlam. He..." and he nodded toward the dead man, "was saddling my horse, him and another guy. Took her away once already this afternoon, and when I challenged him, he pulled a gun."

"Anybody see you? Anybody see it happen?" The Doc raised his voice for the benefit of the crowd.

"The shooting? No one here. His pal ran away. But Lewis there knows I brought the horse in this morning before church with Mrs. Fletcher and her boy, and when we came for her to go home, the horse was gone. I stayed in town to look for her. You know that, I knocked on your door. There was a party going on."

"That you did." He looked up again and addressed the townsfolk. "Anybody know this man?" He indicated the dead man. No one came forward.

Doc looked again and saw George Meachum's head poking out above the others. "Mr. Meachum, I believe you know him. Least you came to my place looking for him few weeks back."

George Meachum strode forward slowly and looked down on the contorted features of the dead man. George clenched his lips and gazed knowingly at Wendy Morgan, then at Zilka.

"That'd be Bill Hendl. I fired him and ran him off the M-bar weeks ago. He took this horse with him once already, the night he was fired."

"Then that'd be your horse?" In the absence of the sheriff, Doc was piecing events together.

"No, although everybody seems to think so. Look at her brand, a T-bar. She belongs to Morgan here. He raised her out of Laramie, so he says."

"That where you from, boy?"

"Yes, sir." The reply was terse. Wendy Morgan knew he was being scrutinized and that but for the word of George Meachum, he could easily have been jailed.

Doc moved his jaw back and forth like a cow chewing cud. "You know the commanding officer?" It was an attempt to verify Morgan's story.

"You mean Major Belden? Colonel McTigue retired last June."

"Went back home to Springfield, Missouri, for a taste of the quiet life. I knew Sam McTigue in '76, quite an Indian fighter he was." Doc stopped his digressions and abruptly returned to matters at hand. "Well, son, I believe you. And Meachum here says you're O.K. Lewis, he seems to know you some.

Lewis spoke up, "Tom Ludlam introduced 'im to me. Says he's right handy with a horse. Even says he been lookin' out for the widder Fletcher. Ole Tom been a match-makin' if'n you ask me." He shot a quick glance at Morgan. Doc had asked and he had said exactly what he thought, the truth. After all, this was a killing, and Morgan would need all the support he could muster even if it meant a little reddening under his collar.

"Well, Morgan," Doctor finally called him by name, "you better stick around town 'til the sheriff gets back. That'd be maybe tomorrow, maybe after the New Year festivities." He turned to George.

"Meachum, you and Morgan here want to help me clear away this body so's Lewis can clean up the mess?"

CHAPTER 30

George Meachum and Wendy Morgan carried Bill Hendl's body to the undertaker's a few blocks away, across the back of the big red mare.

"You solved a problem for me, you know that don't you, Morgan?" George strode slowly beside the horse, holding the body steady across the saddle, while Morgan held the reins, leading.

Morgan shrugged. "You would have done the same."

"Right." And George Meachum thought how the two rivals were really very much alike, and that in a different time, in a different place, he would have walked where Wen Morgan walked. He would have stayed at Nan Fletcher's side instead of watching and hoping and giving from so great a distance. He would have enjoyed a bright little kid like Joey, and he knew that for Joey, he would do all he could even from that distance. He would have blushed purple at the thoughtless remark of Dave Lewis about matchmaking, as he knew Morgan must have blushed in the flickering light of the lanterns.

"You love her, don't you, Morgan?" The words somehow escaped him.

Wendy Morgan stopped like a buck shot between the eyes. Like a boomerang, he shot right back, "Don't you?" The reply was immediate and spontaneous.

George's chin shot up. The two of them stood and stared in the dim moonlight, over the back of the horse, over dead Bill Hendl, their common enemy, like two he-wolves squaring off for battle, jealously guarding their territories.

George was the first to conciliate. "Look, I'm a married man. I won't get in your way, if you treat her right, that is. There's so few women out here and only a few real jewels like her. I'm a married man and I know. My wife's one of the rough cut variety, but if I had it to do over again..."

They had continued walking down the street toward the undertaker's. The snow had crusted with the falling temperature over the daytime melt and cracked crisply under their feet. There was an oil lamp glowing in the window, as Israel Roland, the undertaker, heard the commotion and was waiting for them. George Meachum unloaded the body and left Wendy standing outside with the horse. He was still standing there when Meachum came out.

George finally spoke up. "Well, you're a free man. Sheriff Walsh'll never question my word or the Doc's, and, personally, I think the whole county is well rid of that scum. You might as well go home."

Morgan nodded. Then slowly he lifted his hand from his side, offering it to George Meachum. "Thanks," was all he said. He put his foot in the stirrup, mounted up, and jogged away.

Meachum stood and watched him ride off. He didn't envy Morgan his lonely ride over the rough and frozen roads in the black of night, and he would have to explain to Doc Zilka about sending Morgan home. You just didn't leave a woman with a kid alone in this wild country of Indians and wolves. If there was an emergency, a woman alone had no way of summoning help. If Doc or the sheriff wanted to send a replacement out and bring Morgan in, then that was their affair, but the immediate need was for tonight. It occurred to George Meachum that he was thinking more and more often of Nan, and that he could have gone himself. Instead, he retraced his steps down the street to the hotel.

As he approached the Elkhead Saloon, the acrid smell of teeming humanity pervaded the street around him. He could hear the cheers of drunken well-wishers and smell their stale breath. So many lonely men, lacking homes, families, wives, and the gentling effects of women, celebrated their holiday in the only way they knew how. And there were others, who had families and wives and ran from them, choosing to forget the more intimate moments. They all collected now in this cauldron of male humanity called the saloon. George Meachum slowed his pace as he passed. Then he halted and went in. After all, wasn't he really like all the rest? At least he could have a nightcap with the Rose.

Rose McCartle was glad to see him. Her eyes lit up and she smiled broadly as she elbowed her way through the throng of boisterous revellers.

"Thought you'd forgotten about us."

"I don't forget you, Rose, not when it's Christmas." There was emotion running under this simple statement. "I would have come in sooner, but we Meachums've got a role to play...." He broke off with a sheepish grin. "I went to church."

Rose McCartle burst out laughing. "George Meachum, an honest man!"

He didn't answer, but carefully removed his hat, setting it on the table between them.

She lowered her voice. "But you couldn't or wouldn't make an honest woman out a me." She continued, "So that's where Mose and Dance were, all you Meachums, pillars of the good Christian community!" She giggled some more.

"Don't make fun of us, Rose." His face had gone serious all at once.

"I'm sorry. It's just that salvation is always there for those prodigal brothers a yours, even for the drunks and the killers who come in for their drinks and girls, but never for me." Her eyes were glued to his.

"Rose, please, not now. We've been through all this before. Old Bowden's a bigot. We know that or he would've married us no questions asked. He would've given us a church wedding. Let go the past. It's gone, over." He put his hand over hers.

"Its just that it's Christmas, when ever'body's supposed to be so God-damned happy!" She was almost crying, making a valiant effort to hold back a flood. "Look at them." She motioned at the roomful of men in every stage of inebriation.

"They're drunk. They don't remember." They sat quietly for a few minutes more. "You're their home, Rose. They don't have any place else."

"And you do?" Her words stung. He had no answer to that. He really didn't have any other place. That's why he was here. They had hurt each other, but Rose carried on bravely to the topic of the day.

"Heard there was a shooting."

"Yeah, fella named Bill Hendl, a gunman, used to work for me."

"Hendl? Dark fellow, tall, broad?"

"You know him?"

Her eyes were still strained looking at him, but she was forcing herself to talk, filing off the sharp edges off of her feelings.

"He was one of my best customers these past weeks."

It occurred to George that Rose's best customers required a substantial bankroll. He knew now that Hendl had not left the country when he had threatened him, nor had he even stopped earning his keep. Someone had kept his ample salary flowing.

Just then a spindly mouse of a man came rushing up to George Meachum. He was out of breath and had been running.

"Mr. Meachum! Mr. Meachum, thought I'd find you here!"

Israel Roland, the undertaker, pulled up a chair without being asked. Nervously, he plopped a leather pouch down on the table in front of them. It clinked audibly on the hard surface.

"Mr. Meachum, that body you brought in, look what I found in 'is pocket."

George picked up the pouch and upended it. Twenty ten-dollar, five twenty-dollar, and one fifty-dollar gold piece fell out: $350 — Hendl had been well paid.

Izzy Roland's eyes bulged at the sight of so much money and his brisk entry had attracted unsavory attention.

Quickly, George scooped up the coins, thrust them back into the pouch, and handed them to the Rose. Even these scrubby saloon types would not rob a woman.

"Put this in your safe...now!"

Rose McCartle walked straight to her back room and did as she was told.

When she returned, Izzy Roland was babbling to George, "I just never could have that kind a money around my place. That there is enough to bring the robbers down on me!" The poor little man was talking out his anxieties. George was still seated but Rose remained standing.

Quietly, the gaunt figure of Moses Meachum materialized behind her. His slits of eyeballs were rivetted on his brother and he smelled of pipe tobacco. It was to George he spoke, his blackened pipe clenched all the while between his yellow teeth.

"That thar money a Hendl's, it belongs to brother Harv. He's gonna want it back."

"Just whose side are you on, Mose?"

"Me, George? Why, my own side. Not yours. Not Harv's neither. I like to see peace in the family. I'll take that money back for ye. It's M-bar money. I can give it to Harv for ye. Terms a the truce you could call it." George's mind flashed warnings of Mose's timely interest.

"Thanks, Mose, but I'll do my own dirty work."

"Your pleasure." The small courtesy rang with cynicism. "But yer gonna need a peacemaker." Mose sauntered back to the bar.

Izzy Roland still stood near, twisting the fingers of his right hand in his gold watch chain. His was a good business, and one that isolated him from the toughs of his world until after they were rendered harmless. Small, lacking in physical strength or skill with a gun, he was never at ease in their company.

"Come on Izzy, I'll walk back with you. Maybe I should have another look at that body."

"Sure, sure, Mr. Meachum." The little man had never called any of the Meachums by their first names.

The body had cooled and was stiffening fast. Roland had undressed Hendl's remains and laid him out under a blanket on a stone slab.

"He rode for the M-bar. You gonna give 'im a fancy send-off like you did Grady?" That meant money in the till for Izzy Roland.

"Iz, he was no M-bar rider today, just a common horse thief."

The little undertaker nodded. "Then I won't waste my time on 'im. His effects are over there." He pointed to a neat pile upon a small table.

George picked up the oil lamp and pulled a chair toward the table. Piece by piece, he went over the clothes: a pair of boots, high-heeled, with pointed toes like a Texan would wear; faded jeans; jacket; high-crowned hat; gloves; bandanna: chaps; Colt and holster; a bloodied blue shirt, black leather vest and sheepskin jacket.

"That there pile's what he had in 'is pockets along with the money bag." Roland pointed to a meager pile of a few coins, another bandanna, and the makings for two smokes. He kept talking to fill the silence, "Shame about the jacket. Some poor feller get good use outta it if he could soak out the blood without spoilin' the leather...." He looked quizzically up at George. "You lookin' for more, Mr. Meachum?"

"Maybe." George had picked up the jacket and was running his fingers down the seams. He handed the jacket to Roland. "You find someone can work on this and put it to use."

He took the bandanna and wiped blood from the vest. Running his finger along the inside seam he discovered a pocket, and in the pocket, a letter. The envelope was addressed to Hendl and must have been hand delivered. He opened it and read:

Billings, December 19, 1886

To Bill Hendl:
Your services are still needed if we are to extend the range. Stay close. We will remove the family problem presently. Find replacement for Grady. Contact Murph and Mose. Double pay.

Harv Meachum

And get yourself a good horse.

George knew Hendl would have been instructed to destroy the letter but had kept it for the day he needed insurance against arrest or jail. Harv's word carried weight. And he knew he himself was the family problem. His cheek began to tick and a red mask of anger flushed his handsome face. He would not be "removed." Harv's reference to "extend the range" worried him. This could mean shooting, or, at the very worst, a range war. He wondered how this would affect Nan Fletcher.

Israel Roland saw George's redness mount, his cheek tick, and his teeth clench, and Roland's little eyes bulged.

"Tell no one of the letter."

"No, no Mr. Meachum!" But he sensed it was an indictment of the Meachum clan.

George Meachum folded the letter and tucked it into his vest pocket. Here was written testimony to his brothers' conspiracies. Before, he had repressed the suspicions and ignored the rumors. He could no longer.

Christmas night, December 25, 1886, handsome, poised George Meachum carried his head lower. His broad shoulders sagged as he walked back to the hotel alone. He had exposed shame for the Meachum name and trouble for the Fletcher woman and her boy. He climbed the stairs to a room at the hotel and stretched out on the bed. Exhausted, near morning, he finally fell asleep.

CHAPTER 31

The following week, big Harv Meachum and Dancer Meachum came home from Billings. Sheriff Tim Walsh arrived from Miles City. Mose, Tag, Gabe, and George returned to the M-bar from Red Lodge. Wendy Morgan, Tom Ludlam, and the two Fletchers resumed their homesteading. All were settling in for the cold and claustrophobic winter. News of the Christmas killing, while fodder for backyard gossip, sputtered and went out just as the stable fire flared and died so quickly. One dead cowboy was the evening's toll. And then, of course, Doc Zilka and George Meachum, two very respected citizens, had testified that it had been a fair draw. The *Red Lodge Picket* ran only a short epitaph.

Mose, Harv, and Gabe Meachum, however, thought otherwise. After the New Year, 1887, the three rode abreast up the main street of Red Lodge. They reined in at the Sheriff's office and dismounted.

When they entered, Sheriff Walsh was squatting on his haunches next to a pot-bellied stove, trying unsuccessfully to ignite some damp sticks. He looked up,

"Harv, Mose, come on in. Be with ya in a minute. Kindling's damp. Holiday treat you right?"

"Just fine, Tim. We was up to Billings. Paid a call on Brenda."

"A fine lookin' woman, Harv. Scenery ain't the same now she's gone. How come you let your brother George git her ahead a you?"

"Tim, I'm a cattleman not a ladies' man like you an' George. You know that."

Sheriff Walsh grunted. He looked from one to the other Meachum.

"Can I do something for ya? I'd ask ya both to sit down if it wasn't so God-blasted cold in this place! Can't seem to get the stove goin'. Don't even have a hot cup a coffee."

"C'mon down to th' Elkhead then. Have a nip, git warm. We got some talkin' to do."

On their way down the street, Gabe joined them as the foursome clomped down the boardwalk. Walsh wondered at the presence of Gabe who rarely showed his grotesque face in town. Must be important business.

The four seated themselves at a corner table and big Harv ordered a bottle of the Rose's finest. Ceremoniously, Harv poured each a drink, sipped, and waited to begin. Harv fastened his heavy gaze on the unsuspecting Sheriff.

"It's about the Christmas killing, Tim. Did you know that Hendl was an M-bar hand?" Harv Meachum stared gravely at the affable Irishman.

"I didn't know that, Harv. I got the report says it was a fair fight, four empty cartridges in the dead man's gun. Signed by Doc Zilka and your brother George. No mention a who he was workin' for."

"But you got no witnesses." It was Mose again, biting to the core.

"Folks heard the shots, smelled the fire, then come a runnin'. But no, nobody saw it happen."

Tim Walsh gazed from the iron face of big Harv, to scarred and silent Gabe, to the brutally direct frown of Mose. His blue eyes flickered. His easy confidence vanished.

"How do you know it happened the way this feller Morgan says?"

Walsh gaped, tongue-tied. Hadn't George Meachum said...?

Big Harv raised his voice just a little. "Look Tim, we just want to be sure, do the right thing by our boys. They're good boys, always ride for the brand. You believed Morgan. You worked on these cases before. You're a first class lawman. What did he tell you?"

The fat was in the frying pan now, "I didn't question 'im, Harv. Doc Zilka did that."

The Meachums sat still and let embarrassment worm its way into Walsh's consciousness.

"I'll be glad to talk to 'im if ya want."

"I can't tell you what to do now, Tim, but I think that's in order, don't you, Mose, Gabe? You do that, Tim, seein' as you're wearin' the badge."

"I'll ride out there tomorrow."

Again discussion came to a halt. Again Mose snapped like a wildcat at the truth, "Ya mean he ain't here? He skipped?"

"Naw, but we know where he is, with the widder Fletcher and 'er kid. She needed someone an' he'd only be hibernatin' stayin' in town...no use to no one. The Doc and yer brother George okayed it." Walsh clutched at the feeble excuse. "I thought yo'all knew."

Gabe spoke for the first time. "George gone soft in the city. The women is finally gettin' to 'im."

"You want I should bring 'im in?"

The three Meachums eyed one another. "For questioning, yeah, for questioning by an officer of the law."

CHAPTER 32

W endy Morgan opened the cabin door, and Nan Fletcher's voice cracked nervously, "I worried so!"

"I thought you'd be asleep long ago."

"I couldn't."

She held a candle in her right hand. The yellow glow highlighted the smooth contours of her cheeks and fell softly across dishevelled tufts of light brown curls. Her eyes were red. In the chill cabin, she had pulled a blanket around herself. She looked every bit a wild squaw, except for her pale skin and piercing blue eyes.

"Did you find your horse?"

He shut the door quietly, immediately aware that they were alone in the room. Joey and Tom must be in the back. His every sense was immediately, exquisitely tuned to her presence. How lovely she was in the faint candle glow!

"Yes, I found her...at Dave's." Could he tell her now the awful circumstances? He stopped.

"You came back."

"Did you think I wouldn't?" He remembered, too late, that she had already lost Bo Fletcher in just such a way. He had gone off and never returned, no warning, no explanation. Morgan knew that this was exactly what she had feared. It was in the depth of her eyes and on the vague trembling of her lips. And he was the cause of her fear.

He reached out, took the candle from her hand, and placed it atop the rough-hewn shelf that held the family Bible. And he took her hand. He had no words to describe how he felt for this woman. He loomed over her.

"What happened?" she stammered again.

"Lewis's was full. Someone put her in the stalls behind the school."

His hand was gloved. He had forgotten to take it off. The rough leather scratched. He pulled off his glove and put his hand on her cheek. His touch was gentle like the night air. She did not push his hand away.

"And you found her there?" She was forcing the words. She felt the cool of his fingers. She didn't really want to speak.

"I found her in the livery." He was answering her questions perfunctorily. Words seemed so unnecessary. The snow on his heavy lumberman's boots was beginning to melt and form a small puddle on the floor. They stood there, staring at each other. "Nan, I have to tell you something." But the something stuck like a snag in the rocks of a onrushing creek. He took his hand from her cheek, removed his hat, and clutched it between them. Trying to catch his breath, he heaved suddenly, awkwardly. So many emotions thundered in his breast. The words were there, but after so many years alone, like the snows aloft on the high peaks, they needed light and warmth to melt down and pour forth.

She came up to him then, pushed away his hat, and kissed him gently.

"You came back." She said it again. And he felt the exquisite ache in his heart. How could he not have come back to this woman? Those were awful moments after he had killed, when he stood alone for all to see, over the body of Bill Hendl, waiting for the accusation that did not come, expecting to be bound over for trial, held, and prevented from coming back to her. But for her, he would have run.

The hat fell to the floor. He reached out then and silently drew her to him. They clung to each other, in the cold, in the cabin, by the flickering light of a single shrinking candle. For months they had been together. For months he had watched her longingly. And for months, uncertain, waiting for thieves or gunmen or fate to come and take him, he had not dared. In the end, she had come to him. And even tonight he was still uncertain. He had killed again.

He unbuttoned his heavy parka. She let the blanket drop from around her shoulders. The warmth they sought was deep within each other.

They lay that night, on the pallet where he had lain bleeding, near death, and where she had watched and hoped and prayed for his recovery. They lay wrapped in each other. Tonight, he watched her curl her head on his breast and sleep, and he begged God, if there was a God, that he could soothe her fears and yes, heal her woes.

He lay awake, revelling in this wonderful being who lay against him and filled his being, wrestling all the while with his desire for her and his fears of impending tragedy. He had killed again. He could picture vividly the glassy lifeless stare and feel the dead human weight that he had lifted onto the mare. The passion that he felt for her momentarily snuffed all that out. But the memory rekindled so quickly, like a flame that refused to go out. He wanted to forget the past and return to her, think only of her. And he had come back on the assurances of George Meachum, to life, to hope, to love. Could he now trust the word of George Meachum? Hours passed and she slept. But Wendy Morgan lay wakeful, torn between wretched memories and the wonderful present. Finally, close to dawn, he fell into a heavy sleep.

Nan drowsed in the cold grey dawn. She, languished in the warmth of the man beside her and in what she perceived as his enveloping goodness. The doubts she had were locked deliberately in the back of her mind. How kind he had been to her, how patient with Joey. He had worked so hard beside her when he could have earned a far higher wage elsewhere. He loved her, she knew, but he was so shy of words. And she thought how few men in this wild · country had ever experienced the gentle touch of a woman. It must be very new to him, like a first snow to a new colt. He would back away, hesitate, test with his small hoof before committing his full weight, until he learned to trust, and then he would buck and frolic and glory in it. Such would be the love of Wendy Morgan for Nan Fletcher.

Morning came. The first rays of light pierced the darkened cabin. She did not want to leave the circle of his arms until she heard a thump in the back room. Joey was awake. Carefully, she moved out from under the blankets. She felt neither embarrassment nor guilt, only a pervading joy. Joey should know soon about how she felt, so that he would not be shocked by a sudden discovery. He would be out and looking for breakfast shortly. She moved to stir the fire and heat water for the morning meal. Then she dressed and Joey stumbled in. He recognized the calm in his mother's eyes and spotted Wendy, still asleep. His simple mind did not question. How many mornings before had he seen Wendy asleep in that very place? And they had tiptoed around the cabin so that sleep would heal him.

"Did he find 'er Mom, did he find er?" he whispered. Never had the boy suspected that Morgan would not return, so complete was his trust.

"Yes Joe, the mare's out in the barn."

"Can I go see 'er Mom? Can I?"

"Sure, it'll be a while before breakfast is ready."

Joey hobbled on out and Wendy Morgan raised his muscled shoulder up on an elbow. He watched Joey exit and looked back at Nan.

"Good morning." Nan smiled, determined to wait and not try to read his thoughts.

Wendy's blue eyes twinkled with boyish mischief. "Did he...?"

She giggled, she was almost laughing now.

He found it disconcerting, but it put him at ease. "I mean, did he catch the two of us in bed this morning?" He was grinning broadly, and blushing crimson.

"He didn't, but he may as well have if you don't lower your voice." She laughed at him. The laughter was contagious.

He had risen with the blanket and with his long arms enfolded them both. He loved the feel of her giggling like a teenager and trembling against him.

"We'll have to talk with him." He was rubbing his cheek in her hair.

She nodded. "We'd better talk to him right now."

He rose, pulling the blanket and her with him, to stand beside the warming stove.

The warmth was intoxicating. Suddenly, his tone was serious. "I mean...we have to talk to him about having a new father." It was a backhanded proposal but his eyes and arms said the rest.

She caught the tone. "He...and I...would want no other."

Gently, again, he pulled her to him, stroking the soft brown curls.

"And Nan, there's something you have to know. Promise you won't condemn me?" His hand had tensed and he turned her face so that he looked directly into it. "Nan, I killed a man last night." The dark blue eyes fastened on hers as they had when he lay near death and she had nursed him. Such was the pain in his soul.

Fear, knifelike, struck her then and she backed away.

"They were taking the mare, she was already saddled, and he turned and drew on me...I had to. Nan, please, please don't condemn me. I'm not proud of it." He looked defeated, thinking only of the loss of this woman he had come to love, of a son, and of a home.

"And you're all right? You were not hit?"

"No."

"And you left...you ran?"

He shook his head violently this time, "No, no, I stayed to put the fire out."

"Fire?"

"It was a fair fight. Nan, he was emptying his gun at me!" His mind was racing.

She just looked, and he imagined all the horror that must be coursing through her mind.

"He couldn't see very well. I was in the dark."

Just then, Joey burst back in through the door. Nan went to the steaming pot of oatmeal and silently spooned a bowlful.

The boy looked quizzically from his friend Morgan to his mother. The peace he had read in her pale face earlier was gone. Joey sat meekly at his place. He grinned wide at Morgan, plainly glad to see him. Wendy forced a smile, reached out, and tousled the boy's hair.

Nan placed the bowl of oatmeal squarely in front of Joey and turned away. Morgan caught her by the hand.

"Nan, I love you. I only defended what's mine...and yours...and his. That's what I want. Those horses out there, they're all I have, all I can give you. I'm not ashamed of what I did. He was a gunman, hired, then fired by the M-bar. Meachum himself spoke up for me, and the Doctor."

"George Meachum spoke for you?" She released his hand and backed away.

"Yes...Nan, believe me, I'm innocent. I'll do nothing to hurt you." And he added, "or anyone else."

"Then no one will come to arrest you?" He realized then that it was not the horror of killing but the fear of loss, his loss, and the pain that another loss would cause her, that had made her withdraw.

"Nan, with all my heart, I'm staying here. I want to stay here. I've done nothing wrong."

CHAPTER 33

The following days were idyllic. The weather was warm for late December. The snow cover began to melt and the tips of the grasses emerged again above the whiteness. The animals all went back outside and Nan took advantage of the temperature to air and clean house. And Joey began to get used to Wendy Morgan's open affection for his mother. There was a rosier hue to her cheeks. Her smiles came more easily and almost all the time. For the first time, in her short experience on the frontier, Nan Fletcher actually looked forward to the long isolation of winter.

Morgan, too, thrived in his new-found home. He became more talkative. His blue eyes seemed to dance and the lines in his handsome face turned from worried frown to laughter. He even seemed to have gained a little weight on his tall, slender frame, or was it self-confidence that made him more assured and graceful?

And Joey responded positively too. For they both loved him, helped him when needed, but not to the point of negating his own efforts. Nan and Wendy always had small tasks for him, praised and encouraged him and trained him gently in responsibility and pride. He now had a father, the kind of father he had always needed.

Early one morning, Tom rode in on a black mare followed by Joker. (Old Baldy hadn't survived the trip to the mountain.) The old Indian fighter devined the budding romance in a second and winked at Morgan on the sly. Tom was in fine spirits, although he still stooped and complained of his cold joints. He walked into the barn and cornered Morgan, who was forking hay.

"You done the right thing, young feller."

Wendy looked up and grinned handsomely. He was thinking of Nan.

"I mean about the fire and shootin' that thar thief. You have ta use yer gun, you make it count, that's what I allays says."

Wendy just let him ramble on, as the old loner usually did when he found a willing listener.

"Lewis is surely grateful to ya, I can tell ya that. An ever'body else that had a hoss in that barn. They don't cotton ta thieves, specially hoss thieves that use their town for their pickings. Ya did right, yes sir."

This little speech was balm to Morgan's ears and he beamed.

"Sheriff got back, ya know. An I heard them Meachum boys, not George, th'others, they wanted 'im to bring you in. But Lewis and th' other Meachum, the handsome one, and the Doc, they all says no. Lotsa people backin' you for puttin' out the fire. Boy, I figure you made some friends."

"I need 'em Tom, I need 'em."

The sound of another horse, the squish of hooves on the wet snow, came from the yard. They looked out. It was Tim Walsh, the Sheriff. Wendy Morgan's heart froze. He swore.

"Figured 'e was right behind me." The old eyes fastened on the younger man. "Scared, ain't ye? Stand yer ground boy, an' he'll back off. Too many folks on your side. That's what I came to tell ya."

Walsh yelled from the yard, "Morgan, you here? I gotta talk to you. Walsh here, Sheriff of Gallatin County."

Morgan stepped out from the barn door followed by Ludlam. He could see Nan at the window as her eyes followed him across the yard. She must have seen the polished brass star pinned proudly to the front of the Irishman's coat. He walked straight up to Walsh, who dismounted and hitched his horse. They all shook hands. Wendy motioned toward the house and the three of them stomped up the path. They came in, Walsh paid his respects to Nan and the three men sat down around the table.

"It appears you killed a man last week."

"He was stealing my horse."

"I know the story. Doc filled me in. But he also asked you to stay put and you skedaddled."

"I got work to do for Mrs. Fletcher an' her boy. They can't run this place single-handed. We got stock to tend. You can see them out in the corral."

Walsh looked up, interested. "Good lookin' horses Nan, where'd you come by such a pretty lookin' bunch a horses?" An Irishman always appreciated good horseflesh.

"I didn't, Tim. They belong to Wendy... Mr. Morgan here." She beamed a gratifying smile at the big Irishman. Morgan's prestige had just inflated tenfold to Walsh's way of thinking.

Walsh looked back at Morgan. "Where they from?"

And instead of the grilling Morgan had anticipated, the questioning deteriorated. Their talk was of the various equines in the corral, their sires and dams, training, manners, and fleetness. The Sheriff, it seemed, was once a horse trader. He had failed at the trade. Morgan had a good idea why - he was too nice and not smart enough. He believed people. In the horse business, you had to be able to spot defects at a glance and flesh out the understatements or outright omissions on your own. The conversation drifted back to the Sheriff's visit.

Walsh laid out his position plainly. "Morgan, here's my problem. I got George Meachum back in town who says Hendl was a cur and a snake and got real mean when he drank. Fired 'im under not too nice circumstances. Then there's Harv. That's the big one. He says that there Hendl was a good hand and that he hired 'im back.... What I mean is, I got two sides to this story. Harv is powerful influential in these parts 'an I got to listen, lest he get out a hand, kinda smooth his ruffled feathers. An' George has contacts a-plenty too, especially with th' government an' railroad honchos in Billings and Helena. Now, I'm a family man. I don't listen to him, I can lose my job. So I'm straddlin' the fence bein' pulled both ways. Now I'd like to hear you tell what happened." The "you" rang loud for emphasis.

Wendy launched again into the blow by blow narrative of what happened Christmas night. Nan busied herself near the fire, but he knew she ached at every word. When he finished, Walsh shook his head.

"Tom, you agree?"

"He's what he says 'e is, Tim."

"What I really need's a witness, tell what really happened. You say there was a second man with this Hendl? You recognize 'im?"

"No, sir."

"Tell you what. You come on back to town with me. Lemme write up a report with witnesses, signed an' sealed. That way I cover the law end of it an' big Harv can't say you skedaddled. We have us a little pow-wow an' you come home again."

Wendy shot an alarmed glance at Nan, but Tom Ludlam spoke up.

"He can come home again? We have your word on that?"

"And my hand. Whaddya say?" Out shot his massive right hand.

Tom hesitated a minute, then shook the broad Irish palm.

Walsh turned to Morgan. And Tom interrupted, "He comes back, Tim, I'll hold you to it over my dead body."

Warily, and without conviction, Morgan too, took the big Irish palm.

Nan stood stiffly in the doorway with Joey and Tom and watched Wendy ride off with Tim Walsh. The big red horse stepped out smartly. She was clearly going to lead Walsh's mustang all the way back to town.

Nan busied herself in the cabin, preparing an elk stew and biscuits, which she served them at midday. Tom Ludlam stayed with them through noontime and into the afternoon. He never left until after he had a good, home-cooked meal.

The clatter of hooves suddenly startled them. Nan ran to the door. It was Wendy. He was leading the second horse with Tim Walsh strapped limp over the saddle.

Tom ran out and they both carried the ashen Walsh inside. Nan rushed for her medicine bag as they laid him on the table.

No one spoke. Wendy cut open Walsh's heavy stockman's coat and unbuttoned his shirt. He and old Tom looked on.

"Back shot, stomach wound," the old Indian fighter barely whispered. "He's goin'... better 'e go quick. We ain't gonna help 'im none."

Nan came up with a pot of hot water. Wendy, ashen-faced, took it from her and put it back on the stove. She stood immobile in front of him, gazing at the stricken Sheriff, Wendy's hands gripping her shoulders. Joey had come up beside Tom, his big eyes bulging. They didn't watch for long.

Walsh never saw them. His mouth opened, he coughed once and spit blood, a heavy congealed red mass. He heaved and lay still. For Joey, it was the first time he had seen a man die. No one tried to hide it from him. Death was a fact of life here in the wild. His father had died. Animals died. There were the predators and the prey. The survival of one sealed the fate of another.

Wendy Morgan closed the lids of the mild Irishman's lifeless eyes and crossed his big palms over his chest.

"We got to take 'im in." Tom broke the silence. He looked at Wendy, "It don't look good for ya, son. What happened? Ambush?"

"Ambush. Someone layin' waitin' for 'im. In that cottonwood grove by the bend in the creek. I was ridin' in front - the mare's a walker - and his horse was lagging about fifty yards behind. I heard the shot and by the time I got back to Walsh there, the killer was gone into the brakes along the Creek, and Walsh was laying in the snow. I went to Walsh. He was square with me, least he was tryin' to be."

"That he was... That he was... We'll track the varmint tomorrow in the snow... if'n it don't melt no more."

"I'll take Walsh back to town. I know where to go."

"We all go. That's the Law layin' there, son. Folks is gonna be mad. He was one a them, their own. Joey you go set out a good shock a hay for them ponies an' put yer mittens on. Nan, you too, dress warmly. Morgan needs us to say he done right, an' that he was goin' in with Walsh of his own free will. I'll saddle up. We be back tomorrow."

They wrapped the body of Tim Walsh in an old tarp and lay it over a pack saddle. Joey would ride the gentle little bay. Nan would ride Walsh's horse, Tom, his black. It was still early afternoon when they started out. Wendy led on the red mare, leading the pack horse, then Nan with Joey beside her, and Tom followed behind.

CHAPTER 34

I t was a grim procession. Dave Lewis, at his livery on the edge of town, was among the first to recognize Walsh's horse and spy the bulky tarp on the straggling pack horse. He dropped his blacksmith's tongs and went out to watch. Tom Ludlam acknowledged his friend as they went by, but said nothing. The burly blacksmith followed them up the street. They pulled up in front of the crisp little white house that was the undertaker's. His was one of the few houses that had a coat of paint - undertaking was a lucrative business. This time, Israel Roland was not there waiting for them, but materialized from Nell's Restaurant down and across the street. Lewis helped carry the heavy bundle into the front room and lay it on the table. The minute he saw the little group stop in front of Roland's, Lewis had known what happened and probably the rest of the town knew too.

Morgan pulled the tarp back from Walsh's face. Froglike, the undertaker's eyes bulged. The little undertaker dealt with death often, though it had never become routine to him.

"That's Walsh! That's the Sheriff!" He was looking at Morgan.

Evenly, Wendy Morgan answered, "He was shot from ambush, down the bend in Rock Creek."

"My God...he's got a wife...and a kid!" The excited little man meant no harm, but to Nan the words stung like a whip.

"You want to tell them or should I?"

Morgan's face was somber. He could not take his eyes off Nan. "It may be easier if it comes from someone she knows."

"You want me to go for the Doctor?" Morgan knew from experience that Doc Zilka was Walsh's second in command, also that Doc would not judge him unfairly.

"We'll need 'im." Tom Ludlam's voice was grim and Morgan walked out the door. The urge to run, to leave it all behind, gripped his every nerve. He could go fast and far on the big red horse, just like he had escaped that day along the rim of Deer Creek Canyon. Yet he knew he would not run. These people had treated him justly. George Meachum had returned his stolen stock. Nan Fletcher had nursed and fed him. Old Ludlam had helped him to survive. And Joey, something had to be done for Joey, who had shown him how much he valued a home and children. His palms sweated and his jaw worked anxiously. By sheer power of will, he forced one foot out in front of the other. He would not leave this place, never leave Nan. They would have to kill him first. That prospect festered in his mind.

Doc Zilka answered the door as always, reluctantly and with a grunt. When he saw Morgan, his frown cleared.

"Good you came back, boy. You talk to the Sheriff yet?"

"I talked to 'im."

"Then what you need me for?"

"He's dead, Doc.... Shot, ambushed, out by the cottonwoods at the bend in the creek. I was comin' in with him for questioning, set the record straight. That horse of mine is a fast walker an' I was out in front by about fifty yards. Heard the shot, didn't see it." The wrenching tone of his voice caught the Doctor's sympathy.

"It don't look good, Morgan. You shoot a guy you say is stealing your horse and you leave town. Sheriff goes after you and you bring him back a corpse. People gonna wonder."

"That's why I came back. Nan Fletcher an' her boy and Tom Ludlam will speak for me. I'm hoping Lewis and George Meachum and maybe you will too."

The Doctor reached for his hat and coat.

"You got guts.... Where is he?

"At Izzy Roland's." Was it regret, the horror of killing or something else that burned in this man's dark and handsome face? Doc Zilka read pain there, and fear. But this man was no coward. Nor, he decided, was this man a criminal. He put a comforting hand on Morgan's shoulder and they stepped out into the cold street.

"Come on. Tell me about it on the way."

When they got back to Roland's, a crowd had formed. They were not friendly. But neither were they antagonistic. Morgan caught a glimpse of a thin human form that he recognized. Hadn't he seen it by the light of the fire in the livery, the night he had shot Bill Hendl? He couldn't be sure.

Nan gripped Joey's hand until it hurt. The inquest was complete. The verdict was clear: death by rifleshot to the stomach. The bullet that Wendy thought had come from the cottonwoods by the creek, had come from the other side and from up high. It had been fired at close range, about ten feet, and down at Walsh, as if the murderer had been horsed and Walsh afoot. It had broken a rib on entry, which pierced a lung, hastening what otherwise would have been a slow and agonizing death. Tom had his arm around Nan's shoulders.

Doc, fair-minded as ever, was explaining to Wendy Morgan why he had to stay in Red Lodge. One death, of a horse thief, the town could accept. It happened so often. But this was different. This was their Sheriff. And the path of the bullet, the suggested proximity of the weapon, made it hard to understand how Morgan had not seen anything as he rode in with Walsh. There would have to be inquiries, an investigation, and a jury would have to decide whether or not to press charges.

Morgan could have fled - he had the fastest horse in the county - and the fact that he had not fled should help prove his innocence. Until the jury assembled, Doc Zilka would have to lock him up. And the town would have to choose a new lawman. But he did promise to muster the jury as quickly as possible on the morrow. He was sure they would not bind Morgan over for trial, if he explained about his swift-walker of a horse, and how he was leading Walsh all the way.

Morgan had little to say. His dark eyes flashed toward Nan's worried face and back to the Doctor, then to Joey.

Tom Ludlam spoke up, "You got to understand, Doc, Mrs. Fletcher needs help on that place. There's eight head to feed. Waste of a good man, keepin' 'im here."

"The stock can forage for themselves for a few days." Then, courteously, Doc Zilka addressed Nan. "And you can stay with me for the duration."

"Thank you." She looked at Tom and at Wendy, her expression frozen.

Wendy and Doc Zilka walked out of the pretty white house, through the doubtful crowd, and down toward the jail.

It was a forbidding little building on Red Lodge's only side street, opposite the Elkhead Saloon. Grey, damp, and set apart from the wooden buildings that were its neighbors, the jail was the only stone building in town. It was built of granite and squatted like an ugly wart on the snow-covered street. Thick iron bars, anchored deep into the walls, four feet thick, covered the small high windows. It was cold inside, since no one was there to light the fire. Short of dynamite, escape was impossible.

Nan, Joey, and Tom Ludlam followed to show the good citizens of Red Lodge their faith in Wendell Morgan. And some of the townspeople followed too, out of sympathy for the widow and her crippled son, or friendship for Tom Ludlam, or plain curiosity. Among them were Dave Lewis, beholden to Wendy for saving his barn, Nellie from the restaurant, who had served them Christmas dinner, Rose McCartle, and the youngest Meachum, Tag.

Wendy walked into the chilly cell, heard the bars shut, and the lock clink home. Tom took Joey's hand from his mother's and led the boy outside, followed by the good Doctor.

When Wendy turned around, he saw Nan, tragic and beautiful and alone. He waited behind the bars as she approached and placed her hands on his shoulders. Hesitantly, he stretched his arms through the bars and put a timid hand on her cheek, stroking, caring. He thought only of the soft light and warm blankets of the tiny homestead. She came up to him and their lips met again, longingly, fervently. An exquisite warmth held them there, with only the cold of the prison bars in between.

Softly, she spoke to him, "I'll stay here with you, I mean here in town. We'll find someone for the stock." She walked quietly over and started to light the stove.

Before she left the jail, Nan Fletcher sent Joey home with Doc and made sure a good fire was going in the stove. The jailhouse warmed.

"I'll ask Lewis to take the horses we have with us. Tom said he'd ride over every day and feed the ones at home."

Wendy Morgan had sunk down on his bunk and looked on silently, despairingly, following her with his eyes. Life could be so good and then so cruel.

"Nan," he spoke her name almost tragically, "there's one person might be able to help. I didn't say anything before because

I think he feels about you the same way I do, and I didn't want to lose you to him."

She was bending over the stove and straightened up abruptly.

"Lose me to him? Who? You'll not lose me, Wendy. I love you!" How desperately she wanted him to know this now. "There's no one else!"

"Yes, there is. He told me himself. I mean George Meachum."

Nan laughed lightly and shook her head. "Wendell Morgan, he's a married man!"

"And a rich and handsome one too. He loves you, Nan."

"You crazy man, you're dreaming." She reached out to him, but he caught her wrist and stopped her.

"Nan, we don't know how long I'll be here, or even if they'll let me go. George Meachum admires you. He told me so, and he told me he would help you, wanted to help you, that he'd give me money for a doctor for Joey, and you needn't know where it came from. He loves you too, Nan. Believe it."

Wendy Morgan clenched his teeth and clutched the iron bars until his knuckles turned white. "Nan, go to George Meachum. Tell him everything that has happened. He'll get a stock tender for you until this thing blows over, and you'll have your homestead and a respectable herd."

"Without you? And what will you have?"

"He'll speak for me too." But Wendy Morgan had his doubts.

Moses Meachum had witnessed the bit of drama at the undertaker's house and rode swiftly back to the M-bar before sunset. He arrived just before dinner to find Harv seated by the fire, in serious conversation with Murph and Jenks, the third and last of the Texas gunmen still riding for the M-bar. Mose sauntered to the edge of the fire to get warm. The temperature was dropping again.

"You heard the latest from Red Lodge?"

Harv shrugged and waited. They were lounging comfortably in the best upholstered chairs around the fire and they didn't get up for him. The bottle on the table was only half empty.

"Morgan, that feller that shot Hendl, Doc locked 'im in jail." He looked at the three men in front of him. Was he telling them what they already knew? Big Harv just waited. Murph fidgeted nervously, all the while staring at Harv. Jenks stared at the fire glassy-eyed. They knew. Mose Meachum was sure of it.

"Sheriff's dead an' there's some think Morgan shot 'im."

"Morgan, huh?"

"Yeah, seems Walsh went out there to ask him a few questions, an' out by the bend in the creek, Morgan pulled a rifle on 'im." Mose sensed that the killing of Walsh had been a frame-up, a way to put Wendy Morgan out of the way forever and at the same time to appropriate the Fletcher homestead.

It was a clever plan. Mrs. Fletcher had to live on her land for three years after filing before it became hers. Two years had passed. If she could be persuaded off now, and her survival there was impossible without help, the Meachums could buy cheap. Harv Meachum was losing patience, this Mose knew, and Wendy Morgan was one of the thorniest burrs under his blanket. The other was his own brother, George, with his wild railroad schemes and newfound virtue.

Mose sat down and curled his surly lips around his pipe. "You want we should load the jury?" They understood each other.

"That and pack George back to Billings."

"He ain't gonna go easy, Harv."

"Then he goes hard. Where is he anyway?"

"He's probably hangin' 'round the Elkhead or out countin' 'is nags with old Slim." He blew out a swift stream of pipe smoke. "An' I seen 'im take an uncommon interest in that Fletcher woman...keepin' 'is distance, though."

"We better remind 'im he's married, and 'is lovely wife is in Billings."

CHAPTER 35

The same evening, January 8, Nan Fletcher walked courageously into the Elkhead Saloon. She squinted through the smoke-filled air, gave a little cough, and asked a burly cowboy where she could find George Meachum. The cowboy swept off his hat gallantly and stared at her open-mouthed. Conversations stopped. Heads turned.

She tried again, "George Meachum? Do you know him? If he's here, I'd like to speak with him." Her eyes scanned the room.

Another cowboy approached hesitantly, and another, and another. Nan couldn't see past their broad shoulders in the smoke-filled air. They were a rough-hewn lot, young, tall, lean, but unwashed, some unshaven, their clothing worn, patched, and none too clean. They were all armed. They smelled of beer. They were not ready with words.

Nan waited and looked anxiously from one to the other. She ventured again. "George Meachum?"

Finally, one puncher spoke up. "Ma'am, I believe he's in the back."

"Thank you."

She shouldered her way across the room, pulling her shawl tightly around her. The men hung back, making a natural aisle for her. This was a woman, a real woman, not just another of the bar girls that they were used to. This they sensed, but they were uncertain how to treat her. In the smoky barroom atmosphere, a clear, confident light shone from her blue eyes and brown curls accentuated the creamy skin and smooth contours of her face. The shawl, stretched taught over her shoulders followed the feminine curves of bust and waist. Men stared. Some, who had but recently come in off the range, had not seen a woman like this for almost a year.

She reached the bar. Like all the rest, the bartender gaped too, but he was not tongue-tied.

"Ma'am, can I do somethin' for ya?"

"Please, yes, George Meachum. Is he here?" If he wasn't, it would be an embarrassing retreat.

"He's right over there, ma'am." He indicated a small round table in a corner. Meachum was sitting with his back to the far wall, in conversation with a striking older woman in black silk and lace.

Nan swallowed her apprehensions and reddened at the prospect of having to ask a favor of this man. Wendy had said George Meachum loved her. It was to her a strange, incongruous thought. She had only met him three times, twice at her cabin and once at church. He had been clad for the trail, chaps and a cowman's slicker. He had seemed more approachable. Now she looked at his tanned face, his squared jawline, and the breadth of his shoulders. His tailored clothing, gold watch chain, and waxed moustache formed a striking ensemble. He looked, as he did for the Christmas service, powerful and urbane. This was not a man to love a poor homesteader's widow. This man could have his choice. She laughed silently at Wendy. Surely, he was mistaken. It touched her then that he was also a bit jealous and she smiled.

George Meachum looked up. "Nan! Nan Fletcher! What are you doing here?" His recognition was instant. He was on his feet. Her apprehensions eased.

"I came to speak to you."

He drew out a chair for her, "Please, please do sit down."

"Nan Fletcher, this is Rose McCartle. Rose owns the Elkhead."

Nan stretched out her arm and offered her hand to Rose. George was quick to notice the surprise in Rose's face. It passed almost in an instant. None of the town's respected ladies had ever shaken hands with her before. None of them had ever ventured into the Elkhead Saloon. On the frontier, men could easily hide their past, so many avenues were open to them. For a woman, it was different. There were so few. They were known far and wide, and their reputations, good or bad, followed them. Rose held Nan's hand warmly. Then with deliberation added, "You're always welcome here."

"Thank you, Mrs. McCartle."

"Not Mrs...just Rose." Nan spied just a suggestion of a glance toward George Meachum.

"If you like, thank you, just Rose." And Nan smiled. From the two poles of female society, they would be friends.

Rose fell silent. George looked from Rose to Nan, "What brings you to town?"

"You've not heard?" she hesitated. Then she related the story of the Walsh murder. They had heard about it, as all hear the perennial bits of gossip that titillate a small town, but they had not heard of Morgan's part in it.

"So now you come to me. Why? I can't turn him loose."

"No, but I was hoping you could find me a man to tend my stock. You see," she blushed, took a deep breath and lurched on, "I'll be very frank, Mr. Meachum, Wendy Morgan has lived with us for more than three months, since my husband died. He's become like a father to Joey."

It was what Morgan had become to her that haunted George Meachum, yet he held his eyes on her without a flicker. "You should be able to find someone right here. Plenty of cowboys come in off the range for the winter and plenty of them would be glad to help a pretty lady."

Nan lowered her eyes and pursed her lips. "Don't be gallant, Mr. Meachum, not now. You see, I have no money. Cowboys are expensive in these parts. I can't pay Meachum wages...." The reference did not escape George. It meant Harv's gunman pay was common knowledge. His cheek started to tick. Nan Fletcher continued, "Wendy Morgan said you offered...." She stopped and dropped her head. She was asking for charity and that violated every fiber of independence in her soul. And, God forbid, George Meachum might expect payment in some more intimate way. "I...I shouldn't have asked."

George Meachum stood for a moment, stunned, then recovered quickly. "Morgan told you right, Nan Fletcher." His words came softly. He sensed her uneasiness. "I have two men experienced with horses. One of them will work tirelessly and never breathe a word. No one will be the wiser." He was covering her embarrassment.

Nan felt her doubts diminish. "I'm in your debt, Mr. Meachum. Thank you."

George Meachum sat immobile. The worry lines dug more deeply into his face and a twinge contracted the muscle in his cheek. His doleful brown eyes continued to rest on Nan. "One more thing

I must tell you. This man who will come to care for your stock, don't be afraid of him."

"Afraid? In what way? Why should I be afraid?" The thought flashed across her mind that maybe it was this stockman who would exact the price.

"He's an Indian," and he was quick to explain, "a Crow, Absaroka, friend to the white man."

Relief surged like a torrent into the heart of Nan Fletcher. She thought of the bitter struggle between red man and white, of Sitting Bull and Chief Joseph and Dull Knife. She remembered all the stories Bo had told her of their destruction and savagery. But that was Bo. She thought of her own fears - that Wendy Morgan would not come back. She was a woman alone on the frontier. She did not discriminate in her need.

George Meachum was still talking. "He's a good man, the best with a horse. I trust him and you can trust him. You must not report him. If the army hears he's off the reservation without a permit, he could be thrown in jail. And they may not ask questions, just shoot him down." He sensed the hesitation in Nan. Whites were fearful of Indians these ten years since the Little Big Horn - Hostiles they called them - and from that fear grew the binding weeds of prejudice.

But prejudice was far from the thoughts of Nan Fletcher. Hers were the fears of robbery and rape, of her own feminine clumsiness with firearms, the limits of her physical strength and that of her only son. She struggled with her feelings. George Meachum vouched for this Indian. George Meachum vouched for Wendy Morgan. She was a good judge of men, and from the first time she had met him, when he rode into the yard to return the stolen horses, she had trusted George Meachum. He had never gone back on his word.

"Just treat him fairly and let him do his job. He has different ways from us and may bring his pony into the house, disappear overnight or even longer, but don't worry, your horses will thrive."

"I will trust him," was all she said. She knew she would have to muster great strength to master her fears.

George Meachum got up to leave. "I'll ride out tonight. He'll be there by morning."

Rose McCartle watched him stride, tall and graceful, out through the swinging doors, and Nan Fletcher watched the glow fade from the face of Rose McCartle.

CHAPTER 36

Nan started back to Doc's. As she passed the narrow side street where the jail was, her heart sank. Still, she was drawn into its shadows, to the stubby little cold stone building. Joey would be asleep by now, comfortable and warm in Doc's own feather bed. Fortune had smiled when it had paired Joey with Doc Zilka. How she wished the Doctor could find a way to give Joey strength. But now her mind and heart held a more pressing urgency and she turned her steps toward the jail. A gas lamp shone faintly through the barred window. She knocked and went in. Dave Lewis was taking a turn at guard duty.

"Ma'am, I never expected to see you here this late!"

Nan hadn't anticipated meeting anyone else. "I just came by to say good night."

Lewis knew it was an excuse, that it wasn't for him she came. "He's right in there. He'll be right happy to see ya."

Morgan, who had been lying on his bunk, stood up and came slowly to the front of the cell.

"I just came by to say good night," she repeated, and wrapped her fingers around the iron bars. They were ice cold. "George Meachum will send a man." She was almost choking on the words. He wrapped his big palms around both her hands. "I knew he would!" he said, and the look he gave her went to the depths of her heart. They could not speak what they felt with Lewis there behind them.

"He's an Indian, a Crow," she added, and looked at him expecting a reaction, but there was none. He just nodded as if he hadn't heard.

"I'm staying at the Doctor's."

"You needn't. You should go home now that you have some help."

"We'll see. The Doctor likes Joey, maybe he'll find a way..." She was making every effort she could to say something positive, and strained at the effort.

"Go, get some sleep. The jury will convene tomorrow and I'll be out of here."

She nodded sadly and turned to go. He went back to his bunk.

Lewis came over after she had left.

"Well, I'll stoke the fire and go home to bed. You'll have good dreams, you will, thinkin' a the pretty widder. You need anything, just rattle that thar tin cup on them bars. Someone likely to hear ya. An' here's another blanket keep ya warm, brand new from the Emporium. Coupla days, you be outta here and you kin go back to courtin' the lady an' ridin' yer fancy horse."

Morgan smiled outwardly, but felt only despair. Lewis, he knew had paid for the blanket from his own pocket. His remarks were meant to cheer him. He wasn't at all sure that he would be outta there in a coupla days.

January 9, 1887, the cold wind blew in from the north. It began to snow at dawn and kept snowing heavily all day. The thermometer dropped steadily. The wind picked up. At 8:00 a.m. the snow was two inches deep, at 10:00 it was four inches deep. By noon, a gale was blowing straight down the main street. Pedestrians hunched over and held on to buildings lest they be blown off their feet. Cowboys rescued their horses from hitchrails and corrals and filled every available stall. Cattle sought out the sheds and lean-tos, the rocky overhangs and cottonwood groves, to break the force of wind and curtain of snow. No one ventured out.

Doc Zilka pulled back the curtain in his front room and looked out. He looked guiltily back at Nan. "No jury going to meet today. Nobody going out on a day like this, not even the sick ones. Best to get some quiet work done." Trudy, the town laundress, had prepared a sumptuous breakfast of bacon and flapjacks with homemade syrup. She cooked for the Doctor mornings and evenings. Lunches he took over at Nell's. Joey had wolfed down his breakfast and now lingered in the kitchen with the Doctor's big grey cat and a stethoscope, listening to the cat's heart and then his own.

Nan had nothing to do. Had she been home, she would be milking the cow, cooking breakfast, collecting eggs, stirring the fire, all the myriad tiny necessities every woman busied herself with around a home. Here, she waited. The Doctor had his books, and, she supposed, an occasional nip to keep his blood warm. Joey had the newness of town, the Doctor's instruments and pet cat to tease. His child's brain jumped from item to item around the room, questioning, laughing. Doc patiently answered his inquiries and watched his movements.

All day long the snow fell and the wind blew. Only necessities summoned the townsfolk outside. The Doc made a sick call, to old Mrs. Simpson - to make sure she didn't skimp on her firewood. She'd languished all winter, he suspected with tuberculosis. And then there were the inevitable cases of frostbite. Dave Lewis braved the storm to muck out and feed. His barn was brim full and the horses stamped nervously at the howling wind that invaded the cracks, blowing snow through every peephole into the stalls. Nell rushed from curtained-off kitchen to restaurant counter. Hungry, cold cowboys were arriving in town, driven off the range in the face of the storm, their first craving, a good hot meal. She would run short of supplies if this kept up. She sent over to the Emporium for more flour, sugar and coffee.

That day the mail arrived from Billings, the carrier had started out ahead of the storm, only to ride headlong into it. His horses had floundered in chest-high snow. He had cut them loose, abandoned his wagon, shouldered the mail bag, and continued on foot. He staggered into Red Lodge, cold and spent, at six in the evening. Snow poured through the unglazed, barred window of the jail. Like hoary tapestries, layers of frost crystals and ice blanketed the damp stone walls. It was so cold in the little jailhouse that Nan wondered how Wendy could sit so quietly and keep his teeth from chattering. He looked like an Indian with his dark hair wrapped tightly in the blanket Dave Lewis had given him. Lewis had been there and Doc had looked in, but Tim Walsh was no longer around to keep the fire burning in the little stove. Although Nan eagerly took over this task, it kept on snowing all that day and the next, and the little jailhouse soon became uninhabitable. Dave Lewis took Wendy home with him.

Travelling was hazardous in the extreme. Drifts the size of buildings blocked the railroad from Billings to Laurel and piled over the rutted trails. The Laurel to Red Lodge stage came to a halt after the first day. The snow disguised sharp rocks, roots, and holes that could snap a horse's leg or crack the axle of a wagon. And beneath the snow was a layer of ice, the last vestige of the warm wind that had blown in for Christmas and raised hopes of a mild winter and early spring roundup. The ice was thick, encasing what was left of the summer's green grasses turned gold. Starving cattle gashed their legs and scraped their nostrils in their desperate attempts to uncover food. Nan had not seen George Meachum since that day at the Elkhead and feared for her homestead and animals. She prayed daily that the Indian had arrived.

The north wind never died. It blew colder. Its arrival coincided with the month of January, the Moon of the Frost-Exploding Trees. It was so cold that tree sap froze solid, expanded, and burst open full-grown tree trunks. Cattle left exposed to the elements suffocated. Their nostrils froze closed. When they tried to breathe through their mouths, the cold air froze their lungs. There they stood, dead on their feet, tongues hanging out, like stones in a graveyard, grim testimonies to carelessness and greed. The cutbanks and the cottonwood groves, natural shelters in other milder winters, filled high with their corpses. On the second day, George Meachum arrived in town to tell Nan his man had settled in the nick of time to tend her stock. He and a few half-frozen cowboys were the only people to arrive in town that day. Rose McCartle had seen George ride in. Only she knew it was George. His face was hidden beneath a muffler which was wrapped around his head and had frozen solid with his breath. Icicles hung from the brim of his hat. George had also checked his own herd. Slim had driven them close in under the overhanging rimrock to a store of dry hay and firewood, where they would wait out the storm. George wished him luck. He, himself refused to spend the duration of the storm confined to the isolation of the M-bar ranch house. He could no longer live alongside his brothers. He was sickened by what he saw at his home, sickened at the excesses of certain of his brothers: at the carelessness and cruelty with which Harv approached the business of cattle; at the callousness of Gabe; at the blind ruthlessness of Mose. He preferred to make his bunk at the Elkhead amid the whores and the gamblers. Dancer joined him. Tag, they left behind.

The blizzard raged for eight more days. On the eleventh day, it stopped. The sun shone in a clear blue sky. The snow along the main street of Red Lodge, Gallatin County, Montana Territory, was even with the second story windows. Townsfolk began the prodigious effort of digging out. The paths they dug were narrow alleys between huge walls of white. They dug snow from off roofs to prevent cave-ins, of which there were mercifully few. They attached runners to wagons to make improvised sleighs and even fashioned snowshoes for horses. They shook the dust from the last of the old buffalo robes. They listened to the desperate bawls of starving animals that had survived and wandered into town and tried to eat the bark off trees and the shingles off buildings. These animals they mercifully shot and boiled their bones for soup. Stories circulated of line cabins and lumber shacks where men had perished not from the cold, but, like the cattle, from starvation and asphyxiation. They had failed to lay in sufficient stores to last out the storm, or, buried in their cabins under the snow, they had neglected to keep an air passage open. In the euphoria of warmth at Christmas, like the grasshopper in the fable, they had sung and danced and drunk and gamed without thought for what lay ahead.

Cattlemen were grim. For years they had waxed rich. They bought young cattle in Texas and shipped them north to the lush Montana prairie. It was a prairie they did not own, the range of Indian and buffalo. They waged war on the redman and slaughtered the buffalo. When they needed more pasture, they appropriated reservation land, monopolized precious water rights, and drove off settlers. And they fought among themselves for the use of every acre. They crammed hundreds of thousands of head of cattle, southern-bred, onto stubby, drought-ravaged, low-nutrient grass, and left them to roam without care or shelter. The cattle had developed neither the strength nor the instincts to survive the cold. The cattlemen were deaf to the warnings of Indians, old hunters, and mountainmen. There had been no deep, long-lasting snowfall since the blizzard in March of '78. This kind of snowfall was long overdue. They heeded only their own profits of the last few years, driven by the huge capital investments and ample dividends paid to the big cattle companies. These were wiped out. In this storm, whole herds died off. The days of big companies and big profits were over.

Now, the cattlemen dreaded the coming of spring. Where were the calves and cows that they had bought at thirty dollars a head? Could they have driven them to the foothills where the wind had exposed bald spots? They had decided not to try. In hindsight, they should have. Or, like George Meachum, could they have made a late fall roundup? His own brothers had laughed at him. Fat grass steers sold in Chicago for sixty dollars a head last fall. Now, they dared not think of how many cattle were lost. And they waited helplessly. Only the spring roundup would reveal the full impact of the winter. Only the spring thaw would expose the extent of the disaster.

At the M-bar, Harv Meachum was bitter. He knew his cattle had not fared well. His gunhands, for all their exaggerated wages, were only fair-weather herders. They had come in early off the range at the first sign of foul weather, and whiled away the hours at games of poker and dice. The bunkhouse turned into a game house. Whiskey flowed. Disputes were frequent, fights not uncommon. The roughest among them had even appropriated Harv's whiskey supply and Harv dared not stop them. He could still afford to pay them, but he was using money that would be better spent making up for the winter's losses and restocking his range in the spring. Mose watched him closely. And Mose watched the men in the bunkhouse.

Harv was further irked by thoughts of his brother, George. George Meachum had been right. Harv did not easily stand corrected. The stage road was full of covered wagons bringing settlers, fence-builders, and farmers into the territory, like this Morgan, and the Fletcher woman and her fool husband and scrawny kid. They were filling up the range, filing for their 160-acre quarter sections near the best waterholes and along the creekbeds, and they were ploughing under fine pastureland. Resentment invaded his soul like the worm inside the fruit. But George had left Harv's domain. As the first object of his brother's wrath, he was not available.

Frustrated, Harv turned his anger inward, and toward these hapless grangers, and it grew in intensity. With each passing day, Harv brooded more. He even doubted the loyalty of his brother, Mose. He would pull back the sitting room curtain and gaze out at the whiteness, at the empty corrals and the smoke curling skyward from the bunkhouse chimney. He would often glare at the skeletal form of Mose crossing the ranchyard to that bunkhouse, in the stiffest wind always clenching his pipe between his yellow teeth. He would lie awake nights, listening to the howling wind and thinking of ways to drive the farmers and post hole diggers from the Rock Creek range. He concluded that the very same bitter winter that threatened the M-bar afforded one of the best opportunities to run them out and best his brother, George, if he could mobilize his drunken cowboys. And winter would be his scapegoat.

CHAPTER 37

In the throes of such a winter, shock and indignation at the murder of Tim Walsh receded. Wendy Morgan had moved in with Dave Lewis and had joined in the work of caring for men and horses, clearing snow and keeping warm. Lewis had come to appreciate his quiet, competent aide. Wendy was a common sight wandering around town, frequently in the company of Mrs. Fletcher. He was helpful and kind to everyone. Other folk too, such as Walt Rhenquist at the Emporium and Ty Lamm of Lamm's Feed and Grain, came to know and like this quiet man. Surely he was no murderer. The jailhouse was left untended. There was no urgency to dig it out. Snow covered it inside and out, and it was hidden from view, erased for the duration of the winter by a soft white pillow of snow.

Doc Zilka had never convened the jury. People were too busy with the grueling tasks of survival to worry about justice. This man, whom they saw every day around the town, was good with a gun. But gun skill was normal and necessary for hunters and Indian fighters. He may even have killed, but so had many of their peers. To kill face to face in an even duel was accepted experience in the west. It was the back-shooting, the covert and stealthy actions of the coward, that society condemned. Morgan had not run. He had faced the consequences of killing Hendl. He had brought in Walsh's body and turned himself in. This was not characteristic of a murderer. Toward Morgan, the townsfolk tended to be a forgiving lot. The jury never met and Wendy Morgan roamed at will, a free man. He and Nan started to think about returning home.

Doc broached the subject one night at dinner after Joey had gone to bed. "Morgan, I had some words with Lewis, Nell, and George Meachum. They all see you as an honest man. I"m thinking there'll be no need for a jury. We've all agreed. You're to go free."

Wendy Morgan thought he was dreaming.

Doc continued, "Soon as the roads are fit for travel, you can be going." He looked up at Nan's smiling face but did not change his grave expression. "But my advice to you is to put away that gun, permanently." He hesitated again and drew his lips into a thin line beneath his salt-and-pepper moustache.

"One more thing I think you should consider," he looked steadily from one to the other, anticipating, "now don't take me for a busybody, but I think the boy should stay here."

It was unexpected. Nan's head jerked up. Her face blanched white as the snow that piled in the street outside.

Doc's monotone voice droned on. "Now I know this comes as a shock, but you think a while. Take time and ponder on it. As a medical man, I've been watching Joey. He's a wonderful boy, friendly, bright. But he's weak. I mean physically. And I'm not telling you anything you don't already know." He went on as gently as he knew how. "You're his mother and you've seen other boys his age. You already know he doesn't measure up. You don't admit it, but deep down you know. He hasn't enough muscle for a boy of his age, although one look at those legs makes you think he could climb Sundance Peak in an afternoon." He droned on softly, relating only the facts as he saw them. "I can tell you that his legs aren't normal. And the rest of him is so thin. His joints don't bend radially to the extent they should. His arms and legs just don't have the normal strength and flexibility. And his spine is curved inward, lordosis, they call it. Now, I been searching my books for an explanation and all my old journals for descriptions of muscle disease and I'm not finding anything. But out here I don't have much of a library. Books are scarce. Here's what I'd like to do." He stopped.

Nan was in shock. Never had anyone ever broached Joey's difficulty so openly before. With Bo, it was not even acknowledged, much less ever discussed. Wendy sat grave and attentive. He, at least, was grasping every single one of Doc's words. What was going through Nan's heart, neither knew.

"I can keep him here with me and send him to school. Just opened a little school right up the street last year. He needs to learn to use his head, to read, and do figures. He'll never survive out here on his physical strength. You know it and I know it...maybe you've never admitted it to yourself, but the older he gets, the harder it will be to learn a useful trade...." He paused a moment then forged brutally forward. "Now, when the summer comes and we can have easy travelling, I want to take him over to Miles City or maybe even on to Chicago or St. Louis, and see if we can get a handle on what's the matter with him."

He stopped and looked over at Morgan, whose piercing blue eyes seemed to comprehend. Doc Zilka put a hand on Nan's arm and continued.

"Now, I'm not offering you sympathy or pity. Little good that'll do him in this territory. And I'm not offering you a cure, not even the hope of one, because I just don't know. I am offering him a life of his own, God-willing, a happy one. He needs to go forward with his little life, make some friends his own age, learn to use his head, learn a trade that he can perform within his own limitations so's eventually he can be a man and earn his own keep. He can't do that out there in the woods. He can't ride a horse every day to school. That's why I'm offering to take him in. School's just up the street."

Nan was speechless, her moist eyes staring wildly at the Doctor. Wendy spoke up.

"Thanks Doc. You're going to have to allow us some time to digest all this. I'll talk to Mrs. Fletcher and to Joey."

"Better to make your decision first, without Joey. He's very young, maybe not even aware that much is the matter with him."

Wendy nodded. "And Nan wasn't either."

"Yes, she was. She's his mother."

Nan clenched her teeth and looked up. The shock was wearing off and she was regaining her poise and along with it, her reasoning. "I knew. I've known all along, when he didn't crawl or climb like most babies do, and when he would trip and fall so hard...." Her eyes looked far off into the shadowy corner of the room as if she saw there the shadows of her prior knowledge and fears.

Doc Zilka was not finished. He had yet another arrow to launch.

"I'm being very frank with you, Nan Fletcher. If his legs and arms are weak, probably his heart and lungs are weak too, although you say he rarely gets sick." It was a difficult speech, even for old Doc. He had heralded illness and death so many times before. But Doc, too, had become attached to Joey Fletcher. "You know, Mrs. Fletcher, that he may very well not live out a normal life span, but then lots of men don't out here...if that's any consolation. But they don't know it ahead of time."

"You're saying he's going to die?" Nan's face blanched. Her voice shook. "But he's not sick!"

Doc grunted. "Doesn't mean a thing. Time will tell and I'm telling you what I think. I had a good look at that boy these past weeks. I'll treat him like my own son, and you can come visit or he can go home to visit as much as he likes, except when school's in session or the weather turns bad."

"You're very kind, Doctor." Nan looked straight at him. He was not condescending. His words were straight out practical common sense.

Her husband was dead; her lover, in prison. Now she was losing her son.

"I'm only thinking of what's best for the boy."

"I understand." She mouthed the words.

"No, you don't. You think about it. Think hard. Morgan here'll make a good sounding board. Talk to him - he grew up on an army post and I'll wager his mother wasn't always around. And talk to Joey. I think you'll find he wants to go to school. Curious, intelligent kids usually do. Oh, he'll miss you all right, no doubt about that, but he'll make some new friends and be around people, and play with kids his own age." Finally, he stopped. He couldn't look at the pain in Nan's eyes. He looked at Morgan instead but his words were still for Nan. "You'll miss him more."

Morgan spoke up for the first time.

"Doc, why not start Joey in school tomorrow? Mrs. Fletcher and Joey are gonna be here at least until the trails clear some more. Joe's just frittering his time away. Why don't we take him down to the schoolhouse tomorrow, while Nan can see first hand how he likes it?"

The faintest smile crossed the straight lips of the Doctor.

"Capital idea, Morgan. Why didn't I think of that!"

Nan's heart sank the next morning when she saw the wretched little miner's cabin that was the schoolhouse. From the outside, it looked like an igloo, those strange ice houses she had heard of that the Indians made in the far, far north. The snowfall had completely covered it. Only the entry had been shovelled clear. The inside was lined with boards - Nan firmly hoped that those boards were not the only barrier against wind and weather. She knew that the cabin had been one of the hastily constructed miner's lodgings and a miner's obsession was gold, not a roof over his head. The roof was sod, like that of her own cabin, and probably prone to leak when it rained. She smiled at Joey, but inside she wanted to go home and cry. Still, a sturdy, functioning stove - gift of Eb Krump at the General Store - sat squarely in the middle and provided ample warmth to the squalid little room. A kettle of hot soup simmered on the stove lid and filled the schoolroom with the aroma of boiled chicken. The children would not go hungry. There was a large slate nailed to the wall and someone had painted the letters of the alphabet and the numbers 1 to 10, in bright yellow on the roughened boards. Beside these, was tacked a colorful map of Montana Territory and a picture of Jefferson Davis.

Miss Adelaide Haggedorn, like the Meachums, came from Lexington, Kentucky, of fine, old, albeit now impoverished, Kentucky stock. She had arrived in Red Lodge only one year ago. On meeting her, Nan wondered what she was doing out here. She was a tall woman, regal in her bearing and not at all young. Nan would have guessed her age at about forty. Her hair, which was mostly light brown, now had sprinklings of grey, and she wore it somewhat severely pulled back and netted in a bun. Her eyes were blue, with slightly drooping lids, and her face showed the beginnings of sags and wrinkles. Once, she would have been beautiful. But it was her voice, rich and forceful, yet conveying absolute assurance and ease, that impressed Nan. She addressed Joey cheerfully, seemingly aware that this child was different, yet conveying no false sympathy. She would care for Joey just as she would care for every other child in her care. She would be an exacting but understanding teacher. Adelaide Haggedorn had not simply come west in search of a husband. She was clearly the equal of the task allotted her.

Nan left the school feeling lonely, and not a little fearful. She would have to get along with this woman. Nan wanted sorely to go back to the homestead and take Wendy and Joey with her. Still, the Chinook did not come. The trails remained blocked, the snow frozen and immovable. She busied herself at Nell's each day, trying to make palatable meals for the exhausted men from their dwindling stores. Food was getting scarce. Wendy continued to help Lewis. And Joey went to school.

He thrived. Only two other pupils lived in town. The others all lived on outlying farms and remained home. Miss Haggedorn devoted much of her time to Joey, catching him up to and even surpassing other children of his age. When the time came for a decision, the die was already cast. Joey, himself, elected to stay at school. Doc Zilka shook the boy's hand heartily. Nan Fletcher wept. She kept telling herself it was right for Joey.

CHAPTER 38

The little Fletcher homestead had weathered the winter successfully in the care of the Crow, Lame Bull. The Indian had swept the snow clean from the walkways and shovelled some off the roof. The wind had done the rest. He had hardly disturbed the interior of the cabin. He had slept on the floor in his own robes, making use of only those things, pots and knives, for which he had a direct need. He had milked the cow and fed the chickens and horses. They were thinner, but not so much from lack of nourishment, as from lack of exercise. They had lost muscle during the enforced inertia of the heavy snowfall, but they would soon regain it when the snow melted, the ground softened, and they could again gallop and play. He brushed them down and trimmed their hooves.

His days rolled by like waves off a shoreline, and after tending the animals, he would sit for hours watching the coals in the fire, at times lost in memories of laughter in the lodges, when the Absaroka people did not fear the Sioux raiding parties or the whims of the white trader. He despaired that the laughing times would never come again, but he was not lonely. He lived at one with animals, domestic and wild, at his side, and the tall mountains, the ancestral home of his people and of his gods, at his back. He longed to escape to their fastness for his dreaming, but the snow was still too deep. In the spring, he would lose himself in the land of the Bear's Tooth, far back in the white-capped peaks, where no white man would dare to follow. The old Colonel was dead. His debt was repaid. Slim, his only friend, was old. It was time for him to return to his people. Only the horses held him here.

One morning, in the second moon of his stay, he heard rumblings in the earth. Four horses were coming slowly across the southern hills. The woman whose house he tended would have been coming from the east. He grabbed his rifle and quietly crept out around the far corner of the barn. The ground rose a little at this point, giving him good cover as well as a good view of the cabin door.

Four men rode up brazenly. The going was still treacherous. The horses were noisy and snorting from the effort of wading through drifted snow. Where they had broken through ice, their legs were bruised and scratched. It had been a rough ride.

When Bull saw the skinny man with the pipe clamped in his teeth, he recognized Mose Meachum immediately. He cocked his rifle. The slight noise split the frozen air. The four riders stiffened visibly.

It was obvious that the visitors never expected to find anyone. They were all armed with rifles and pistols and their horses stamped with impatience. A rider pulled a cork from a jug that hung by the side of his saddle and took a long swallow, slathering drops of the yellow liquid down his black, broomthatch whiskers. He smacked his lips.

"Don't see no gold, no likker neither." The words were directed at the two riders on his left, away from the sullen Mose. "You want we get shot up fer nothin' Murph?"

"We know the widder woman ain't here. Now who's playing housekeeper I like to surmise?"

The Indian writhed. He was a hunter and a fighter, not a squaw, as Mose implied. But he said nothing, made no move. The horses snorted impatiently, sensing the tension of their riders, while Mose took a few minutes to reorganize his thoughts.

"Murph, you go see who's throwin' down on us. Probably, old man Ludlam. He taken a shine to the widder."

The Indian remained silent and hidden. The other men were three of Harv's crustiest gunmen, frustrated with the boredom of the bunkhouse and eager for diversion. They lacked all scruples. Knowing Nan Fletcher was in town and Wendy Morgan in jail, Mose Meachum had led them to the Fletcher homestead for easy loot. He wanted the horses. They would burn out the homestead and steal the stock. The Fletcher woman would fail to prove up on the 320 acres and presently the Meachums could take over. Harv would be delighted, George would be outsmarted. Mose had not anticipated resistance, especially the shooting kind. Old Tom Ludlam was the closest neighbor and Mose knew Tom had been ailing and wasn't as fast as he used to be. The Fletcher place should have been an easy take.

Mose steadied his mount and leaned his forearm across the horn of his saddle. "Ludlam, we don't want you. Go crawl in yer own hole. You too old fer playin' Robin Hood to a piece a skirt."

He motioned Murph forward. One shot cracked and knocked the horn right out from under his arm and off his saddle. A second shot sprayed icy splinters into Murph's whiskers. The two cowboys spurred their horses behind the watering trough to reach cover on the other side of the barn. Mose was shaking his hand. A big splinter stabbed through his palm between thumb and forefinger. He plucked it out.

"Fancy shootin', Ludlam. We know it's you. I heard yer eyesight was gettin' blurry. You ain't gonna slam down on the four of us, ya know that, at your age." He kept talking while two cowboys steered their horses around the corner of the barn.

Lame Bull had seen the deployment and knew that they planned to come around the building unseen and up behind him. He backed off around the zigzag of pine logs piled one on the other that made the corral barrier and gave good cover to a shooting man. He fired again, just as the two cowboys came around the end of the barn.

"Thought you said this was easy pickins Mose?" Jenks was annoyed and it showed. "I ain't gettin' my pants wet over an ole man and bunch a nags."

Finally, Murph spoke up. "You promised 'em shine, Meachum. I don't smell no shine in some scrawny widder's hut an' I ain't gittin' shot up without no whiskey." He was mad.

"I smelled a still up the road, Murph. That was back December." They were walking right past Mose now, who still held the pipe between his teeth. "I'd reckon t'were ole Ludlam's still at that." He stopped for effect. "Smelled soooo sweet, like good Kentucky corn with a Texas kick....must feel like velvet on a man's tongue."

"You 'member where you smelled that still Jenks?"

"My nose don't never forgit."

Murph nodded toward the other two behind the barn. He raised his voice so it could be heard past the corral.

"Ludlam, just you hold yer fire. You kin tell the widder we just come by to pay our respects, friendly like." Murph backed his horse slowly away, reined around, and started to ride off. Jenks and the other man followed. They were all laughing.

"You comin', Meachum?" It was an afterthought.

Mose Meachum had no choice.

Lame Bull watched impassively. Three days later, he was haying up and a black dog trotted into the yard.

CHAPTER 39

Late in March, the thawing southerly wind finally arrived. Gentle Annie, they called her, and softly as a maiden lover she caressed the rangeland. But it was too late.

Cattlemen all over the prairies rode out to count their losses. What they found was catastrophe. The cattle had drifted with the storm and the few that were left alive were hundreds of miles from their home ranges. They looked like ghostly skeletons with gossamer skins stretched thin over protruding bones. The bones and rotting flesh of their peers littered the range. Whole carcasses, frozen in the winter ice and released with the spring flow, clogged the rivers and creeks. Vultures loomed above. For many a rancher, bankruptcy threatened. The big Niobrara Cattle Company failed and took along with it the most powerful bank of the St. Louis stockyards. Some cowmen, sickened by the winter's slaughter, sold out the remnants of their herds, vowing never again to own an animal they could not feed and shelter.

The wolfers brought in a record number of pelts. The skinners scavenged the range, and the hide-buyers crowded the towns, eagerly bidding for whatever was salvageable of the big herds and could be sold on the open market for profit back east, after the wolves and the vultures grew fat.

In the confusion, Nan and Wendy saddled up for the ride home. It would be a grueling trip through slush and mud, but they were reasonably certain they would get through. They rode the horses they had arrived on, the sorrel mare and the bay. Dave Lewis had lent them two mules to pack in supplies. Some of these were intended for Tom Ludlam. Lewis was worried about his old friend. Tom was not in good health.

Nan had steeled her nerves for the good-bye to Joey and waved stoically as the horses trod, heavily laden, out of town. George Meachum saw them off with a parcel for Lame Bull, the Indian, and instructions for him to rejoin Slim under the rim. Between George, Doc Zilka, Lewis, Joey, and Nellie, the parting was not at all sad. Even Rose McCartle watched from the steps of the Elkhead. George, she noticed, was staying in Red Lodge.

Nan would miss Joey, of that she was sure, but the prospect of a life with Wendy Morgan filled her with hope. Once the final parting with Joey was over, she rode along not unhappily. Wendy would clear his name and they would be married. She marvelled at how much she trusted this man, at how that trust had evolved so that she could now ride off alone into the wild country, unwed, with him who was, only a short time ago, a stranger. And she marvelled at how quickly the townsfolk, too, had come to believe in him, and how quickly, out here in the wild, reputations ebbed and flowed. It was good to be on the trail. There was an eagerness in her soul to be going home. She thought of the crude chairs and rope bed and big stone hearth. She remembered each animal from chickens and cats to Blazer and the cow that had served them so well. She would be glad to be with them again, among her own.

They rode on across the flats and past the cottonwoods near the bend in Rock Creek where Tim Walsh had been shot. No incident marred their gentle pace. Rocks lined the creek for which it was named and a highwayman could easily lie waiting, unseen. They rode on up the creek into the folding hills within sight of the mountains. And nearing home, they saw smoke curling from the chimney.

A black dog emerged from behind a snowdrift, wagging its tail, and Nan's heart warmed at the expectation of seeing Tom. Trust him to come over and check on things. The Indian was nowhere in sight. But the hay was neatly stacked, the paths swept clean of accumulated snow and several of the horses, their shaggy coats gleaming in the sunshine, were turned out in the corral. The stock had been well cared for.

As they dismounted, a tall, buckskinned figure stepped out from the doorway. Nan had not known what to expect. She had met few Indians and these had usually come to beg. This man was different, and she thought of the stories she had heard Bo tell of the brutalities of warriors, stories that he used to justify the Indians' expulsion and extermination. This man had been a warrior, she was sure. He was tall, easily more that six feet, and muscular. His copper skin stretched taut over prominent cheekbones, squared jaw, and long, straight nose. His black hair hung in two braids fastened over each ear and he wore a necklace strung with bone and bear's claws around his powerful neck. His black eyes looked at them unblinking. This man could easily inspire fear. Nan understood George Meachum's concerns. She expected the Indian to say something, a word of welcome, as is white custom, but he simply stood there, stoically. And she stared back at him.

Wendy seemed to know better what to do. Quietly, he dismounted and ground hitched his horse. He did not offer a hand. But, as Nan watched, his arms and hands were moving fluidly with the universal greetings of the plains tribes.

"Mrs. Fletcher and I are grateful to you."

The Indian nodded. Wendy waited patiently for an answer.

"Lame Bull is happy to serve woman of Fletcher." The answer came slowly, articulated in rich, deep intonations, and accompanied too by similar movements, but his were more graceful, more a part of his mode of communicating. They went inside. Joker, too, charged in through the door. He sniffed a pot of something stewing on the stove.

"I see you've met Tom Ludlam." Wendy wondered how the old Indian fighter had taken to this former foe. He obviously liked his dog, and Joker seemed very much at home.

"Tom Ludlam?"

"Our neighbor, he lives close back in the hills." The Indian was staring uncomprehendingly at Morgan. "That's his dog, Joker, right here. He won't go anywhere without him."

"The dog arrived one moon ago. He comes when the snow covers the forest and the wind blows...he was cold."

Nan was fascinated by the majestic sweep of Bull's arm that coordinated so well with his solemn description of natural events. But she had not grasped their full meaning.

Wendy Morgan shot a glance at Nan. He knew Tom was not here, just Joker. He asked again. "There is no one here with you, no man came with the dog?"

The answer was swift and firm. "No man."

Nan was alarmed now too.

"I'll ride over there right away. Have to take the pack horse anyway." This was to Nan, to allay her fears. Then to the Indian he added, "Stay with her 'til I get back."

He shifted his saddle to a fresh horse, the pack to another, and headed out. Immediately, he noticed the depressions in the melting snow where the four Meachum horses had passed weeks ago. They had ridden in over the hills from Deer Creek and the south, not from the east and town. He would have to ask Bull about that.

The wind had swept some of the trail clear. He made good progress. The four horses had trampled down the rest of the snow weeks ago. He urged his fresh horse to its utmost, tugging all the while at the pack horse to keep up, hoping, fearing what he would find ahead. He passed the standing rock where the trail to Tom's headed down toward the creek, crossed on the ice, and came on Tom's sheltered hollow from the creekbed below the bench. As soon as he reached the creek, he recognized the stench of wet ashes and death.

Tom's dugout was in ruins, every rail of every fence was broken or burned. The home and stable had been pulled apart, its supports roped and heaved out from under the roof, which had caved in. The hay that Tom had so prudently cut for winter had become fuel for a huge bonfire, and everything had been thrown in to fan the flames. Peculiar moccasin tracks, blurred by the melting snow and with deep heel impressions, surrounded the burning. Wendy saw the blackened end of the watering trough sticking out, a piece of chair, a charred saddle, wasted. What had become of the horses, Wendy did not know. Joker somehow, had escaped. And where was Tom?

Wendy dismounted, stunned. In one short winter he had seen more of death than in all the rest of his young life. His father, Hendl, Walsh, and now Tom Ludlam, for Tom could not have survived this. Bitterly, he kicked at the mound that had been home for the old scout. Horses had trampled everything. The sheer brutality of the destruction sickened him. Joker, he needed Joker, for the dog, with its acute sense of smell, would unerringly find his old master. As if sensing his thoughts, Joker appeared coming up the trail. The playful antics of the young pup were gone. He had lost the bounce in his gait, his head hung down, and his tail curved between his legs. He trotted not to the house, but to a crumbling embankment that must have been the side of the stable. There lay Tom. He had been scalped and mutilated in a grotesque and crude imitation of an Indian raid. His upper body was exposed, skin dead grey and cold, eyes staring blindly at the mountains he loved so much. His lower torso and legs lay buried under a rough pile of earth. His arms had frozen in the grotesque and unnatural angles of death, but he still held his rifle. It had never been fired. No Indian had done this. They would have taken the rifle. Inadvertently, Wendy shut his eyes as if he could blot out the ugliness. Then he lifted the grizzled head. Tom had been shot once in the back of the skull and must have fallen right there. Death came instantly. Scalping must have been an afterthought, a crude attempt to lay blame elsewhere, when the crime was discovered. His attackers had not bothered to dispose of the body, but had pulled down house and barn on top of him, burying the body in the cave-in.

Wendy Morgan stooped down, closed the glassy eyes, and removed the rifle from the dead man. Then he got up and lifted the canvas cover from the packs. This he threw over old Tom. The destruction was so great that he could not even find a shovel to dig a grave. He would have to ride home again and come back on the morrow to bury old Tom. The body must not lie forever exposed. That it had not already been scavenged by animals, Wendy attributed to the terrible cattle losses. This year, the wolves had tastier pickings. It struck him too, that the outlaw, Hendl, would have a fitting stone and tended grave on Boot Hill, but that this honest old scout and friend, who had given his life to the opening of the frontier, would lie in his grave unmarked and lonely. The mountains would stand his vigil and the wolves howl his dirge. But then, Tom Ludlam would have wanted it that way. Wendy Morgan wondered why, and then he saw the broken still. So that was it. Old Tom had had his pleasures and for this they had killed him.

He arrived back home after dark. Nan was waiting as she had before, but this time without the eagerness. The Indian was sitting stolidly by the fire. A poignant glance, eye to eye, and Nan knew the horrible news. She had expected it. He said it anyway "Tom's dead." And Wendy had to turn his head away. He was crying.

Even Lame Bull understood. The set of his facial muscles changed minutely from stoic passivity to anger. He remembered chasing this very man into Deer Creek so many moons before. Yet this man had treated him more fairly than any Meachum except

George and maybe Tag. And Lame Bull understood this man's
sorrow for the loss of a friend. Years ago, he, too, had lost many
friends. What he did not understand was the indifference of Harv to
his own brother, the day he left Tag hurt and alone on the trail by
Bleeker's Rock. And he did not understand the role of George
Meachum, who had sent him to care for and to guard the very horses
that Harv Meachum had stolen. An Indian never forgot a horse.
These were the same horses right here in this corral. He suspected
the skinny pipe-smoker had come for them, but did not dare openly
cross the three gunmen. Did George know he was guarding the
horses from his own brothers?

Bull broke the anguished silence. "They come here, four
men. The Meachum brother, skinny like the thorn, who smokes a
pipe, he bring." And then he added, "They want firewater."

Nan knew immediately of whom he spoke and with a quiver
uttered, "Mose Meachum."

Wendy had never seen Mose Meachum - Mose did not go to
church even for Christmas - but now a vague recollection was
forming in the depths of his brain. Skinny, spidery, he remembered
a spindle-legged man in the light of the gas lamp, Christmas night,
standing next to Bill Hendl in the livery barn, the night he died. He
could picture the form clearly, holding the bridle by the big red
horse. Could this "skinny" man who had escaped be one and the
same with Mose Meachum? What a queer family they were! Gifted,
wealthy by frontier standards, one driven by munificence or guilt to
kindness and generosity toward this widow and her crippled son,
another impelled by greed, coveting every inch of range in the name
of family and appropriating it by whatever dreadful means. And a
third, if this was the third, scheming, cowardly, and evil.

At dawn, Wendy and the Indian rode back to Tom's. Bull
watched every turn of the trail, every depressed pocket of melted ice,
every thicket broken by the passage of the four. He studied the
shape of the horses' imprints in the snow, one, large and wide,
whose rear hoof overstepped his fore by nearly two inches, another,
shortened in stride, whose rear print covered the fore exactly.
Another horse seemed pigeon-toed in the rear. Lame Bull filed all
these and more clues in his mind, ever watchful for a hair stuck to
a clump of sage or a small pile of tobacco ash where Mose Meachum
had emptied his pipe.

By the time they reached the standing rock, Lame Bull had
a clear idea of each man's habits. He even knew how heavy each

rider was, and how he sat his horse. They crossed the creek by a ford upstream from the icy crossing Wendy had used the day before, but much safer, now that the spring thaw was advancing. The stench of death persisted. Wendy walked the mare slowly forward, up from the creek to the edge of the bench, where they could see the full breadth of the destruction. Bull followed and then stopped his horse. They stood there silently, while Wendy proceeded around the ruins to where Tom's body lay. He took the pick and shovel from his horse. They would only be able to dig a shallow grave, and this with difficulty, because the ground was still frozen hard close under the surface. He set to work.

Lame Bull dismounted too, but took up no tool. His bronzed face and dark black eyes looked disdainfully at Morgan.

"Indians did not do this."

"I know." Wendy looked up from his work.

"How you know? When men die, when horses stolen, when homes burned, soldiers blame Indians, punish Indians, chase and kill them, come and take our land. These men wear moccasins, like Indian. They scalp and burn, like Indian. They lie. They write their lies in the ashes of this lodge and blood of this man, but who will see the signs of their lies, and who will believe them? Lame Bull saw tracks at the creek, melted now, where they changed their boots for moccasins. Lame Bull saw ends of ropes they use to pull down. They lie charred in fire. He sees tracks where they ride away, driving horses, not toward Absaroka Reservation, but south toward Meachum Ranch. He remembers their faces when they came to the Fletcher Cabin seeking firewater. Lame Bull remembers like he remembers the summer warmth that browned the prairie grass and starved the rivers, like he remembers you when he tracked the white blaze horse to the entrance to Deer Creek. And Lame Bull shot you. He does not lie. This he did not do." He stretched his long arm over the desolation in that slow and graceful movement that lent such majesty to his speech, and he repeated, "This he did not do." He stopped solemnly, then continued. "They would blame Lame Bull for this. They would offer Lame Bull whiskey to make him forget. And they would give him gold. Lame Bull has no need of gold. Lame Bull never lie. Lame Bull and Absaroka never drink. Lame Bull should have killed them when they come to Fletcher homestead. You, white man, tell Absaroka no kill." He paused, his copper face immobile, then added, "Those white men need killing."

The Indian was right. The quiet redman's poignant speech held Wendell Morgan in awe. For once he understood the Indian. He felt exactly the same.

The Indian continued, "Lame Bull go now, no more will he work with the big one and the thin one who blacken the name of Lame Bull and the Absaroka people. He goes to the very nice place in the beckoning mountains, there to build his lodge among his gods and make up for the wrongs that he has done in the name of Meachum, and the shame he has caused himself and his people." And then he added bitterly, "He paid his debt to Meachum long ago, and that Meachum dead. Now Lame Bull curses the name of Meachum." He turned his horse south and west toward the tooth-shaped mountains.

Wendy watched him go. There went the only witness to the hideous crime, yet Wendy Morgan knew the Indian was right. No one would believe him. No one would admit that white man would kill white man, and maim him, for a drink, only to stunt the boredom of winter. No one would believe him against the word of a Meachum.

Brutally, Wendy Morgan heaved the iron pike against the hard and frozen ground. The muscles of his shoulders, back, and biceps contracted ever more violently. Sweat coursed down his face, even in the cool breezes of the April morning. Meachums had done this. Meachums had killed his father, robbed him and left him for dead. Meachums had brought Bill Hendl onto the range and deprived a woman of her husband and a boy of his father, all because of their blind belief that they owned the range. Now, without motive, not for more land and not for better horses, they had struck again. The pick struck the brittle sod in loud and resounding blows that echoed like thunder rumbling against the rim of the mountains in the distance, and like the anger crashing ever more loudly against the confines of his soul. And gradually, as he worked, a plan of action solidified in his mind. At first, when his father had died, he had been physically too weak and alone to fight. But now, struggling against the vagaries of winter, he had recovered his strength and made friends. He had waited long enough. Tom Ludlam would not go unavenged. Time now to confront Harv Meachum.

Carefully, he freed the body of Tom Ludlam from the debris and carried it to its last home, under the bench by Rock Creek. The old scout's face was blue, his fingers gnarled with arthritis. He remembered the old man complaining about his joint disease. He remembered Tom's simple appreciation of a meal shared with his friends. He remembered gathering hay in the meadow beneath the Silver Run Plateau, the encounter with the grizzly, and old Baldy cast on the mountain slope. And he remembered Tom's not too subtle way of pushing him on Nan, and Christmas dinner. And Tom had made him stay with Nan. He filled in the grave with the chunks of frozen soil and piled a few aged rocks at the head. When he finished, he uttered a prayer, one of two that he knew, the Twenty-third Psalm.

"The Lord is my shepherd, I shall not want...."

When he finished, he thought how really inappropriate the Psalm had been. Tom Ludlam had done his own shepherding. But the prayer had quieted the violence of his anger, although it had reinforced his resolution. He mounted to ride back to Nan, but he would not stay with her, not this time. There would be no living peacefully, honestly, without fear, until Harv Meachum was exposed for the murderer that he was and driven from the range. He wanted nothing more than to be with Nan, marry her, be a father to Joey, build a home and a family, and run a few horses and steers, but he knew now that Harv Meachum would never allow him to do this. Die he might, but if he was to live a free man, he must bury Harv Meachum.

Joker followed him home.

CHAPTER 40

Nan watched him ride in as she had so many times before, as she had watched Bo before him. She paled when she saw the grim set of his features. She did not ask what had become of the Indian. Wendy did not take the mare to the stable, but ground hitched her in front and walked stiffly up to the door. There was no loving greeting, no loving glance, only a few hard-bitten words.

"I'm not staying." And then an order as if barked by an army sergeant, "I'll need a rifle, some ammunition and a couple of days' rations."

Nan had never seen him like this. He stood before her, healed in body and armed in spirit. He had faced the winter's storms and in the struggle had grown in virility and courage. This was a man who stood before her now, firm in his resolve. She did not question. That he loved her, she did not doubt. That he must leave her, she knew, and that he would return, she could only hope. For his leave-taking was no escape. It was a willful effort to make a better life for himself and for her. It was something he must do.

He had just entered the room and stood blocking the door. He dared go no farther lest his resolution weaken. She bowed her head and went for the provisions. Shoving food into a sac, she took Bo's rifle from its rack on the wall near the hearth. The ammunition she fetched from a store in the root cellar. When she handed him these, she touched his arm.

"Come back safely."

"Yes," he nodded, but there were no guarantees. And then he added, "When it's over, you may not want me back."

"I'll want you, no matter what!" Instinctively, Nan knew he was about to set out for the Meachum Ranch. "You go there, in their midst? They'll kill you!"

"Maybe. If I'm not back tomorrow, go to Dave Lewis. He'll know what to do with the horses, sell them for a good price, and you'll have money to carry on...start over." He was giving her everything he had left in the world. He bent down suddenly and kissed her on the brow. And, just as suddenly, turned on his heel and marched down the path to his horse. He did not look back. Joker started to follow but Nan called him back.

Wendy Morgan urged the red mare almost to a gallop until he lost sight of the Fletcher homestead. Then he slowed his pace, and rode on at the mare's long swaying walk. The Meachum Ranch lay across the Meeteetsie Trail to the south of Red Lodge, east of the Beartooth Mountains, along the Wyoming border. From the Fletcher place west of town, he cut southeast diagonally, across open country. It was a country of dry, rolling hills with some rock outcroppings and an occasional tree here and there in the depressions and wallows, where now, in April, the melting waters ran. For the first hour, he spotted little life. Only the skeletal remains of the winter were scattered hideously in every possible nook and shelter. These he ignored. He was a man bent on his purpose, not aware of the dying, not aware either of the rummagings of rodents, the chirping of birds, these portents of new life that would come later.

When he spied a bunch of skinny strays, he knew he was nearing the M-bar. Evidently, not all of the Meachum's vast herds had been lost. Harv Meachum was still paying his gunhands. He had gruesome proof of that. How many more cowboys, forced from herding by the ravages of last winter, would turn to their guns for a living?

He looked down on the ranch buildings from the valley rim. It was a big spread, bright and prosperous in the glaring noon sun, bigger than many of the ranches he knew, with several large barns and outbuildings. And the main ranch house was two stories high, a rare sight on the Montana plains at this date. This was the place that had spawned the Meachum brothers.

He spurred the mare down the rocky slope and rode on into the yard. A fat man in overalls came out of the barn with a pitchfork in his hand and a chew in his cheek. Wendy rode up to the front door of the main house. From behind him a voice sounded.

"Kin I he'p ya mista? You lookin' fer someone?" It was the fat man in the overalls. Wendy had paid him little attention at first, he was so obviously not a gunman.

Now he looked again at the florid face and clear blue eyes. "I'm lookin' for Harv Meachum. You know where he is?"

"He expectin' ya?" The question was simply curious. Nothing about this rounded figure, from the straw cowman's hat to the big mucker's boots, was threatening.

"Maybe." Wendy was not going to give away his intent.

"Well, you're no different than some o' th'others that come ridin' in here. Harv's still hirin' this spring if'n what you're hankerin' for is a job, although what you need all them guns for to herd some skinny cattle, is way past my thinkin'. Go on in. Harv ain't there but his brother Tag is."

Tag Meachum, hearing the voices in the yard, had come to the door. Smaller, slighter than his brothers, he had the fair hair and soulful eyes of George and Dan. Wendy drew up short at the sight of him. Tag still stooped from the gunshot wound of last fall. This was the Meachum Wendy had shot. There was no malice here.

"Morgan, isn't it? I know your horse. What can I do for you?"

"I'm looking for your brothers, for the murder of Tom Ludlam."

"Murder? You sure?" He hesitated. A few seconds of silence intervened. "They're not here. I'm not frontin' for 'em Morgan, I'm tellin' you straight." The two men stared deeply, straight at each other, eye to eye. "They left this mornin' to count cattle, but I expect they'll end up today or tomorrow in town. Ain't too much to count after last winter except bones."

Morgan nodded. Any other Meachum, he would not have believed. He turned the sorrel mare away. Locating Harv and Mose Meachum was not going to be so simple. He could ride into town and wait, but the good people in town, the Doctor and Lewis, would probably try to stop him or slap him into protective custody. And Joey was in town. He decided reluctantly to try to find the Meachum brothers on the range. Here, he could make a clean kill, and make his escape across the border into Wyoming. He rode east, knowing the western pastures through which he had already ridden to be mostly empty.

By nightfall he had circled most of the eastern M-bar range in vain. There were several scrawny bunches of cattle, tended by a few battered and demoralized cowboys who had not seen their boss in weeks. And there was the old man they called Slim, with George Meachum's horse herd. These horses, with an ample supply of hay, protected under the rimrock, had weathered the winter quite well. Wendy looked for Tom's horses among them and thought he spotted two of the mares. Slim eyed him suspiciously, remembering the time he and George had returned the stolen horses to the Fletcher place.

CHAPTER 41

Tag Meachum, meanwhile, did not waste time. He did not know where to find Harv or Mose, but he knew exactly where to find George. Willie saddled him a fast horse and he started for Red Lodge, arriving at dusk.

George was seated at his usual table in the Elkhead, with Rose McCartle at his elbow. He looked haggard, but smiled, surprised when he saw Tag. Of all the Meachums, Tag was not a regular in the saloon.

Tag pulled up a chair without uttering a word. Rose understood that they needed privacy and excused herself.

"Wendy Morgan is gunning for Harv and Mose."

"Morgan? How do you know it's Morgan? You only met him once."

"Twice, Christmas and the time he shot me, and I know that flashy animal he's ridin'."

George nodded, and Tag talked on.

"Says they murdered a friend, that old gopher, Tom Ludlam."

"What did you say?"

"I told him, I wasn't frontin' for them, that they were out ridin', countin' the cattle that are left after the winter. He believed me."

Tag stopped, but his jaw was still working. He was still very pale. "George, they did it. I've been home these months. I've watched. I've listened. There's been trouble in the bunkhouse, fights, shootings. It's those toughs Harv's been hiring. He thinks the whole damn range belongs to him, and the older he gets the more greedy he gets...and the more violent. I suspected before, but it wasn't 'til that chase with Morgan, when Harv insisted Morgan was a thief and we went after him and Morgan shot me. Then you came along and gave the horses back. Harv boiled over that one. He was wrong and you called him. When I was ailin', recoverin', I had long hours to think. Harv's gone bad and Mose is worse. He plays Harv like a fiddle, tunes him to his likin', excites him, soothes him, plucks his strings 'til he has the whole ranch dancing. And all winter, Mose has been bootlickin' those gunmen, promisin' them money and good times and loot."

George was nodding his head gravely. The tick in his cheek was hammering steadily. "I know, I know. I've known ever since that man Hendl crossed me. Why do you think I've stayed here in town? Not because it snowed and I couldn't get home."

"Not much of a home any more, George. Not like when we were kids." Tag was nostalgic.

"Tell me more about Morgan."

"If he doesn't find Harv on the open range, I think he'll come in here and call him out."

"He was that mad, you say?"

"He looked dangerous, George, angry, yes, but controlled, like a bloodhound on a scent. He's not gonna swerve one inch.... We want to save Harv, we should warn him."

"Why? Why should we?"

"He's our brother, George."

"He the son of the same father and the same mother, and that's all, And that goes for Mose too...and Gabe." He stopped only for a moment and Tag blanched at the bitterness in George's voice. "They've run the M-bar to ruin. Harv calls himself a cattleman. He's no better than the guns he hired. Countin' head, you say that's where they've gone? Tag, look at the range, there's hardly any stock left...only my horses, and only because they were close herded and fed. There's no cattle out there, not enough to make a decent herd. And they probably drove whatever poor beasts survived to the railhead at Laurel, got rid of them cheap so they could pay off the gun hands before they start gunnin' for us when they haven't been paid..."

He put his hand on Tag's shoulder. "We been foiled, little brother. Come on up to my room. You look like you need some sleep."

Wendy Morgan woke next morning refreshed. There was a certain security in knowing precisely what you have to do and setting out to do it. The doing was not the hard part, the anticipation was. He lay in his bedroll under a huge lodgepole pine that shaded his eyes from the early morning sun and dissipated the smoke from his campfire. The mare was picketed not far away on a rolling bed of bluestem. He had overslept. Calmly, he ate a breakfast of jerky and coffee, pulled his saddle off the fallen log where it had rested for the night, and went for the mare. She was as eager as he to be off. They headed for town. He wondered what news of his intentions had preceded him. Had Tag or Fat Willie spread the alarm? He approached Red Lodge this time from the south, from the far side of the creek, and his horse's hooves clattered loudly across the wooden bridge. He came up the side street perpendicular to the river and entered Main Street, around the corner from the jail. Here he stopped, looking up and down the street from atop the big horse. The town lay grey and sleepy in the morning sun. The general store, the livery barn, the restaurant, the saloon, the barber shop, and the few houses, all were quiet. He turned toward the Elkhead, turning his head only to give the Doctor's house a fleeting glance. Then he focused his eyes forward. The mare marched on. He felt like she was marching straight to hell.

CHAPTER 42

Across from Eb Krump's Dry Goods, Wendy Morgan stopped. He looked up and down the street, reconnoitering. All was still. The sun was rising behind the livery barn at the east end of the street, its rays sliced the gloom. He looked closely at the long shadows it cast against the angular buildings, engraving these firmly in mind. It would be a fine, clear day. In a gun duel, he would need the light at his back. He turned his head east and tilted back his hat to let the sunlight flow over him. He felt a sense of imminent loss. The simplest things, the sun on his face, the animal smell of his horse, the dust puffs in the street, moved him like never before.

The mare glowed a golden red in the dawnlight. The few people who were already stirring could not help but notice her, proud and lithe, like the man who rode her. Dave Lewis, hands stuffed in the pockets of a giant blanket coat, gave Morgan a salute and a nod but got no response. Lewis went to light his kiln and his sharp eyes took in the gunbelt, buckled and tied down at Morgan's hip, the hunched shoulders and drawn lips. Morgan hardly saw Lewis. He planned in his mind how to confront big Harv Meachum. He could go into the Elkhead and wait for Harv to bluster into the saloon, as sooner or later, he was bound to do. Or he could stop fifty yards short in the alley by Aunt Nell's Restaurant, where he had a good view of everyone coming and going. He opted for the latter more cautious approach. Tethering his horse with a nosebag full of grain well back down the alley, he headed for Nell's, aware that this could be his last good hot meal. He felt empty and nervous.

Rusty hinges squeaked as he entered and unbuttoned his long canvas stockman's coat. He took a table by the window, pushed back the curtain, and looked out. Some of Nell's flapjacks and stiff black coffee would settle his nerves. It was still early. Nell was glad to see him and humored him as if he was her son. She saw the gun and knew its purpose. She asked no questions.

Nan Fletcher was alone again in the early dawn. She looked around the cabin at all the little reminders of past companionship. There was Bo's favorite seat on the settle by the fire, his gun hanging loosely from its peg on the wall, her family's Bible on its shelf near the door. Bo had really left so long ago, shortly after Joey was born. She remembered him and their happier times in Iowa like the blurry images of an old watercolor. There was the big iron kettle on the stove, and a stew simmering. Tom Ludlam used to stomp in at the faintest whiff of her cooking. She had depended on Tom and his neighborly additions to her larder, especially after Bo had retreated from his role as provider. Sensing her distraction, Joker came up and put his head on her knee. The memory of Tom hurt.

And there were the cats, Joey's favorites, three of them curled in front of the fire. She thought of Joey, her only son. A mother had a right to think of a son as lifelong human connection, but not here on the frontier. Values were different here. His pet cats were curled up and sleeping comfortably in front of the fire. Here, they were his only friends. Intuitively, she knew he was happier in town, with schoolmates and under a doctor's care.

Finally, there was the pallet where she and Wendy had slept. She averted her eyes. These were the most vivid images of all, great passionate frescoes splashed across the reaches of her mind. So many times he had come and gone and come again. She looked again. The blankets were rumpled and the bed sagged where they had coupled. Would he ever be back? Or would outlaws or Meachum henchmen or the weather's fury or accident, or worse, death, keep him away? He could die. He probably would die where he had gone. She wanted him back most of all, but this cold morning she despaired and she cursed the cruelties of life on the frontier. How she had slaved to create a home in this far place, in this humble cabin, to be a devoted wife who knew her place in the Victorian scheme of things. The place was striking, probably the most beautiful natural setting she had ever seen, the rolling foothills spread out in front, with the bench and the snowcapped mountains at her back; the home was clean and tidy though poor; the barn was sturdy and the animals well-fed and sleek even after this worst of winters. The dry wind had chapped her face and the sun bleached her brown hair. The grit had scratched and reddened her hands. For what? For whom? They were gone, all gone. Tears came and streaked her cheeks and swelled her eyes. She tried to stanch their flow with her hands. The dog came up and licked her salty hands, bringing her back from her darkening dreams. She scratched his ears affectionately. He was the only one left.

CHAPTER 43

Wendy watched as two cowboys drifted in and dismounted in front of the restaurant. They came in and ordered breakfast. A cart bumped out from behind the doctor's house, the Doc on a call. Krump was raising the blinds before opening his dry goods store. Miss Haggedorn clomped down the boardwalk on her way to opening the schoolroom. Joey and the other children would be coming out soon. Morgan, intent on watching the street, did not see a tall form enter the dining room from behind the curtain that separated the cooking from the eating area. George Meachum came directly up behind him.

Wendy started. Meachum did not sit down nor did Morgan offer him a chair. He glanced at Meachum a moment, then held his eyes on the street.

The tall cattleman was blunt, "You hunting Meachums, I hear." And when Wendy did not answer, he pushed further. "Tag beat you in. He told me."

Wendy Morgan nodded. "I'm hunting Meachums all right, bigger ones than you."

George ignored the insult. "Tell me about it." He pulled out a chair.

At that moment, a distant dust-devil rose on the horizon beyond the buildings at the end of the street. It grew and expanded until presently Wendy could make out Harv Meachum and two other riders. Harv was unmistakable on his big bay, but at this distance not even George Meachum could make out the identity of the other two. Wendy Morgan felt a knot in his gut and shoved back his chair. George Meachum reached out and grabbed his right arm like a vise.

"You know what you're doin', Morgan. You're gonna die. What about the woman and her kid?"

"She's why I'm doin' it, Meachum. Seems your family won't let an honest woman live." The riders moved closer. "Old Ludlam was the reason she survived last winter and your brother and his cronies shot him down."

"You got any witnesses?"

"Yes, your very own Indian. They came to Nan Fletcher's first, thought it was empty 'til he emptied a couple of barrels, wounded one. Then, they left for better pickings elsewhere - Tom kept a still - bunch of whiskey-frenzied killers. Bull knew where they went. He doesn't lie...but who's gonna believe an Indian?

"I do. Where is Bull anyway?"

"He's taken off for the mountains. You'll never see him again."

George Meachum held Wendy's arm in a vise-like grip. Morgan got up from the table, shook off George Meachum's hand, shoved on his hat, and walked toward the door to the street. "Stay out of it. She ain't yours and he ain't your kid."

George Meachum went white. The sudden reference to Nan Fletcher and Morgan's knowledge of his admiration for her cut him to the core. He watched a haggard Wendell Morgan tramp out the door. There he stood, George Meachum, looking like a prince in his wild kingdom, and wishing against all hope that he could walk out that same door in the shoes of the other man. Life had not dealt him happiness. The door slammed. George Meachum stood very still and watched Morgan's receding back through the window. Morgan was walking to his death, of this George Meachum was sure. He should have been out earlier, quietly choosing a position, lining himself with the sun at his back and a clear unobstructed view of the street in front, judging the light and shadows, the line of the projectile, assuring himself every advantage. A professional would have. Morgan was an amateur. Now it was too late. Harv Meachum was riding steadily down upon him. Morgan did not draw his gun. He would challenge big Harv, convinced he could beat him. George was not convinced. It would be a fair fight. Morgan was brave. George would concede him that. He was also compulsive and foolish.

Suddenly, George stiffened as Morgan froze in his tracks. Joey was crossing Main Street on his way to school. Joey was hobbling to school right through the no-man's land between Wendy and the oncoming riders. George Meachum and Wendy Morgan would have known his stiff-legged gait anywhere. The road was muddy, and sucked at the boy's feet as he struggled to lift his heavy boots and put one foot in front of the other. Now, he spotted Morgan on the opposite boardwalk, grinned, waved, and waddled over.

Wendy Morgan stepped back into the shadows and cursed. Harv Meachum, the rider called Murph, and the other called Jenks rode on by.

Joey had reached the boardwalk now and stooped over to climb up the high step on hands and knees. As he pulled his small body erect, he stood facing Morgan.

"Aren't you glad to see me?" There was an edge of doubt in the words.

"Sure, sure. It's good to see you!" He tousled the boy's hair as was his habit, but the clip in his voice and the forced smile belied the show of affection. There was a lapse. He had not called Joey by name. The grin faded.

"Is Mom with you? Where's my Mom?"

"She's home...she's fine." Another pause. The ease and flow in conversation was absent. "How's school?"

"Fine." Joey did not elaborate but tilted his head slightly sideways and looked quizzically at Morgan.

"Be a good boy, work hard." The words fell like dry leaves on sand, the uninspired wish of an adult who is too preoccupied to listen to a child. The boy nodded, sensing the distraction in the older man. Then his eyes settled on the gun and followed Morgan's gaze to the grizzled gunmen hitching their horses in front of the Elkhead. Joey had nothing more to say. He hobbled on up the street.

This brief exchange gave George Meachum just the few minutes he needed and quietly he crept out of Nell's via the kitchen and the back door.

Morgan waited until Joey had gone on down the alley to the old log-cabin school. He heard the school bell ring. He stepped out into the street and walked deliberately west toward the Elkhead, where Harv Meachum's horse was tethered. Jenks had stayed outside. The horses stamped their hooves, splattering the mud up to their knees. Jenks was loosening their cinches.

Morgan could waste no more time.

"You there, M-bar, go in and tell your boss Wendy Morgan is waiting for him outside. Tell him it's about Tom Ludlam and I want to talk."

Jenks looked lazily over the back of a horse. A broad Texas hat shaded his eyes. "Who? You talkin' to me, mista?" He took in Morgan's dark handsome features, his blueblack eyes shrouded now in deliberation and anger, and recognized the name as the man who killed Bill Hendl. But he gave no sign. He noticed the heavy Colt weighing the belt at Morgan's hip. The flap was open. He turned on his heel and went inside.

Morgan stood like a pillar of stone in the middle of the street. He took a gulp of his own saliva and it went down hard, wrinkling the sinews in his neck. His palms were sweating. He wiped them on his shirt, hooked his thumbs in his belt and waited.

Presently, Jenks came out. "He says Ludlam's dead an' he got nutthin' to say to a lily flower named Wendy."

Morgan's face did not even flinch. Deliberately, he took measured steps, one after the other, in steady rhythm toward the saloon. His lips closed evenly in a grim line, eyes staring not at Jenks but at the saloon doors. His thumbs were still in his belt. The tension had left him.

"Morgan, stop right there. You want to get killed? That one there is as deadly, maybe deadlier than any of the rest of them." The voice came from behind and to the right. The bass was unmistakable. George Meachum was standing behind him about four paces to his right.

"Mind your own business, Meachum." Wendy fastened his gaze intently on the swinging doors. During the interval with Joey, George Meachum must have moved into position.

"It's my family you're fightin' and I'm sidin' you, Morgan." And he repeated, "Against my own brothers." Then George Meachum raised his voice, "Jenks, you hear me! Tell Harv I want to talk to him, that he's a thief and a killer and I'm ashamed to bear the same name. Tell him if he doesn't show, I'll go in there and haul him out and the only lilies he'll be seein' are black ones at his own funeral!"

His voice reverberated up and down the street. Heads popped out through shuttered windows then shrank back in and slammed the shutters closed when they suddenly realized the deadly intent of George Meachum. Doors slammed. A woman called her mongrel into the laundry. Rose McCartle and Dan Meachum watched bravely from a window of the Elkhead. Ty Lamm watched from a corner of the Feed Store across the street. Dave Lewis had led the horse he was shoeing inside the livery barn and watched warily from behind the huge smithy's kiln. Harv Meachum and Murphy stepped through the swinging doors. The three hitched horses, the only barrier between the opposing camps, stamped their feet and swished their tails. Jenks looked coldly over their withers.

Big Harv moved forward to the edge of the boardwalk in front of the Elkhead Saloon. His broad chest was visible over the horses' saddles. His hat sat on the back of his head. The lanky and silent gunfighter, Murph, stood to his right.

"Speak up, little brother. I'm listenin'."

"You're a small man, Harv Meachum. For all your bluster, you've a shrunken heart and narrow brain. The big man with the big spread hires big guns to do his killin' for him. Think back, Harv, think of Crowley, Walsh, Ludlam. I'm just beginning, Harv."

"I didn't kill Ludlam."

"You paid for it. You disgust me, Harv. You don't stand and do your own killin'. You pay your gunmen, Harv, like that pistol packer standin' next to you right there on the porch. Most of the guns in this town are workin' for you. There were others before that they killed, that you killed, Harv... Heidelberger, Crowley, Tim Walsh, but I can't prove that, and Morgan here, and his Pa. Morgan was lucky - you didn't quite kill him." The words were rolling off his tongue smooth and resonant as a seasoned politician running for office. "You run a pack of freeloadin' gunmen for cowhands, and pay 'em to kill and loot by sellin' the cattle that's Tag's and Dance's and mine."

He stopped, suddenly aware that he had gained an audience. The whole town was listening. On the periphery of his vision he knew Iz Roland was there, Dave Lewis and Nell and the Doc and Parson Bowden. Eb Krump from the Emporium watched, cowering from behind a barrel of flour. Ty Lamm was with him. And there was Tag over by the Chinese laundry. George Meachum commanded an audience. Only Nan was not there. He wished she were here listening. He was doing this for her, for the Fletchers and the Morgans, the herders and the grangers, and all the decent folk who came to fill this vast expanse of earth. The tick in his cheek was pounding like a hammer.

"We want the ranch back, Harv, Tag and Dance and me. We want to run it honestly. We want to hold our heads high and make neighbors and raise families and build lives. You don't get through a winter like the last one without neighbors, Harv." It was a lovely speech, better than anything the Parson could offer of a Sunday, the testimony of a man who knew he would probably be dead in a few more minutes. "There's no more cattle left after last winter, Harv, and you're still stealin' your brothers blind and hasslin' the newcomers from behind your gunmen's skirts. Do your own fightin'. Tell Murph and Jenks to back off."

"Tell Morgan to back off."

"Scared of Morgan, Harv? He's just a lily flower. You called him that yourself."

Harv Meachum's jowled face was purple with rage. His eyes levelled on the tall Stetsoned figure of his brother. "You bastard!" someone heard him mutter. Large man that he was, he jumped right from behind a porch pillar and reached for his gun. George saw him leap and fanned his Colt from his holster. The two fired in the same moment, Harv's bullet clipping George in the right forearm and George's thudding into the center of Harv's middle. A third shot, almost indistinguishable in its report from the first two, hit George from the right side, in the neck, below the ear. Morgan leaped and rolled and was firing too, under the horses' bellies at Jenks. Harv was down and George, and Murph was hit, but still on his feet. Bullets spit up dust all around him, yet Murph had not yet fired. Harv had fallen in front of him and he was using the big man as a shield. The animals bucked and jerked as Murph, left arm flapping like a dead fish, took cool and careful aim at Morgan over their backs.

Suddenly, a rifle cracked from the Elkhead window and another gun skidded clattering off the roof of the Feed Store with the thin form of a man, a sniper, right behind it. They landed together in the dusty street.

The gunmen froze, and Wendy Morgan rolled to a stop.

"There's three men bleedin' out there, now cut that out!" Rose McCartle, screeched. Stepping out from the swinging doors, she cocked her rifle and fired another shot at Murph's feet. He backed away, dancing on his tiptoes and leaped for his frightened horse. Jenks was already mounted and galloping away down the street.

Morgan rolled up on his feet, miraculously unhurt, and walked over to George Meachum. Rose McCartle was already there. George's face was ashen, and blood pumped from the hole in the side his neck, over his white collar, and down the front of her blue silk dress. He was conscious, although not able to talk or hold up his head, regal even in death. His eyes fastened on the Elkhead's Madame. The Rose held the handsome head against her breasts as his life poured out in her lap. She was mumbling and wailing something about never being an honest woman, and tears were streaming down her face. The townsfolk and Wendy Morgan knew enough to leave her alone. Nothing could be done for George.

They busied themselves with Harv and Mose. Harv was coughing up some blood, but he was alive. Mose, who had shot his brother George in ambush from the shelter of Ty Lamm's roof, was dead. Rose had aimed at his eyes and had come amazingly close. The rifle bullet had torn away the side of his face and he was dead when he fell. His pipe had landed at his side, unscathed.

CHAPTER 44

They carried the bodies of the two brothers, George and Moses Meachum, to Iz Roland's casket works. The undertaker cleaned the bloodied corpses and placed each in identical oak coffins, the best he could supply. He walked to the telegraph office and wired Brenda Meachum in Billings. She would come as soon as she could clear her social calendar. The Doctor, returning from his house call an hour later, signed the death certificates. Rose sat immovable, with the rifle still in her hand, by the bier of George Meachum. Tag, Dance, and Amelia Craven came later that afternoon to pay their respects and lead her away.

The ladies of the Elkhead came out into the muddy street to intercept their Madame. Her blue silk dress was wet with blood, her dark hair dishevelled, and her makeup streaked with tears and mud. They led the bloodied, hysterical woman back into the barroom. There the bartender poured her a slug of the best brandy to dull the pain. The girls made her drink it, bathed her, and put her to bed. More brandy made her sleep. Her silken clothing, they burned. They kept watch all night, each one taking a turn, lest she waken and try to take her own life.

They carried Harv unconscious, but alive, to the Doctor's. Doc laid him out on the same oak table where Bill Hendl had lain a few months before, and bathed and cleansed his wounds. The bullet had lodged in his spine. Doc Zilka could not probe for a bullet in that location without doing further damage. With good care, Harv would survive. Whether he would walk again was a question. Whether, if crippled, he would want to survive was yet another question. Doc patched the wounds as best he could, rolled down his sleeves, and left an unconscious Harv Meachum in the care of Nell.

He was walking down the street toward the Elkhead, as much for a drink as to see about Rose. In the absence of a lawman, he and George had decided what to do with wrongdoers. Now, there was only him. He grimaced at the thought. He'd need help. Dave Lewis might help, but he was getting old and the town couldn't get along without a blacksmith. He thought of Wendy Morgan, likeable enough and good with a gun, but he had too many scrapes already and he'd been right in the middle of the gunplay this morning. Better to keep him out of this. Besides, he'd have to question Morgan about the morning's events.

Doc kept walking and started to mutter to himself out of habit. "Three Meachums left, Dance and Tag and Gabe. Harv's ringleading days are over." He thought about George's impassioned last words and shook his head. George had been speaking on behalf of his brothers as well as on his own behalf. He mentioned Dance and Tag. Doc would never forget those words. "Dance Meachum's well-liked, somewhat irresponsible, likes the ladies, but then so'd his brother." George had only acquired respectability after he was married with a home of his own. "Dance Meachum," the Doc corrected himself, "Dan Meachum - married and settled, might yet make a lawman, given the chance to carve his own niche. An he's been seein' that little tart for some time now. Have to think on that. Might make an honest woman of her. Ya never know. And young Tag, he'd take over the M-bar now or what's left of it, not ruthless like Harv, and with more brains." The Doc came out of his reverie several strides past the Elkhead, pivoted and walked back the five steps to the swinging doors. He was rubbing his eyes as he walked into the saloon and grumbling all the way to the bar. "Tired, so tired, and it isn't even bedtime." The bartender poured out a drink.

"On the house for you today, Doc."

Doc nodded. "Where's Rose?"

"Asleep. The girls are watchin' 'er."

"Good. Anyone seen Morgan?"

"Came in after the shootin', with the girls bringing Rose. I gave him a bottle an' he walked out again. He's around. Probably drinkin' it off." Doc Zilka knew what that meant.

Doc nodded, shoved his hands back into his pockets and walked, still mumbling, across the smoky room and out into the bright noon sunshine. The temperature had warmed. He yawned. Morgan could wait. He was going to look in on Harv and Nell, then go to his room and take a nap.

CHAPTER 45

N an Fletcher arrived in town about mid-afternoon. Wendy Morgan had not returned, and she remembered his admonition to go to Dave Lewis if he didn't return. Lewis had gone back to his job of shoeing and was hammering away on his anvil when she drove up. The noise was deafening and he didn't hear the clatter of the buckboard traces as she pulled up in front of the livery. She had braked the wagon and fastened the horse to the ball and chain before he looked up. The old man smiled forlornly and she knew the news would not be encouraging. Hesitantly, she explained why she had come.

"He tell ye thet, Morgan, to come to me? Why me?"

"It's about his horses...he said if he didn't come back, you should take them and sell them, that you would know what to do. I have no way of caring for that many head."

For the first time, Lewis stopped what he was doing. His old eyes squinted intelligently at Nan. He shoved the thongs and the red hot shoe he'd been working on into a tub of water. The water sizzled and steamed; the horseshoe cooled and blackened. Lewis took his time.

"You lemme put Blackie back in the barn. You can unhitch your horse." He unfastened Blackie's tie and slowly led the half-shod horse back into his stall. There was no rushing Dave Lewis.

Nan did as she was told and started to unbuckle her own harness. Presently, Lewis came back to help her and led her little bay to a clean stall spread with sweet straw. She waited. Finally, he spoke. "Now Morgan said to sell them horses, if he don't come back. You know where he went?"

"He went hunting Harv Meachum." She straightened and added, "With a gun."

Dave Lewis smacked his lips twice and nodded. "Jest arrived, didn't ye?" He shook his head. "No one told ye, did they? He found Harv Meachum right here." He stopped, waiting.

Nan prodded. "He's all right?"

"Lady, that man a yorn is one coow-rage-geous feller!"

"Mr. Lewis, Wendy Morgan is not my man. I am not married to him or anybody else. Is he all right?" Exasperation wracked her voice.

"Mebbe not hitched to 'im, but ye may as well be, I seen it. Coupla times, he couldda left, but 'ee didn't, cause a you an' that young calf a yorn." He winked and grinned through his whiskers. "He's fine...lucky man." Lewis should have noticed the blank relief on her face, but he just kept talking.

"Oh, he's alive. Around somewheres. You jest got to find 'im before 'ee does somethin' foolish, like start that shootout this mornin'. He ain't left town, I'd a seen 'im. An when you find 'im, tell 'im I'd like to talk to 'im. Old Ludlam left somethin' fer 'im." Then he added with a lascivious wink, "and fer you, too!"

Nan blanched and finally old Lewis filled out the story of the morning's events, slowly, scrap by tiny scrap. And she thought of George Meachum in death and her mind blanked. The handsome, solicitous stranger who had come to her door and stayed for dinner seemed the essence of life and virility.

"Now, I don' know where he's at," Dave Lewis's voice was droning on. Nan was only half-listening, "but you might start at the Doc's an' you might check the schoolhouse. 'ee was mighty fond a thet kid."

Nan walked away in a daze, painfully aware of her own frailty, not sure where to turn next. Of the men who had helped her, George Meachum was dead. Wendy Morgan was alive, but nowhere to be found.

Nan walked nervously down the street past the Elkhead to Doc's house. She rapped on the door lightly. There was no answer.

She rapped again, this time more loudly. A rumbling and shuffling came from the interior.

"I'm coming, I'm coming, a man can't have a nap and a snort around here, except he's interrupted!"

"Doc, I'm sorry, it's Nan Fletcher."

"Nan! Why didn't you say so. Come to town to see Joey?"

"That, and I'm looking for Wendy Morgan."

"He's been here, I mean in town, parading around on that fancy horse of his again and just about getting himself killed. Making more work for these old bones."

"I heard." She hesitated, not wanting to seem too concerned. "Dave Lewis told me."

"Shame about George Meachum. A good man. Bad blood in the family. That Morgan started it and Meachum horned in, took on the fight like it was his own, and maybe it was."

Wendy Morgan was not usually a drinking man, but today was an exception. He unhitched the mare and led her quietly to the livery barn at the end of the street. Lewis was not there, he'd probably gone to fetch water from the creek. He closed her in a stall and shovelled in a helping of oats. She chomped contentedly. Then he rambled out the back of the barn, took his bottle, and found a comfortable piece of sod and an old cottonwood to lean on in a gully down by Rock Creek.

He hadn't intended it to happen that way. Blood, there was too much blood. Six men shooting and one woman. Meachum, George Meachum was dead. He felt a peculiar remorse. He took a swig of the whiskey and it burned his gullet. George Meachum was not supposed to die. He, Wen Morgan was. His rival was dead, shot by his own brother. Nan Fletcher was his. Yet he could not bring himself to claim her. He could not ride up to the homestead a hero. George Meachum had made the sacrifice. He was the hero. He had the strangest feeling that Meachum had known exactly what he was doing, had planned it. Why? His whiskied brain thought on that for a long time. His conclusion shocked him into a new respect for the character of George Meachum. He concluded that George Meachum really did love Nan, hopelessly, distantly, and secretly. What exquisite torture had been George Meachum's. He took another swallow of whiskey. Now the exquisite torture would be his. He would have to live with it. He was feeling tired now that it was over. He should be leaving, but could not bring himself to get his horse and go. Even in death, George Meachum stopped him. George

Meachum hadn't wanted him dead, he had intended that Wendy should care for Nan and Joey. Wendy's original plan was to challenge Harv Meachum and, before the dust settled, to flee and start over somewhere else where he had no reputation with a gun. George Meachum would care for Nan.

As the whiskey fogged his brain, he knew he could not leave on the sorrell and he had no other. The red mare had been a beauty ever since she was foaled.

She stood out, against grass, against snow, like Nan. On that horse he would be watched and admired, like when he was with Nan. Men coveted that horse and fought over her. Again, like Nan. And so he sat against the gnarled tree, maudlin, dreaming, and just a little drunk.

At dusk, he roused himself. He had slept. A keen sense of loss wracked his soul and, like the jaws of some immense predator, held him immobile. His head pounded. After a while, he went back to check on his horse. Lewis had already extinguished his kiln and had gone to dinner. He stood there in the gloom of the stable, elbows on the stall door, looking at his beautiful mare. He had decided. She was a great horse, but she would have to stay behind. Dusk was falling. He would leave in the morning.

He didn't hear the footfall that came up alongside him. He did hear the match strike to light the lantern. It was Nan. Wendy Morgan had not considered what he would say to her. It would have to be good-bye.

"You. Here? What are you doing here?"

"It was you told me to come...to Dave Lewis if you didn't come back."

True. He had. He wanted her to be safe, secure, happy. That her happiness also depended on his presence, had not occurred to him.

"Where is Dave?" He mouthed the words, making simple conversation.

Wendy Morgan looked back at her quizzically. "What would he have for me?"

"From Tom Ludlam." She sensed his self-doubt, his deep and immediate need for affirmation. "He should tell you, but I will." She stopped again, gazing directly into his glazed eyes. "It's the deed to his property. He must have suspected what was going to happen, his joint disease and his lungs going bad after that accident with you on the mountain. He left the deed with Lewis last Christmas, 640 acres, a whole section, and it abuts mine. Tom wanted you to have it."

"Why? Why me? I don't think I want it."

Nan shrugged. She bit her lip and he knew she was holding something back. She repeated the obvious. "You were leaving, weren't you?"

"Yes." He couldn't hide it.

"Now you are Tom's legal heir, horseman to horseman, old to young. It's fine land with good watered pasture."

He took off his hat and ran his fingers through the dark mass of hair. A quiet rationality was returning after the fury and inebriation, like the spring thaw after the fogs and storms of winter. Her beauty stirred him. Her nearness excited him. She kept talking, hesitantly. "You have what you came for, land to build on and graze your horses...that is why you came." Then she added, "You almost died for it."

"More than once," he said weakly, as he loomed above her. Suddenly, he broke his reserve and his words burst out as if shot from a cannon, "I would have died for you!" Nan didn't think she was hearing quite right. But he went on, "Know that, remember that! But now I can bring you nothing but pain. Sell the horses! Stay here with Joey!"

Another lantern lighted the opening between the great barn doors and shed streaks of light down the aisle. They both looked up, startled.

"Morgan, there you are! We been looking all over town." Lewis and the Doctor were coming down the wide aisle between the stalls. "So Nan found you first. You gonna do it?" It was Doc Zilka doing the talking.

"Do what?"

"She didn't tell you...the terms of Tom Ludlam's will?"

A flood of confusion muddied Morgan's thoughts. He stared back at Nan, who was shaking her head at the Doctor.

"He's made up his mind to leave. I can't."

"You tell 'im, Dave."

Slowly, as was his fashion, big Dave Lewis reddened even in the lantern glow and shuffled his boots uncomfortably. He looked off in the darkness for an escape, and his eyes settled on the big red horse. He would not meet their questioning eyes.

"Doc's a coward, leavin' the grit and core to me." He kicked at the dirt floor. "When Tom there give me thet paper writin', I couldn't read, so I give it to Doc and he..."

"Goddam Lewis, get to the point!"

"There's a hitch, ya see. Whaddid ya call it, Doc? Anyways, that's the way old Tom wanted it." They all waited.

Doc could stand it no longer. "Deed restriction, that's what he means. Old Tom gave you the land, but only if you get married first. You run out, you lose!"

1045
96